The Navaho leaned down and peered into the darkness inside the wag

"Tell him to watch out," J.B. called. "Could be grens or anything in there."

But the warrior was already climbing down, feeling with his feet on the steel ladder. "Tell my brothers I count the first coup," he said. Now only his head and shoulders were visible. "This is a good day to—"

With a startling violence, the young man disappeared, cut off in midsentence.

"Fireblast!" Ryan cocked the SIG-Sauer and stared into the dark interior of the war wag, helpless to do anything to save the young Navaho from what had seized him.

Out of the stillness, floating up to the listeners, came a bubbling laugh, gentle and loathsome.

"Nice trick, you 'pache butcher. Suck on this."

They heard a cry of pain and two bodies struggling with each other...then the voice of the warrior, sounding thin and strained. "He's got a gren. Pin pulled!"

Ryan was stranded, literally sitting on top of the bomb. He kicked out at the open hatch, watching it fall in almost slow motion, and rolled backward into a clumsy somersault. When he landed on the ground, the breath was driven from his body.

Life was s ime.

Also available in the Deathlands saga:

Pilgrimage to Hell
Red Holocaust
Neutron Solstice
Crater Lake
Homeward Bound
Pony Soldiers
Dectra Chain
Ice and Fire
Red Equinox
Northstar Rising
Time Nomads
Latitude Zero
Seedling
Dark Carnival
Chill Factor
Moon Fate
Fury's Pilgrims
Shockscape
Deep Empire
Cold Asylum
Twilight Children

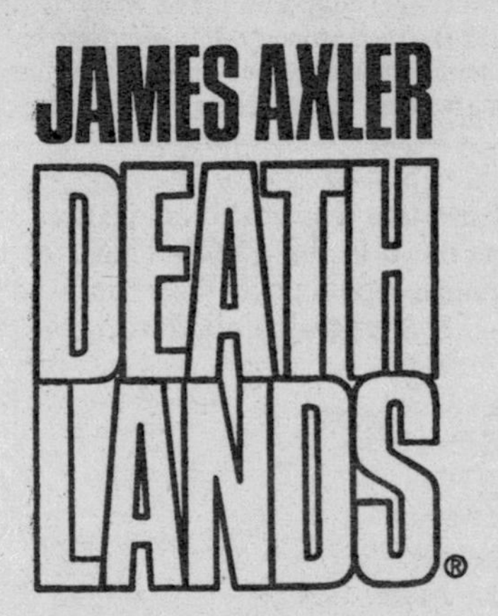

Rider, Reaper

TORONTO • NEW YORK • LONDON
AMSTERDAM • PARIS • SYDNEY • HAMBURG
STOCKHOLM • ATHENS • TOKYO • MILAN
MADRID • WARSAW • BUDAPEST • AUCKLAND

Nobody deserves a dedication more than Joe J. Sirak, Junior, so this is for him. With thanks for all the hours of reading he's put in over the years. And with every possible good wish.

First edition August 1994

ISBN 0-373-62522-7

RIDER, REAPER

Printed in U.S.A.

Happiness dwells within each heart,
Until it's stolen by a thief.
We all know well that villain dark,
Whose wretched name is grief.

—From *Lives of Quiet Desperation,*
by Mary Lynn Britton, Bishop's Press, 1888

Chapter One

Ryan opened his good eye and blinked up into the early-morning sky, a bright blue band etched between the high sandstone walls of the New Mexico canyon where he lay resting from the glare of the sun.

The bird was a blur for a moment, its large wings flapping lazily. Then his sight cleared and Ryan recognized the creature as a snowy egret, rising from a bunch of cottonwoods a hundred yards to the south.

At his side, Jak Lauren hadn't stirred.

A light breeze brought the familiar scent of sagebrush from farther down the trail.

A tiny lizard scuttled out from under a frost-riven boulder, looking for a moment toward the two motionless figures. It decided they represented no threat and moved out into the band of sunshine, vanishing into a patch of Indian rice grass.

Ryan glanced at Jak, as the youth stirred in his sleep, his arm flung across his pink, light-sensitive eyes. The familiar mane of snow-white hair was markedly longer than in the old days when they'd ridden and fought together, spilled out over the dusty, cropped grass.

The albino teenager had always been a hardened survivor, but the dreadful events of the past few days had etched fresh lines of pain around his deep-set eyes and thin-lipped mouth.

The bottom of the canyon was cool, barely in the eighties. Out in the open it was way over the hundred-degree mark.

The two men had come alone, drawn by a common purpose. By a remembering and by a sadness.

The rest of the party of friends were camped among a bosk of aspens, by the clear stream that trickled steadily from the higher ground. The stream had become the main water supply for the spread where Jak Lauren had settled with his wife, Christina Ballinger, and where the recent joy of their marriage had been the bright little Jenny.

A gopher snake slithered from its hiding place and coiled itself, its delicate tongue probing at the morning air, tasting the two human beings. It found the vanishing flavor of the small lizard, balancing caution against hunger.

Hunger won and it moved out into the open, following the tiny reptile.

Ryan watched it go.

Time was passing. His wrist chron showed that they'd been away from the others for well over the hour. Krysty would already be worrying. J. B. Dix, the Armorer, would probably be checking his own chron every now and again.

Mildred Wyeth, the black doctor they'd thawed in a cryocenter, would be resting, maximizing her strength for the ordeal that they all knew would be starting very soon.

Dean Cawdor, Ryan's eleven-year-old son, might be throwing pebbles into the fast-flowing stream, or sleeping, or hunting for snakes to chill.

Doc Tanner, the oldest of the group of companions, born in 1868 and time-trawled to the bleak postholocaust world of Deathlands, would likely be asleep, flat on his back, his eyes covered with the distinctive swallow's-eye kerchief he always carried. The massive gold-plated commemorative Le Mat pistol would be holstered at his hip, and the ebony sword stick with the silver lion's-head handle lying at his side.

Jak stirred and sighed, then looked sideways at Ryan. "Time to move?"

"Guess so."

The young man stood, stretching, showing the feline grace that made him one of the finest hand-to-hand fighters that Ryan had ever known, though he had to admit that Michael Brother had the edge on anyone for sheer combat-reflex speed.

"It's like time never existed."

"How do you mean, Jak?"

"Like I'm still with you. Like quiet months were dream. Like dark's always with me."

"Least you had them, Jak. Krysty often talks about us settling down like you and Christina. Says how she wants to stop the running and the fighting."

Jak nodded. He took a long, slow breath, running a finger around the collar of his denim shirt. His right hand rested easily on the butt of the huge satin-finish .357 Colt Python Magnum, with its six-inch barrel. Ryan and J.B. had used to tease the white-haired youth about carrying such an enormous cannon, but Jak had shown repeatedly that he was able to handle it.

Christina had never liked the gun, and on their last visit she'd insisted that Jak put it away.

"Never really took to us," Ryan said.

"Chris?"

"Yeah."

"She appreciated how you saved her."

"By chilling her brothers and her father. Sure. Good way to become friends."

They'd encountered the Ballinger family many months earlier—R.G., the father, the triple-stupe, vicious brothers, Jim and Larry, and their sister, limping with a built-up boot on her crippled left foot. Her blue eyes would never look at anyone, in case she got a fist in the face for rudeness. The girl's brutal world had been low on childhood and love, and high on violence.

"Best say goodbye." Jak looked around the canyon. "Favorite place."

"It's beautiful."

"Others not want to come?"

"Don't think so, Jak. Not really anything left for any of the others to say."

"Suppose not."

The wind fell away, and the steep-walled canyon became totally silent.

They walked together through the hot, deeply crimson sand, toward the three graves. Each of them had a marker, carved from wood, the letters burned neatly into the slab of beech.

The two men stood side by side, silently united in grief.

Two of the graves were large, the middle one much smaller. All three lay in shade, beneath a wall of red rock that rose vertically and vanished into the deep blue of the morning sky.

It was a place of great quiet. Jak and Ryan glanced up as the ghostly egret floated above their heads and vanished away toward the ruins of an Indian cliff dwelling.

None of the markers carried any date or age.

One read Christina Lauren, Beloved Wife of Jak and Mother of Jenny. Murdered.

The small grave bore the legend Jenny Lauren, Dear Daughter of Jak and Christina. Murdered.

The third marker claimed Michael Brother. Good Friend from Another Time.

That was all.

Ryan laid a hand on the slim shoulders of the teenager and stood with him in the stillness while they both remembered everything that had happened in the previous few weeks, since the companions had arrived unexpectedly in New Mexico after the last jump.

Chapter Two

Michael was weeping, which was the first sound that Ryan heard as he started to come around from the jump.

His eye opened, slowly and painfully. It felt like something had been spitting hot sand under the lid. Ryan closed his eye again, aware that he had a ferocious headache, situated behind the empty socket of his missing left eye.

"Fireblast!" He groaned in pain, wishing that Michael would stop crying. The rasping noise was already starting to get on his nerves.

In between the throttled, choking sobs, it seemed like the youth was trying to say a name. It sounded to Ryan like "Dorothy." The name was vaguely familiar, but he couldn't quite work out where he'd heard it before.

Ryan risked easing open his right eye again and saw that the walls of light purple armaglass had vanished, which was the last thing he'd seen as they started the matter-transfer jump from the buried military redoubt. Where had it been?

"New England," Ryan croaked triumphantly. This was good. The scrambling of the brain that was always a consequence of a jump was healing already.

Now the walls were a pale silver. That color also rang a dim and distant bell in the far-off reaches of Ryan's mind. But too dim and distant for him to claw it out of the shorted memory banks.

The silvered disks in floor and ceiling had all lost their brightness, and the last tendrils of ghostly white mist were disappearing above his head.

Michael was doubled up in a fetal position, tears streaming down his cheeks, still repeating the name Dorothy.

Now Ryan remembered. That was the name of the young woman Michael had fallen in love with and who had been about to join them on the jump and then changed her mind at the final moment.

Correction—*beyond* the final moment. She'd opened the door of the gateway and risked the destruction of the triggering mechanism that could have sent all of them into a whirling, infinite oblivion. There was no way of knowing whether Dorothy had survived, and there never would be.

Ryan wriggled himself into a seated position, his back against the wall. His mouth felt like a stickie had been sick in it, and his stomach still churned. There was a sore place on his neck that he couldn't recall injuring.

Other than Michael, no one else had recovered from the jump.

Next to Ryan was Krysty, lying on her back, hands neatly folded in her lap, her flaming red sentient hair packed tightly around her nape. The woman's green eyes were closed, and she was breathing steadily. Her legs were crossed, the cuffs of her pants ridden up to reveal her dark blue leather Western boots, with the chiseled silver points on the toes and the silver spread-wing falcons embroidered on the fronts.

Dean sat next to his father. He was stirring, mumbling to himself, a thin string of yellow bile dribbling from his lips. His head rocked back and forth, and his fingers kept opening and closing. He was as pale as wind-washed ivory.

J.B. lay on his side, as though he'd tipped forward during the jump. Ryan's oldest friend, the Armorer, had joined the legendary Trader and his war wags about the same time as the one-eyed warrior. His fedora had rolled across onto the far side of the chamber and lay by the door. Ryan could just see the folded glasses protruding from the top pocket of J.B.'s jacket.

Mildred was next in the circle. She had been born on December 17, 1964, into a politically active Baptist family. She hadn't even been a year old when the good old boys of the KKK rode out of the night with their burning crosses and murdered her father.

Three days before the end of the year 2000, Mildred had gone into a hospital for minor abdominal surgery. She had been an expert in the field of cryosurgery and cryogenics, and it had been logical, when something went wrong during the operation, to have her traumatized body deep frozen.

Then the nukings of the following month had devastated the entire world, decimating the population.

Millions died during the sky dark, and tens of millions more of the rad sickness during the long winters. Civilization vanished, never to return.

The United States of America reverted to a number of scattered communities, some of them small villages of a few dozen, some of them larger villes with up to four or five hundred souls, run by gun-carrying barons.

It became Deathlands.

For nearly a century, Mildred had slept on, dreamless and dark. Then she had been jerked back to life by Ryan and his companions.

The last of the group was Doctor Theophilus Algernon Tanner. In November of 1896, Doc had awakened to another normal cool, bright morning in Omaha, Nebraska, and kissed his beloved young wife and two children goodbye. Then his world had ended at the whim of blank-faced scientists of 1998. They were working on an ultrasecret time-traveling project, picking victims—or candidates, as they were known—and plucking them from their past into the uncertain present. Operation Chronos.

Now Doc lay on his back, with his chin on his chest. His mouth gaped open, revealing his excellent teeth. His white hair brushed the shoulders of the frock coat, and his cracked leather knee boots were stretched out in front of him. He was snoring with the steady pounding of a steam-powered reciprocating engine.

Krysty opened her eyes and groaned, staring at Ryan, her vision out of focus. She licked her lips.

"Gaia! We made it." She touched the cold armaglass walls with her fingers. "Silver. Been here before?"

"Think so. But I can't remember where."

"What's wrong with Michael?" Memory illuminated her face. "Dorothy? She got out of... Did she get out?" Krysty looked around the hexagonal gateway chamber. "Yeah, looks like she got out just in time."

"Not sure. Last thing I remember was seeing her kind of transparent in the doorway. Guess we'll never know. Unless we pressed the instant return control."

In the long blackness that followed the nuking of the planet, most technowisdom disappeared, including how to work the matter-transfer units. Ryan had stumbled upon the first of them in a long-buried secret redoubt, and had found that the closing of the chamber door was enough to trigger the operation. You became unconscious for a brief period of time, and when you came around again you were elsewhere.

Doc had worked briefly on the system, during the couple of years he was an unwilling captive of the scientists. But he had become so difficult and emotionally unstable, constantly seeking a stolen opportunity to try to get back to his own time and his lost family, that those who had trawled him from the past used the experiment to push him forward, nearly a hundred years, into what had then become Deathlands.

But even Doc had no idea how to actually set coordinates on the gateway to be able to control where you jumped. All the codes and comp information had vanished in the rad-violent months after the holocaust.

"Silver walls," J.B. commented, coughing as he struggled to sit up, nearly losing his balance. "Been here before."

"Michael!" Krysty called out to the teenager. "Michael, come on."

But there was no response, just the racking sobs that seemed unstoppable.

"Dad, I feel awful."

"Sit still, Dean, or lie on your back. Sometimes helps. It'll pass."

"What's wrong with Michael?" Dean managed to sit up, staring worriedly at the hunched figure of the teenager.

"Think that nearly having Dorothy come along, and then the way she freaked out and nearly chilled us all, has tipped him over the edge for a while." Ryan glanced at Michael. "He wasn't all that well after the last jump. Seemed real depressed. Don't worry, Dean. He'll get over it."

Michael uncoiled like a striking rattler, making all of them jump. His dark eyes were wide and staring, and there were flecks of white froth clinging to the corners of his mouth. Ryan found that his own hand had fallen to the holstered SIG-Sauer, easing it half out and cocking it before he even realized that he'd reacted to the sudden movement.

"Get over it, will I, Ryan?" The voice was harshly mocking.

"Yeah."

"You'd know about getting over things, wouldn't you?"

Ryan nodded. "Everyone here's had loved ones that they've lost, Michael."

"So what the fuck does that mean to me? Why should I be interested in other people losing their loved ones? Why should I, Ryan?"

"Take it easy, young fellow," Doc said, recovering and sitting up. "Ryan's correct about us suffering loss. Few more than myself, I daresay."

Michael stood, staggering to his left, and steadying himself with a fumbling hand. "Damn it!"

Ryan and the others were all up on their feet, ringing the young man.

"She made her choice in the end, Michael."

"Fuck choice, Ryan."

"Sure. I'll drink to that any day of the week. But it won't change a damned thing. She's gone back to Quindley and her own people."

Michael punched at the wall, his knuckles cracking on the armaglass. Then, before anyone could stop him, he deliberately head-butted the silvered wall. There was a sickening damp thud and he staggered, hands going to his face. Blood flowed fast from a gash across his forehead, into his eyes and dripping off his chin onto the floor.

"Michael!" Mildred stepped in close, lifting a hand. "Let me put something on that."

He waved her away, grinning through the mask of blood, his white teeth smeared with crimson. "No, thanks, Dr. Wyeth. Save your medicining for others. I don't need it and I don't fucking well want it."

Ryan glanced at the woman, who caught his eye. "Surface cut. It'll bruise up some. Lot of blood near the surface of the skin around the eyes. Nothing serious."

"Let's get out of here. Can't stand being closed in like in a grave."

"Wait!" Ryan's voice cracked out like a buggy whip, freezing Michael in his tracks, a half pace from the handle of the massive armaglass door.

J.B. had been polishing his glasses. Now he perched them on the end of his bony nose and peered at Michael. "You want to chill yourself," he said quietly, "then that's your right. Everyone's right. But you don't take others with you. You understand me, Michael?"

"Yeah, yeah. All right. Guess you'll probably shoot me if I don't do like you say, won't you?"

"Possibly." The armorer turned to Ryan. "Ready to move out of here?"

"Guess so. Wish I could recall which of the gateways we jumped to that had walls this silvery color."

"I can remember."

Everyone looked at Mildred, except Michael, who'd begun to cry again. This time it was far more gently, small pearl tears easing out of his swollen eyes and cutting uneven pink furrows through the fresh blood.

"You can remember which redoubt had this gateway?"

"Sure, Ryan. I'm honestly surprised that you can't. And surprised at Dean. Didn't expect old farts like Doc to recall it, but the boy..."

Dean scratched the side of his nose, his face a study in concentration. Suddenly he smiled. "Yeah. Course."

Then it came to Ryan, as well, and to Krysty. "Might not be the same place," he said. "Could be several gateways with the same color of armaglass."

Krysty shook her head. "No, lover. Now I remember and I can feel it. I'd stake a bootful of jack we've jumped to New Mexico. We can see Jak Lauren again."

Chapter Three

The redoubt had been extensively damaged during a huge explosion on their first jump to it, blowing away half of the red-baked mountain. The battered, rusted communication dish at the bottom of the slope, where they'd all sheltered to save their lives, still stood there.

Fortunately the gateway and the control room hadn't been damaged, secure and safe behind the massively thick vanadium-steel sec doors.

J.B. checked his lapel rad counter, finding that it was flickering faintly between the yellow and orange bands, but nowhere near the red.

"Safe enough," he said, breathing in the warm air, as he looked out across the expanse of desert.

The pocket nav comp had confirmed that they had, indeed, landed once more in New Mexico. They all emerged into a narrow, dusty passage that ended in a gaping hole, where the earth had been sliced away, destroying virtually the whole of the redoubt concealed above it.

"Wonder how things are with Jak and Christina," Dean said, wiping away beads of sweat with the sleeve of his coat. "And their baby. What was..."

"Jenny," Krysty replied. "Jenny Lauren."

THE ONLY MOMENT OF DRAMA on the trek to the Lauren spread was when Dean spotted a mutie rattler.

The snake was one of the biggest that any of them had ever seen. At least fifteen feet from poison sac to bony rattle, its vivid colors stood out against the gray sand.

"More scared of us than we are of it," J.B. said, drawing a cynical laugh from Mildred.

"Now how do you know that, John, dearest? Firstly I'm so petrified I'm nearly pissing in my pants and, secondly, that snake doesn't look scared of us at all."

The rattler reared up, nearly as tall as a grown man, its head weaving slowly from side to side. It was coiled square on top of a narrow ridge, in the partial shade of a big flowering cactus.

"Could put one through its brain," Mildred offered. "Happy to do it."

"Best not to set the echoes ringing with a bullet," Ryan warned. "Keep watching it, and we'll go around."

"Fine with me," Mildred said.

"I will most heartily lend my acquiescence to that motion." Doc looked around at the others, pale dust folded into the creases around his eyes and mouth. "All in favor indicate by saying 'Aye,' in a loud clear voice." Nobody spoke. "Carried by a policy of silent acclamation."

"Shut the fuck up, old man." Michael turned and spit toward Doc, narrowly missing the toes of his boots.

"Peevish boy." Doc stared at the teenager, forcing him finally to look away. "It's time that you revealed more evidence of maturity, Michael."

"Fuck you, and fuck the world!"

They circled around the patiently watching rattler and kept heading for the Laurens' home.

THEY WERE, by Ryan's calculations, nearly halfway to the homestead, which nestled in among the low hills northwest of the redoubt, when, without a moment's warning, Michael seemed to stiffen. He then crashed facedown, raising a cloud of dust and sand around his prostrate body.

"What?" Ryan queried, turning to look back.

"Keep off him a minute," Mildred ordered sharply. "Might be some kind of fit. Let me check that he hasn't swallowed his tongue." Michael's whole body was arched backward, and one of his arms seemed to have become trapped behind his head. Mildred knelt by him, still not touching the young man.

"Arm's dislocated at the shoulder," J.B. commented, looking down at Michael.

"I know that, John. Trapped it when he fell. Airway's clear. Some kind of clinical shock felled him, I think. Better try and get that damaged shoulder returned into place as quickly as possible. Turn him on his back for me. Slow and careful, please."

Michael's eyes were wide open, each reflecting a perfect shrunken image of the golden sun. His breath was slow and steady, his heartbeat slightly slower than normal. The arm was out from his side at a crooked, unnatural angle, the fingers hooked into claws.

"Hold his head still, Ryan. John, take his legs and try and stop him from moving."

"What're you doing?" Dean asked.

"Watch and learn," Mildred replied. She sat alongside Michael, carefully placing her right foot into the unconscious young man's right armpit. The toe of the calf-length boot pressed snugly under the limp arm.

Doc turned away, studying the distance that expanded around them. "Forgive me if I avail myself of a rain check on watching this," he said. "I once had a severely dislocated knee while on a walking vacation, and the memory of the pain is still quite peculiarly fresh."

"Now," Mildred said, taking Michael's wrist in both her hands and bracing herself. "Hold tight. May make him jump some."

She pushed her foot down hard, simultaneously jerking with all her strength at the arm. There was an audible click, as the joint relocated, the head of the bone popping back into the socket. The young man gave a whimper of pain, but Ryan and J.B. held him still.

"Good." Mildred stood and dusted herself off. "Be a bit sore for a day or so. Muscles shouldn't be too badly damaged. Tendons and ligaments'll have stretched some, but he's fit and strong."

She smiled across at Dean, who had gone slightly pale. "There. Not a thing to try if you don't know what you're doing."

Michael came around a few minutes later and got up without a word to any of them. He rubbed at his shoulder, easing it a couple of times, wincing in pain.

"How's it feel?" Mildred asked.

"Like a clumsy, bloody-bones butcher's been working on it," he replied.

"You ungrateful, miserable little shit!" Krysty took two steps toward the youth, making him back away from her bright-eyed anger.

"Touch me and you'll regret it," he roared. "Just leave me alone."

"Be glad to, Michael. When you start behaving like the Michael Brother we've known as a friend, then I'll be glad to see you back again."

Limping slightly, muttering to himself, Michael set off, leading the way toward Jak's place.

THE FOOTHILLS WERE appreciably closer, and the day was wearing on. Michael had, at one point, gone two or three hundred paces ahead of the rest of them. J.B. had commented on it, but Ryan had shrugged.

"We can see all around. No dead ground. No real risk of an ambush. Rad counter's showing safely into the green. Tell the truth, J.B., but I'd rather be without his company when he's in this kind of foul mood."

Mildred walked beside the Armorer, her quilted denim jacket slung over her arm. "I'm seriously concerned about Michael, you know, Ryan."

"What do you think's wrong?"

"The last jump seemed to slide him into a depressed state. And that made him vulnerable to the approach from Dorothy. Then, when she vanished like that, out of the mat-trans chamber, it pushed him another few notches down the slope. I don't see the good signs of him climbing his way back up the slope. Mebbe it's still a part of the trauma from being time-trawled."

"I could greatly sympathize with the poor lad over that." Doc sniffed. "There have been occasions—many occasions—when I have doubted my own fragile grasp on the rudiments of what sometimes passes for sanity."

"Woman back in Harmony ville when I was a girl got depressed." Krysty brushed an insistent wasp away from her face. "She had great mood swings, weeping one minute and laughing the next."

"What happened to her?" Mildred asked.

"Slashed her wrists during one of the bleak, black dog nights. In a warm bath. Time her father found her it was way too late. Nothing anyone could do."

"You think Michael's permanently crazed?" Ryan whistled between his teeth. "Can't go around in Deathlands with a triple stupe. Get us all chilled."

Mildred shook her head, the tiny beads plaited into her hair making a faint clicking sound. "Can't tell, Ryan. Ask me about all the subtle effects of low-temp surgery and I'm your woman. Psychology never was one of my strong points. Sorry."

Doc was beginning to find the long hot walk through the hundred-degree day a strain. "I don't suppose that a rest is anything of a possibility, is it?"

"Not all that far now." Ryan stopped and squinted ahead of them. "Yeah. I can see the place. Pale roof. Better catch up with Michael in case he goes charging in and Christina puts a long-nose .45 round through his skull."

THE SHIMMERING HEAT of the deserts of the Southwest, combined with the clear air and enormous distances, made distance judgment difficult. Even Ryan, for all of his experience, underestimated how much farther it was to the Lauren ranch.

The sun was sinking away to the west and they'd finished all of their water, and the white roof still looked to be a couple of miles off.

Doc was finding it harder and harder going, stumbling and twice falling into the soft sand. Michael had rejoined them and seemed to be making more of an effort to be friendly, helping Doc, and even carrying Dean on his shoulders for a quarter mile or so despite the boy's amused protests.

"Someone coming toward us." It was Krysty who spotted the pale rider. "Jak?"

"White hair," Michael said, shading his eyes against the lowering coppery sun.

"Jak." Ryan glanced behind them, making sure from ingrained habit that nobody was coming up from their rear. For a moment he thought that he saw someone duck out of sight into a furrowed arroyo, but he stared hard and nothing moved.

"Yeah," J.B. agreed. "It's Jak."

CHRISTINA LAUREN didn't share her young husband's delight at the visit of his old companions. She was standing on the porch, wiping her hands on an apron as they arrived. Little Jenny was beginning to walk, toddling from the open door, then hiding behind her mother's long skirts when she saw all the strangers.

"Knew you'd come back one day, Ryan Cawdor," the woman said, as she walked down to meet them. Ryan spotted the butt of a small revolver holstered at her belt, something he'd never noticed on his previous visits.

"Sheer chance, Christina," he replied. "Can't control jumps. You know that."

"Sure, sure. You come out of the desert like a one-eyed storm crow."

Jak turned on his wife, eyes glowing like hot rubies. "No way speak to friends, Chris." He faced Ryan and the others. "Stay few days?"

"Few. Good to see you, Jak. And you, Christina. And the little one."

"We were doing well without you, Ryan," the woman stated. "Not saying you aren't welcome to stay a few days. We both owe you, the Good Lord knows. But just for a few days, all right? Then you move on."

"Sure," Ryan agreed. "Few days, and then we move on."

Chapter Four

The first of those few days were wonderful. The weather was excellent, from the cool clarity of the dawnings, through the cloudless mornings and bright afternoons, into the mild evenings where they all sat outside and listened to Christina singing along to an inlaid guitar that she'd bought from a traveling pack-man a few weeks earlier.

It was a time for healing of wounds and injuries, those of the body as well as those of the soul.

Ryan found that his neck was better, the wound finally clearing up, leaving only a small, puckered scar. Michael's shoulder also mended quickly, his efforts at exercise earning him Mildred's approval.

Four days slipped past so quickly and painlessly that it hardly seemed possible that they'd been at the ranch for that long. Christina's fears seemed to have eased away and she sat among them, Jenny on her lap, laughing, joking and sharing in their memories of some of the good times gone.

The food was wonderful. After the vegetarian fare that they'd been given in Quindley, this was fine ranch eating—loin of pork and a sauce of apples laced with cloves, sweet potatoes and a blended mix of buttered carrots and corn. Jak had traded some furs he'd hunted in the high country behind the spread, bringing home several dozen green bottles of a sweet white wine. Doc delightedly pronounced them to be better than a half-way decent Piesporter Michelsberg.

The fourth evening found everyone on the porch. Only half of the setting sun remained, a corridor of gold leading to it across the desert. Jak cuddled the sleepy baby, while Christina sang quietly.

Mildred was lying down, her head resting in J.B.'s lap, her right hand folded into his. Krysty sat on the edge of the stoop, leaning against Ryan's shoulder. Dean was on the other side of his father, silently playing jacks with the tiny black pebbles that are sometimes called Apache tears. Doc lay stretched out on the swing seat, rocking himself back and forth in time to the music.

Michael stood at the far, northern end of the porch, whittling a piece of wood with one of his twin daggers. While not joining in the singing, he still seemed to be a part of the group.

Far off, a thousand feet above the house, a single coyote howled at the setting sun.

"Coffee anyone?" Jak asked, getting a chorus of "yes" from everyone except Michael.

"How about you, Michael?" Christina peered along the porch, in the gathering gloom.

"No. Nothing for me. I want for nothing. When you got nothing, then nothing's what you want. Sorry to be a downer, Mrs. Lauren. Can you go on singing, please?"

"Sure."

Jak handed the child to Mildred. "I'll put kettle on stove."

Doc stood and stretched. "A man could get used to living out here."

"We like it," Jak said, vanishing inside the building.

Christina took up her guitar again to sing the final verse of the song. Her strong, true voice ringing out across the desolate wilderness:

> The light departs and night comes fast,
> All life and love will soon be past.
> And darkness follows after day
> Over the hills and far away.

Hesitantly, following on Doc's lead, the others repeated the melancholy chorus.

The last plangent chord faded slowly, and the night seemed to crowd in a little closer around the fragile oasis of light and warmth.

"By the Three Kennedys!" Doc exclaimed. "But I think that some specks of grit have entered my poor old glims and made them water most fearfully."

"Sure is sad," J.B. agreed. "Reminds me of the hymns those Amish folk used to sing. You remember, Ryan? Time with Trader when that sickness hit the war wags?"

"Yeah. I remember. Who was it said that the Amish were open people with closed minds? Can't recall."

"Think that Abe will ever find Trader, Dad?"

The little gunner from War Wag One had become preoccupied with rumors that the Trader still lived, despite a considerable body of evidence that said that he'd gone off into the forests to die from the stomach rad cancer that often made him puke blood. It had seemed like Trader to crawl away like a dying animal to end his life in solitude.

But the stories kept coming about a grizzled man with a battered Armalite rifle. They saw him in Portland, Maine, then a day later there was a word of him up in Portland, Oregon. He was spotted down on the Gulf and up in the Canadian tundra.

So, Abe went looking. Ryan couldn't precisely recall how long ago it was now. Months? There hadn't been any message, but communication within Deathlands tended to be, at the best, erratic. At worst it was nonexistent.

"Dad?" the boy repeated.

"Abe find Trader? If the old son of a bitch is still to be found, then I'd back a hatful of jack on Abe being the man to ferret him out."

"What's that you're carving, Michael?" Mildred leaned forward, carefully holding on to Jenny, one hand supporting the tousled little head.

The teenager walked slowly from the end of the porch, tucking the knife back into its sheath. "Been whittling away at my future."

"Show me."

Jak had lighted three oil lamps, hanging along the veranda. They gave off a gentle, yellow glow, attracting a number of death's-head moths that fluttered around the hot glass.

The young man had his right hand clenched tightly in front of him.

"Show us your future, Michael," J.B. urged, smiling up at him.

"Here."

He opened his fist and turned it over, allowing dozens of tiny white chips and splinters of wood to fall onto the ground by his feet.

"Michael." Krysty half rose, then sat down again, closing her eyes and putting a hand to her forehead.

"There's my future," he said, very calmly and very reasonably. Then he turned on his heel and walked away from the house.

LATER THAT NIGHT Krysty lay in the double bed she shared with Ryan. She was on her left side, facing the wall, with Ryan pressed hard against her from behind, one hand cupping a breast, the other guiding himself between her thighs.

They both hesitated as they heard the click of the back door opening and closing, then the steel sec bolt being firmly pushed across.

"Michael?" Krysty whispered.

"Guess so. Muties wouldn't lock the door behind them, would they?"

"Where's he been?"

"Walking and thinking? Fireblast! I don't know, Krysty. It's really getting to the point where I'm seriously worried about the lad."

"Had some double-bad shocks since we brought him around in the trawl."

"Life's never easy."

Ryan had resumed the slow, thrusting movement, the springs on the narrow bed squeaking in unison. He reached around Krysty's hips and touched her with the tip of his index finger, making her moan and push back harder against him.

Their conversation faltered away as they both became deeply preoccupied with the lovemaking.

Ryan set his teeth into Krysty's nape, with infinite gentleness, while she stretched her arm up and pushed a moist finger into the corner of his mouth, letting him taste her own arousal.

The door of the adjacent room to them opened and closed softly, where Michael was sleeping in a bunk bed next to Dean. For a brace of heartbeats Ryan checked his movement, but he could feel his own climax gathering force and he carried on.

"Oh, Gaia!" Krysty sighed the word into the sweat-damp feather pillow. Her body arched against him, her strong stomach muscles fluttering with the power of the release, repeatedly gripping and releasing his hardness, sucking him deeper into her at the climactic moment, so that they came within a second or so of each other.

Moments later Krysty slipped easily into a dreamless sleep. Ryan slipped out of the bed, washing the stickiness from his body in a bowl of clean water, using a rough linen towel to dry himself. The night was warm and still, and he pulled on his blue denim shirt, picking his careful way, barefoot, across the ragged tufts of the oval rug. He opened the door and walked out onto the porch.

There was the click of a hammer being cocked and he spun, cursing himself under his breath for leaving the SIG-Sauer behind him in the room.

Trader's words came to him at that moment. "Man doesn't have to be careless more than once. Once is all it takes to get to be deeply dead."

"Can't sleep, Ryan." It was difficult to tell whether it was a statement or a question. The spurred hammer on the long-barreled .357 Magnum eased back down again.

"Right, Jak." The blaze of snow-white hair like magnesium flared at the far end of the veranda.

"Figured on going for a hunt."

"When?"

"Tomorrow. No, gotta mend fences tomorrow. Day after. Get us some deer meat in hills."

Ryan nodded as he considered the suggestion. "Sounds good."

"Saw fire."

"Where?" He took a few steps to bring him closer to the teenager.

Jak wore a cotton nightshirt in dark blue material. He lifted his arm and pointed out into the velvet blackness of the desert, to the northwest. "That way."

Ryan caught the feral scent of sweat and sex, realizing that the young man had been doing the same as he and Krysty. Oddly he found that mildly embarrassing, guessing that the same rutting odor would hang about himself.

"Can't see anything."

"Might be lightning strike. Saw chem storm that way. Didn't last long."

Ryan leaned on the smooth cottonwood rail. "Air's heavy. Could be a storm here."

"No. Reckon not. Passed away behind hills."

"You should know, Jak. Lived here long enough now. Still enjoying marriage and fatherhood?"

"Sure. Beats anything. You and Krysty should do it."

Ryan smiled at Jake. "One day."

"Wait for happiness and find old age and sadness."

"Deep thoughts for a kid."

"Don't call me, 'kid,' Ryan."

Now they were both smiling at the familiarity of the old, shared joke.

"Times we miss having you riding with us, Jak. But, I guess you know that."

"Sure. Times I miss those days."

They shared a companionable silence together, each allowing his mind to roam back through their shared memories. Times past.

Ryan straightened. "Guess I'll turn in, Jak."

"Me, too." He paused. "Ryan?"

"Yeah?"

"Michael? Christina reckons he's got sort of black boil festering inside him. Got to be cured or she thinks one day it'll burst."

"She's right. He lived a strange and enclosed life before he got jerked into this world. Seemed to have coped with it well. Much better than Doc, most of the time. But lately things been setting badly wrong."

"He get better?"

"Sure. Sure hope so."

"Man pulls blinds down over his brain...triple danger to everyone."

"Can't argue with that, Jak."

There was a brilliant streak of silver light, touched with purple at the trailing edge, hundreds of miles above the heads of the two men.

"Another chunk of rad shit," Ryan commented. "Amazes me that parts of the old Star Wars hardware's still up there. Never did any good when they were new. Certainly not doing any good now, dropping out and burning up."

"Jenny likes them. Thinks real pretty."

"Me, too." Already the smooth flare was fading away, back into the darkness, allowing the surrounding stars to break through again with diamond clarity.

"Michael needs cure." Jak turned toward the door, a slight figure in the night. Ryan guessed he hadn't put an inch on the five four he'd been when they first met.

Though the one-ten pounds could now be closer to one-twenty. With Christina's cooking that wasn't surprising.

"Mebbe hunt, day after tomorrow? Could be just the cure he needs."

"Kill or cure, Doc used to say." Jak's teeth were white in the blackness of the porch.

"Yeah. Kill or cure. Sleep well, Jak."

"You, too, Ryan. G'night."

"Good night, Jak."

Chapter Five

"Well, I'll be hung, quartered and fucking dried for the crows!"

Abe woke up with a start, his hand fumbling for the stainless-steel Colt Python under his bedroll. "What is it, Trader?"

"I don't know." He blinked up at the moon, guessing that they were still an hour or more from the first light of morning. "Something woke you?"

Trader was sitting up, his blanket crumpled over his knees, cradling his much-traveled Armalite across his lap. The cooking fire had long died, and only a wisp of gray smoke rose between the surrounding trees.

"Yeah, something woke me, Abe. Want to know what it was, do you?"

"Sure."

Even in the relatively few weeks since he'd tracked down the Trader, Abe had learned quickly that his former leader's temper hadn't improved with age. It was a whole lot better to try not to argue with him.

"I woke up because I was having a real bad dream." He stretched and pressed his right hand against his stomach, stifling a groan of pain.

"Guts bad?"

"Yeah. Been better for a couple years or more. Used to be like having a pair of starving rats fighting in my belly. Then it got better, after I walked away from the war wags. You remember when I did that, Abe?"

"Course I do, Trader."

"Yeah." He nodded. "Went into what a Mescalero shaman called 'remission,' whatever that means. Think it means it got better for a while. Least, it didn't get any worse. Last few weeks I been feeling it again."

"Anything help it?"

Trader shifted position, farting noisily. "Help it? Heard that milk and stuff was good for it. True that liquor burns like fucking napalm. Some fruits seem to make it worse. Way I see it, I'd rather go out walking tall and piss-drunk and hurting, rather than ten years on down the line, flat on my back, with a bowl of warm milk and bread to suck on."

"Yeah. Me, too." There was a long pause. "Trader, you said some dream woke you."

"Don't remember."

Abe sniffed. "Don't matter."

"No. It don't."

THE BEAVER TAIL was skinned and sliced thin, then cooked in a skillet over the revived fire. Trader had shot the animal as it emerged from the nearby pool, dripping after its lumbering swim from a large lodge of tangled branches.

Abe had dug up some potatoes from an ancient cottage garden, nestling off a side trail, the ruins of the holiday home barely visible through the brush. There were also some massive, mutated turnips, woody and coarse, but edible after they'd been parboiled and then fried.

"This is the life," Trader said expansively, lying back and picking his teeth with the point of his slim-bladed dagger. "Beats working, don't it?"

"Sure does."

"When are we moving from here, Abe?"

"We can go farther up into the Cascades. But we gotta stay close by the ruins of Seattle. Ready for when Ryan comes up here after us."

"He might not get the message."

Abe nodded. "Could be."

From where they sat, it was possible to see miles down a V-shaped valley, heavily wooded on both sides. A lake lay at the bottom, invisible beneath a white coiling bank of early-morning fog. The dark place that had been Seattle itself was invisible, about twelve miles to the west.

Over the past few weeks, Abe had been thinking a lot about the messages that had been sent. A large number of travelers and packmen had been given a scrap of paper, the words written by Abe. Trader didn't have the way of letters or numbers.

> Success. Will stay around Seattle for three months. Come quick. Abe.

There was still plenty of time left, and the men and women who carried that message were spreading all over the wastes of Deathlands. Like a drop of oil poured onto a bowl of water, they would cover the continent, visiting nearly every ville and frontier settlement. They were urged—threateningly—to look for the one-eyed man and his red-haired woman, a small guy with the hat and glasses, a black woman, a kid, an old man and a teenager who moved faster than a speeding bullet.

One of the messages should get through.

There'd been a number of times since meeting Trader again that Abe had experienced doubts about the wisdom of what he'd done. It didn't seem at all like he remembered it. Or how he'd expected it would be.

Trader had always been hard. That went without saying. You could walk into a frontier gaudy and say you rode with Trader. Folks might not love you for it, but they would, by the living God, show you respect!

But the hardness had been tempered with wisdom and with a sense of what was fair and what was not. Nobody looked to cheat or lie to the Trader and get away with it. At the least you'd crawl away from a good smacking. At the worst you lay in the dirt with rain pounding into your open eyes.

Now it was different.

The man still had the same hardness, but now it seemed to Abe to be overlaid with a brutality that was at best casual and at worst considered.

"Want another helping, Abe?"

"No. Yeah, thanks. I will. Good meat."

"Better than rattler?"

"Yeah."

Trader nodded. "Better than the baked tongue of a baby puppy, Abe?"

"I guess so."

The older man lay down, staring up into the moving branches. "Better than... better than the earlobes of Mex virgins, slow-boiled and served on a bed of saffron rice with young peas and a cream and butter sauce?"

Abe laughed. "Can't recall ever eating a dish like that, Trader."

But there was no answering laugh from the other side of the fire. "I thought you was with us when we raided them horse thieves in Juarez, Abe."

"No. Don't believe I was, Trader. You mean you..." He picked his way through the potential mine field. "You telling me that you ate that food you said?"

This time Trader did laugh, throwing back his head and roaring out his merriment. "You triple-stupe sucker, Abe! Guess you fall for any dead trap I lay."

"Yeah," Abe agreed, wiping grease from his long mustache. "Figure I do."

THEY GOT AMBUSHED on the way to the lake. Two skinny old men, wearing a mix of rags and filthy furs, each carrying an incredibly antique flintlock pistol, stepped silently out behind them from the cover of a huge tumbled chestnut, taking Abe and Trader by surprise.

"Move them blasters and get to be dead," said the taller of the pair in a thin, reedy voice.

Trader had the Armalite across his shoulders, and Abe's big Python was holstered. In Deathlands you didn't look too much at the age or pedigree of the blaster that threatened you. The man or woman holding it was far more important. Both the ancients looked like they knew how to handle their pistols.

Abe and Trader turned slowly around, taking care not to make any sudden moves.

"Smelled your smoke a couple of days. Seen you got pretty blasters. Figured we'd have them." The muzzles of the flintlocks looked as big as railroad tunnels.

"Never met a man yet able to take my blaster away from me," Trader stated.

"But you ain't met Mick and Pat. We'll do that. Pat and Mick'll do it quick." He giggled at his little rhymes. "So you best lay the blasters down and then strip off them fancy clothes and you get to walk away."

"Yeah, two naked jaybirds danglin' off into the woods," Mick cackled. "Don't take too long to decide, strangers. Or old Liza here might bark at you. And we might think about takin' us some funnin' with you before you go."

Abe was waiting for Trader to make a move. He was as certain as he could be that the two old bastards would chill them the moment they put down their guns. They'd have done it from cover, but this way was safest of all. Trader himself used to say that when you killed someone you tried to get two hundred percent of the action on your side.

"Quick," warned the shorter of the pair.

They were only twenty feet or so apart. Safe range even for unreliable flintlocks.

"No," Trader said.

"How's that?"

"You deaf as well as stupe?"

Abe felt his balls struggling to climb back into his body with terror. Any second and the pistols would show him a burst of flame and black powder smoke.

"Lay them down, outlander, or—"

"Know who I am?"

"Don't give a midnight fuck with a flyin' squirrel, mister. Just know you're cold meat."

"They call me the Trader. Heard of me now? I got two war wags with fifty armed men and women within a mile of here. They know me and Abe are camped out in the hills here for a day or so, getting us some fresh air. They hear a shot and they'll ring the place. Give you a hard passing."

"He's bluffin', Pat."

"I reckon so, Mick."

But Abe could hear the doubt, riding herd on their voices. The initial boasting confidence had slithered away from them in twelve seconds of talk from Trader.

"Then do it." Trader spread his hands wide.

"I figure I *did* hear of the name of Trader, Mick. Around and about."

"He tellin' us the truth, stranger? You with the hair trickling down your chin?"

Abe nodded, swallowing hard. "You guys better believe it. I've ridden with Trader for fifteen years and never known him to call a bluff or tell a lie."

Now the doubt was so strong it might have been tattooed across the low, brutish foreheads.

"Easy to make a mistake. Damned shameful thing is to leap into eternity on account of a foolish moment." Trader's voice was low and intense, kindly and filled with honest trust. Now Abe saw the old Trader. Saw the man's unique power.

"Mebbe we'll let them go, Mick."

"Mebbe we can, Pat."

"Nobody gets hurt this way." Trader pointed at the flintlocks. "Those are beautiful blasters. Man like me could take them away from you, but I won't. Sun's shining and the day's filled with promise. Ease down on the hammers. Shake hands and we all go about our business and make believe that this is just a half-recalled memory of a midnight dream."

Abe thought it was like watching rabbits hypnotized by a weaving rattler.

The callused thumbs took the pressure off the ribbed hammers and let them slowly down to nestle snugly in the pans. The pistols were tucked into belts, and there was an instant relaxing and a surge of friendliness.

Mick stepped forward and shook hands with the Trader and Abe. "Sorry about the misunderstanding, Mr. Trader," he said. "Glad it got sorted."

"Sure," Trader agreed. "Sorry business to spoil a fine day with blood."

Pat shuffled his feet. "Me and my cousin here are sure glad we got the mistake sorted. So long, boys." He paused. "There's good beaver to be had up at the pool, yonder. Though I guess you likely know that already. So long."

"So long," Trader called as the two old men turned their backs and started to walk away from them, along the trail. They were ten yards off.

With unhurried, practiced ease, Trader unslung the Armalite and raised it to his right shoulder, winking sideways at Abe as he did so. He squeezed the trigger twice, the flat snap of the explosions muffled by the surrounding forest, putting a bullet through the back of each of the old men's skulls. The exiting full-metal-jacket rounds blew most of their faces into a mist of blood, bone and brains.

Trader looked across the clearing at the twitching corpses. "Like a couple of stupe rabbits," he said to Abe. "Let's get on. Day's wasting."

Chapter Six

"You sure you don't want to come along with us, Michael?" Dean was astride a little pinto pony.

The teenager was sitting on the swing seat, a foot trailing on the weathered boards. The baby dozed in his lap, wrapped in a swaddling patchwork blanket. "Guess not, Dean. Thanks. I'll stay here and play man of the house. Milk the horses and walk the pigs, or whatever it is. Look after Christina and Jenny. It's a tough job, but someone has to do it."

Over the past day and a half, Michael seemed to be making a serious effort to pull himself together.

He'd joined them at the table for all the meals, obviously trying to enter into the conversations and the plans for the hunt.

But the strain was clear.

There was a tightness across his cheeks, and the youth seemed to have lost a startling amount of weight since their arrival in old New Mexico, though he hadn't appeared to be eating any less than usual. Dean had told his father, a day earlier, that he'd seen Michael out behind the smallest barn, on his hands and knees, finger down his throat. He'd puked up the entire eggs-and-ham breakfast he'd just eaten.

Now Christina stood next to him, wiping her hands on her apron, a smear of flour on her right cheek.

"You don't want to make a real expedition of this?" Krysty called from the back of a speckled roan. "Could still take a picnic and all go."

Jak's wife smiled and shook her head. "You got a good day for it. Jenny'd slow you down some. No, we'll all three stay right here. Michael's got plenty of chores. Barn needs sweeping out and the hayloft could do with some attention. We'll work the day away while you people all play." But she still smiled as she said it.

Jak stood quietly by his midnight-black stallion. He handed the bridle over to J.B. and went to kiss his wife goodbye.

"See you later, dearest," he said.

They didn't embrace. There was that ease of love between them that generally comes to couples who've shared each other's company for many years. Jak kissed her once on the cheek, and she touched his face with her fingers.

"Come back safe, love."

"Will do. Bye."

Taking the reins back and swinging agilely up onto his mount's back, Jak kicked his heels into its flanks and moved off at a fast trot toward the nearby hills, the rest of the group trailing along after him at their best speed.

Ryan glanced back once.

It was a vision of perfect peace and happiness—a thread of smoke from Christina's cooking oven; Michael waving to them, the child asleep in his arms; the woman, taking off her apron to wave it over her head, stepping with a clumsy grace down the three wooden steps to the yard.

THEY WERE STRUNG OUT over a hundred yards, Jak leading, and Doc, on a raw-boned gray gelding bringing up the rear. Ryan allowed his own horse to fall back off the pace to accompany the old man for a while.

"Enjoying this, Doc?"

"Do you wish for the truth or for the diplomatic lie, my dear fellow?"

"I thought you'd done a fair bit of riding, Doc, way back in...in..."

"My past life? My idea of riding, Ryan, was a gentle canter along Rotten Row in London's Hyde Park on a well-schooled, broad-backed ambler, raising my bowler to the many elegant courtesans, admiring the fetching way they set their silver spurs into their spirited stallions, allowing my thoughts to wander away along rather forbidden lines, I fear." Doc grinned at the salacious memory. "Though my suspicions at the time were that every single one of the sporting chaps watching the pretty little fillies at exercise were fancying themselves prancing between their thighs.

"But you were a respectable married man, Doc. I'm shocked at you."

"I was shocked at myself, my dear Ryan. But as for this creature—" he slapped the horse on the neck "—I shall be damnably glad when we reach our destination and resort once more to the legs God gave us. Walking doesn't involve bouncing along on this articulated sawhorse of an animal."

"Be at the place Jak mentioned in about an hour, Doc. Can you hang on until then?"

"An hour is approximately fifty-nine minutes too long," Doc replied. "But I shall relish the pleasure of ceasing this painful mode of transport all the more when we stop."

THEY FINALLY STOPPED about an hour and a half later. Jak had led them upward on a winding trail that gave them a view across the scrub plain below, the gray dust vanishing away to the shimmering blur of the horizon. The house and the slant-roofed barns stood out, seeming to be surrounded by rectangles of finely ground emeralds, where the irrigation had brought fresh life to the desert.

Then the path wound higher, snaking around the flank of the mountain, rising higher, and taking them out of sight of the Lauren spread. The trails finally leveled out again in a clearing among some live oaks.

Doc swung his leg across the pommel and nearly fell as he reached the solid ground. "Praise the Lord and pass the ammunition," he said. "For this relief, much thanks."

All of the horses were tethered to a rawhide rope, stretched between two trees.

"How about Indians?" J.B. asked, slinging the scattergun across his shoulder.

"Lot of tribes," Jak replied. "Hopi, Zuni, Navaho, Mescalero and Chiricahua. Get on well with all. Christina tended sick Navaho kid few months back, and we gave failed hunting party young steer. They give furs and bring meat and fish. Know us. We know them."

"Wouldn't steal the horses?"

Jak shook his head at J.B.'s question. "No way. Renegade breeds and whites. Mex raiders. Heard about gang up toward Sangre de Cristo mountains."

"What sort of gang?" Ryan asked, tucking the weighted ends of his white silk scarf inside his coat.

"Wags, they say."

"War wags, Jak?"

"Sure, Ryan. But talk's talk out on frontier. Never seen no war wags all time down here."

"What sort of armored vehicles, Jak? We talking tanks or PAVs?"

The white hair blew in the fresh breeze. The red eyes turned toward the Armorer. "Told you, J.B., it's talk. Probably old truck with sheet of iron stuck up on it."

"How far to where we're going to get the deer, Jak?" Dean was carrying a single-shot homemade rifle that he'd been lent for the hunt, and he couldn't wait to get up into the higher country and use it.

"Hour. Bit more, bit less."

The weather was glorious, unsullied blue stretching from east to west and north to south. Jak knew the countryside around his spread like the back of his hand

and drew them higher, into the shadowed brush-lined canyons.

The late-morning air was still and sultry, making all seven of the companions sweat as they climbed upward between the stark walls of red rock.

"Christina loves it here," Jak said, pausing to allow Doc to catch them up. He laughed. "Said she'd like to be buried up here."

"It's a lovely place." Krysty sat down on a rounded boulder. "Wouldn't mind too much if I had to pass eternity here myself. Reserve me a spot, will you, Jak?"

"Sure. Just for family and friends."

"When do we get to the deer?" Dean asked, eager to get on with the hunt.

"Soon. Pass old Indian ruin, then trail gets out into open, above stream. Find them there."

"What kind of a ruin is it, Jak?" Mildred asked. "Anasazi?"

"Old ones. Heard called that, Mildred. Pueblo people. Like joined houses with small doors and windows, under overhang, farther up canyon."

"I have been fortunate to visit many of the great Anasazi ruins of the Colorado Plateau. The Three Mesas and Acoma, Chaco Canyon and the wonders of the great Pueblo Bonito." Doc sighed and wiped perspiration from his forehead.

Mildred nodded. "Don't forget that my minor was Native American Sociological Groupings. I forded Chinle Wash to look at the White House, back before they stuck those seriously ugly link fences all around them."

"I've seen a lot of those places, as well." Krysty sighed. "Sure is hot here in the canyon. Thing that surprises me is that they were mostly built around the year 1000, up to 1200, and loads of them still survive. Our cities were modern and strong, and should've lasted a million years. Yet they were all gone within a few sky dark days. Gone forever."

"How about the deer?" Dean asked plaintively. "We didn't climb up here to talk about old ruins."

"No," Doc said gently, "but it would be a vile heresy to pass such wonders by without at least the most cursory glance in their direction."

EVEN DEAN WAS SILENCED by the ruins. They were concealed beneath the lip of the cliff, the rock above stained by the countless cooking and heating fires. The sandstone was also discolored by the rain-leached desert varnish. The adobe was cracked in a few places, and one of the interior walls had collapsed. The site had obviously been carefully explored and excavated by professional archaeologists sometime, back before the long winters, and there were no potsherds or other human artifacts in the buildings.

The only evidence of occupation was a scattering of animal remains, mostly deer, but with some sheep and even a few horse and cattle bones.

"Cougar," J.B. guessed.

"Coyote?" Jak offered.

"No." The Armorer shook his head. "Coyote wouldn't climb this high. Not dragging haunches of a carcass behind it. Got to be something bigger."

Doc wandered from room to room, ducking to squeeze through the oddly narrow T-shaped doorways, his grizzled head protruding unexpectedly through dark windows.

"This is wonderful," he proclaimed. "Pure Anasazi. Look at the kiva down there. And another one farther along."

"What were they for, Doc?" Dean asked. "They look like sort of wells. Or some kind of storage rooms for wheat and olden-times stuff like that."

"No, dear boy. The kiva was the center of the religion for these ancient people. They believed, simplistically, that the underworld was literally that—existing just below our feet, like a dark mirror of our own universe, so they descended into the kiva for their spiritual ceremonies to be nearer to this other world. This is wonderful, Jak. But I confess some surprise that they have not been occupied."

The albino youth was sitting on a low, crumbling wall, looking bored. "Scared shitless, Doc. Ghosts of ancestors. Seen scratchings on walls. Spirits like Fluteplayer, Kokopela. Locals call themselves Dine. Just means sort of—"

"The People," Mildred said. "Lot of Native American tribes call themselves by their own name for 'the people.' I used to know them all once—"

"You still got your throwing knives, Jak?" Dean interrupted. "Haven't seen them."

"That's point, kid," Jak replied.

"Don't call me—" Dean began, stopping and grinning as he realized that he was being teased.

"If you can see knives, so can enemy. That's why I keep them hid."

"Still practice though?" J.B. asked. "Now you got the family?"

Jak looked around the site of the Anasazi ruins, pointing with a bloodless finger at one of the desiccated beams that supported a wall, about fifteen yards away. "See poison bug?"

They all looked, seeing the sickly yellow back with leprous silver spots across it, the barbed horns on the insect's head and the curved stinger, like a miniature scorpion. It was crawling slowly across the rectangular section of wood. From horns to tail it was less than an inch long, though capable of giving a painful wound from its hooked sting.

While they were all looking at the bug, there was a blur of movement from the albino teenager. His wrist snapped, there was a whirring sound like a diving hornet and a thunk as the needle point of the leaf-bladed throwing knife buried itself in the oak beam, clean through the middle of the poisonous insect's soft body, killing it instantly.

A tiny trickle of colorless liquid seeped from the twitching corpse.

"Holy shit!" Dean breathed.

"Good," J.B. said. "See you keep your hand in."

RYAN DID THE SHOOTING. The powerful 7.62 mm round from the Steyr SSG-70 made short work of a couple of young deer, picking them off from the outside of a small herd that Jak had tracked down. The animals had gathered around a shady pond, near the head of a narrow box canyon. Ryan had used the laser image enhancer to select his prey, working the bolt action with fluid ease.

The first animal went down to a brain shot, and the rest of the deer froze for a vital moment. The second round was a direct hit through the spinal cord, clean and finite.

They quickly gutted the dead animals, the blood steaming on the ground.

It was a little after one o'clock in the afternoon.

Jak had brought along poles and cord, making it easy to string up the two limp, lolling carcasses and take turns in bringing them back down the mountainside, toward where the horses were tethered.

They had passed the Indian ruins, with Krysty leading the way, when the fire-haired woman stopped, putting her hand to her mouth, her eyes glazing in the shock of "seeing."

"No," she whispered. "Oh, Gaia, no!"

Chapter Seven

Ryan was carrying the end of one of the poles that supported the smaller of the deer carcasses. He stood close behind Krysty when she stopped dead in her tracks, and he instantly lowered the carcass to the dirt and went to her.

"What?" he said, unable to conceal his own shock at the horror etched on her face.

Krysty turned slowly to stare at Ryan, her eyes blank, as though she didn't even recognize him. "What did you say, lover? Sorry, didn't hear properly."

"You've seen something?"

"I thought for a moment.... It was like someone projecting a lantern slide on a sheet, right inside my skull. Picture of a bloody skull and raw bones."

"Who?"

The others had all gathered around, the bodies of the animals already attracting the attention of a number of greeny-blue blowflies.

Ryan repeated his question, laying a gentle hand on Krysty's shoulder. "Who did you see, lover?"

"I can see you, Ryan. And there's your little boy, Dean. Good old Doc. Mildred and J.B., together. And—" she paused as her emerald eyes hesitated on

Jak's bone-white face "—and someone else," she finished, haltingly.

"I'm Jak," he said. "You know me, Krysty. Known me ages. Known me years."

"Oh, this is... It's awful. Death and corruption!" Her voice was raised, close to a scream.

Mildred stepped in and gestured for Ryan to move away. "Sit down, Krysty. Could be the heat's got to you. Just sit down and take a short rest for a—"

Krysty jerked violently away from the woman. "Don't touch me! I know what I saw. It was Death. Dark rider on his dark horse. Ring of bones around his waist. Eye sockets brimming with maggots. Mouth open and a tongue like burnished copper. Teeth like spilled tombstones."

Jak looked around uncertainly. "You ever known her wrong in seeing, Ryan?"

"No. But...but she sort of feels danger or a threat. Generally can't say exactly when or where it comes from."

Krysty arched her back, so that her face was looking directly toward the bright sky. Her burning hair tumbled back off her shoulders, like spilled lava.

"'When the Lamb brake the seventh seal, there was a great silence in the heavens for about the space of one half hour. And I saw the seven angels that standeth before the Lord God Almighty and to them were given seven trumpets.'"

"It's the Book of Revelations, from the Bible," Doc said.

" 'The first angel made the trumpet to sound and there fell hail and fire, mingled with blood. And they were thrown down upon the earth. And the third part of all the forests were burned and the green grass shriveled and dried.' "

"Ryan?" Mildred looked at him. "It's like she's become possessed."

"I know. But I don't know what the fuck to do about it, Mildred."

" 'The second angel sounded and the blazing mountain was cast into the deeps of the ocean and one-third part of all the waters became as blood.' "

Jak punched his right fist hard into his left hand. "Come on. We best get back. Leave venison. If all right, can come back for it later."

Krysty swayed from side to side, barely retaining her balance, as though she alone could hear the far-off sound of weak piping and a little drum.

" 'The third angel sounded and...and there fell a great star from the heavens, blazing as though it were the heart of fire. It fell upon the third part of all rivers and fountains. The name of that star is called Wormwood.' "

Her eyes rolled up, white in the sockets, and she stiffened and fell straight back into the waiting arms of Doc, who caught her and laid her very gently on the ground. "By the Three Kennedys, I think that the poor lady has been overtaken by some sort of a fit."

Jak had started to walk toward the tethered horses, a couple of hundred yards farther down the narrow canyon. But he stopped as Krysty dropped like a board, calling out, "She all right?"

Nobody answered him.

Mildred had knelt immediately by Krysty, putting a finger against her neck to check the pulse, peeling back an eyelid. She looked up at Ryan after a few moments. "She's all right, I think. More or less a faint."

Krysty's eyes opened and she gazed blindly at the circle of faces above her. "Everyone is here," she said doubtfully. "Then it was wrong what I thought I... Where's Michael?"

"Back at the ranch with Christina and little Jenny," Ryan replied.

"The ranch," Krysty said slowly. "We should get back there, fast as we can."

Jak had rejoined them again. "What you see, Krysty? Trouble at home?"

"Yeah. But it's fogged. All kinds of people and all sorts of things happening. Just can't see clear at all. But I think we should get going."

"Come on!" Jak shouted over his shoulder, running down the slope, his feet kicking up great swimming clouds of vermilion sand behind him. His white hair flowed behind him like a banner of war.

"Yeah," Ryan agreed. "Mildred, you and Doc help Krysty. J.B. and Dean, with me."

He'd lived long enough with Krysty Wroth to be sure that her strange, almost-mutie power was rarely wrong. It often lacked a sharp focus, failing to point out precisely where a danger might be. But if she thought there was something wrong at the ranch, then Ryan knew, with a sickly certainty, that she was likely to be correct.

Jak was already in the saddle by the time Dean, fastest over a short distance, joined him. Ryan and J.B. were only a few paces behind.

"Hold on, Jak!" Ryan shouted. "If there's trouble, then four of us are better than one."

"Quick, then!" He jerked so hard on the reins that his mount whinnied in shock and reared up onto its hind legs, pawing at the air.

They all spurred together, stirrup to stirrup, moving down the trail at full gallop. Ryan wasn't the best rider in Deathlands, and his heart was in his mouth as they charged toward the open plain, knowing that if one of the horses put a hoof wrong or rolled over a boulder, then they'd all go clattering down together in a tangle of broken bones.

But the gods favored them.

Gradually more and more of the limitless desert opened before them. The canyon walls gave way, and the trail grew wider.

Being an albino, Jak found bright light difficult to cope with, though he saw excellently in dusk or darkness. But he was still the first to spot the band of horsemen, eight or ten miles away from them, moving toward the south, surrounded by a veil of roiling gray dust.

"Look." He reined in, standing up and shading his ruby eyes with his ivory hand.

They all stopped their mounts and looked down. There seemed to be about twenty or so in the group, riding at a good speed. Ryan and the other three were still about a thousand feet higher than the strangers four miles from the ranch.

It was only guesswork, but it certainly looked as if the horsemen were going directly away from the Lauren spread.

"You make them out?" Jak asked. "Way they ride I figure them Navaho."

"Could be," Ryan agreed cautiously.

"No sign of a fire or nothing bad at the house." Dean's horse was almost beyond the boy's control, whirling around and around, stamping its hooves, kicking up a spray of sparks from the bedrock beneath it.

"No sign of Christina or Michael, either," J.B. added. "Nobody."

Behind them they could hear their friends' horses, coming closer.

"No point in going off like a bat out of hell, now, Jak," Ryan warned.

The teenager swallowed hard, taking in several long, slow breaths. Nodding. "True, Ryan."

They allowed the other three to catch up with them. Krysty had been swaying in the saddle, her face almost as pale as Jak's. Ryan rode alongside her at an easy canter, ready to reach out a supportive arm if needed.

"I'm feeling better, lover," she said.

"Sure?"

"Yeah. Who are those riders we saw from higher up in the foothills?"

"Mebbe Navaho. Were they the trouble you saw?"

"Can't tell."

They were now roughly a mile away from the farm.

Ryan scanned the area, hoping against hope that he might catch a glimpse of Christina, or Michael, standing shy and silent in the shadows, possibly holding little Jenny in his arms.

But there was nothing.

And nobody.

"Dead animals," Dean said, riding close to his father.

"Where?"

"By the small barn." He pointed with his right hand, nearly dropping the reins as he did so.

The rest of the horses were gathered in a tight nervous group at the back of the corral.

"Three cows missing and some pigs," Jak commented. "Dead ones are goat and two sheep. Lotta blood there."

Without a word being said, they all reined in at almost exactly the same moment, about two hundred yards from the house.

There was a stillness in the afternoon. The horsemen had vanished away south, though the pillar of dust that marked their passing could still just be seen. Off behind them, in the foothills, Ryan glimpsed again the snowy egret that he'd noticed around the area since they'd arrived there a few days earlier. The sun was sinking slowly in the west, and the sky was still totally clear of any clouds.

Krysty caught Ryan's eye and made a slight, imperceptible movement of the head. He nodded, knowing what she was telling him, knowing it himself.

The stillness told its own story.

"Christina!"

Jak's voice made all the saddle horses start, Dean nearly losing his seat and falling to the dirt. The cry echoed off to the mountains, coming back to them, the last syllable, "Tina," rolling back and forth until it had faded once more into the stillness.

"We going in, Ryan?"

"Guess so, Jak."

"Hold a perimeter?" J.B. asked, but the flatness in his voice answered himself, even before Ryan said anything.

"Don't figure there's any point, do you? Whatever's happened here has happened. Done." Ryan slid down and looped the reins of his horse over the picket fence that bordered the neat orchard.

One by one, they all dismounted. Jak stayed last in the saddle, as though he were single-handedly holding off the bad news that lay around them. The air seemed to taste of the bitterness of hot iron.

"Want us to go in first, Jak?" Ryan suggested as gently as he could.

"My house. My wife. My baby."

"Sure."

"They could have got away when they saw trouble coming," Mildred suggested.

Jak shook his head, his face cold and calm. "Nice idea. But doubt it."

In the corral, one of the horses snickered. A door in the hayloft of the largest barn blew a few inches open, then closed again.

"Best get it right." J.B. looked around at the others. "Go to double red. Blasters out and cocked."

Ryan went to the right, around the house, followed by Krysty and Dean. J.B. led Mildred to the left. Jak chose to go straight on in, onto the porch and through the open front door.

Christina Lauren was in the kitchen.

Chapter Eight

Christina had died hard. Her dress was torn across the shoulder, revealing her breasts, and her skirt was around her waist, her thighs showing the bruises and the other sickly evidence of how she'd been used. Krysty stooped and pulled down the thin gingham material, covering the woman's nakedness. She then took a cloth off the table and laid it over the woman's chest and head.

Her face was severely bruised, blood clotted around the mouth and nose. More blood seeped from both ears, indicative of an injury to the head. Both her wrists were badly broken. Her left eye was swollen shut, the other staring blankly up at the low ceiling of the kitchen. A crimsoned knife lay in the corner of the room, its tip snapped off.

"She did some damage," J.B. said quietly. "There's far more blood around than came from her. She wasn't stabbed." He bent and reached under the towel. "Looks like someone in heavy combat boots kicked in the back of her head, after they'd..." The sentence trailed uneasily away into the silence.

"You reckon she killed some of those Navaho?" Dean asked.

"Likely," J.B. replied. "There's a trail of blood into the other room, soaked into the floor. Then it's smeared, like someone was dragged away."

Jak had said nothing since they entered the charnel house. He stood by the stove, idly brushing crumbs from its black iron top. His face was totally without emotion, drained of all life.

"Jenny?" Mildred queried.

The thought of the baby had been on everyone's mind since finding Christina's corpse.

Ryan coughed, clearing his throat. "Doubt she'll be too far away."

"Is it beyond the bounds of possibility that young Michael might have escaped with her?" Doc asked.

Nobody answered.

It was all too obvious that the killers had been in the home for some time, with the leisure to take their pleasure with the helpless woman.

So, where was Michael Brother? The only realistic answer was that he was dead, his stiffening body lying somewhere around the spread.

"How come they left the way they did?" Krysty asked. "They didn't break anything or start a fire or steal food. Just butchered some stock."

"They saw us coming," Dean said.

Krysty shook her head. "No, they didn't. When we first spotted the riders, they were well off the spread. It's like something interrupted them."

"Michael?" J.B. suggested. "Then where is he? He must be somewhere close by. He'd have seen us ride in."

Once again they heard the loose door on the barn banging in the light breeze.

"Find Jenny's body," Jak said. The first time he'd spoken.

THE SEARCH didn't take long. Jak himself found the pathetic bundle of crimsoned rags, lying at the base of the wall of the feed barn. At about the height of a man's shoulders, there was a dark patch on the wooden planks, dried blood and a sickening trickle of brains, with a few hairs stuck in it. Splinters of bone gleamed like metal in the late-afternoon sun.

He stooped over it, head bowed, saying nothing. The rest of the friends stood in a half circle. It wasn't a time for words. Dean was the only one to speak, hissing between his teeth, "Bastards! Little girl like that!"

Finally Jak put his hands beneath his daughter and lifted her up, tenderly arranging the sodden blanket around her.

"Didn't have to do that, did they?" he whispered.

They didn't look for Michael. Not then.

The important thing was to be there for Jak. They followed him slowly back into the house, into the cool, airy living room, where he sat down on the long sofa, still cradling the little corpse on his lap.

"Jak?" Krysty said.

"What is it?" The voice was like ice water over obsidian.

"There are things to be done for Christina and for Jenny. Will you let Mildred and me help you?"

"Why not? Won't make difference. Not now. Should've been here."

Mildred sat by him, putting a hand on his arm. "That's the road of madness, Jak," she said softly. "Blame won't bring them back. But it'll suck you into the pit of desolation. You did nothing wrong. Nobody did. Just that you can't anticipate when evil and chaos are going to slink out of their holes."

He nodded, his stark white hair drooping and covering his face. "Yeah," he said flatly.

Krysty glanced at Ryan and the other men. "Want to go look around outside?"

"We can wait here," J.B. replied. "No hurry. What's done's done."

Mildred looked at him. "John, go outside and take some time. We have things to do in here, with Jak. It wouldn't be proper for all of you to be here."

"Oh, yeah. Sure."

Led by Dean, they went out onto the porch.

DOC AND THE BOY sat quietly together on the swing seat, both deeply shocked by the unexpected horror of their return to the spread.

Ryan walked out into the crimson light of the sun, beckoning J.B. to join him.

"Something not right," he said.

"Krysty saw it," J.B. agreed. "If it was those Navaho, then I don't believe they'd have just up and ridden away like that. Not with the rest of the horses and stock still here. They'd take it all."

"They could have had someone on watch who saw us coming back."

The Armorer shook his head. "Don't think so. We would've seen him breaking to join the others. No, the timing's all wrong on this one, Ryan."

"We take a look around?"

"Sure."

They moved out in opposite directions, working their way toward the edge of the spread. It only took a couple of minutes to start finding tracks that told a very different story.

Ryan and J.B. stood together, near the main gate onto the property, looking down at the soft, churned-up earth.

"Unshod ponies," the one-eyed man stated. "That'll be the band of horsemen we saw."

"Sure. But their trail's on top of whoever came to the spread earlier. Likely the ones that did the killings and butchered the animals."

"Then the Navaho came along and interrupted them, and they vanished, while we were still working our way down the canyon out of sight of here."

J.B. stooped. "Two wags. Broad tires. Look to me like the marks of something like the old LAV-25s. Designed to carry a crew of three, but they could easily be adapted to carry a dozen or more."

"Definitely two?"

"For sure. See here." He pointed with his scattergun. "They overlap."

There were clear marks of two wags, looking like the eight-wheeler light armored vehicles that J.B. had suggested. Ryan straightened and stared around.

"Two wags come in. Christina sees trouble, but for some reason it's too late for her to do anything. Mebbe she was cooking and didn't hear them."

J.B. sighed. "They chill the baby. Rape and chill Christina. Start slaughtering some of the stock to take along for food supplies and then someone spots the horsemen coming. They would've been visible a ways off. Then, everybody leaves and we arrive. That the way you read it?"

"Guess so. Leaves one question without an answer."

"Michael?"

"Yeah. Where's Michael?"

The only answer was that the teenager was gone.

They both knew that there was no point in undertaking a close search of the spread and all the outbuildings. There were only three possibilities, and one of those wasn't all that likely.

His body lay somewhere close to the ranch. It only took Ryan and J.B. about twenty minutes to confirm that there were only the two corpses there. Christina and the little girl. A glance into each of the barns showed no sign of life.

Or of death.

The attackers could have taken him as a prisoner, bundling him into one of their vehicles.

"Don't reckon that," J.B. said. "Apart from the tracks of the wags there's plenty of combat boot marks around the place. Looks to me like the Navaho simply rode on by without dismounting or even hesitating. Knew who they were chasing. No other sign of bare feet or moccasins anywhere."

"So, we agree that he might have seen danger coming. Realized he was way, way outmatched and took a runner. Hiding in the hills."

The Armorer looked down at his own feet, considering what Ryan had said. "Way I see it, there's only one thing wrong with that third option."

"What?"

"By now he'd have seen us and come out to join us. He hasn't, so where the dark night is he?"

"I suppose that there's just an outside chance that the lad could've taken one of the horses and gone off after the killers. Before the Indians got here." Ryan shook his head. "I don't know. He's gotta be someplace."

WHEN THEY RETURNED from their recce, the evening sun was almost gone. The shadows of the house and the barns stretched out, stark and black against the pale earth, reaching their way toward the foothills to the east of the property.

Helped by Mildred and Krysty, Jak had finished the melancholy task of washing and laying out the stiffening bodies of his wife and firstborn child. They now rested together in the big double bed, covered with a faded patchwork quilt.

Christina's hair had been washed and brushed, and it fanned out across her shoulders. Jak had insisted that she should be dressed in her favorite nightdress.

"Was her gran's," he said matter-of-factly. "Goes back almost to long winters."

It was bleached cotton, with a high scalloped neck, embroidered around the bodice with posies of tiny flowers.

Her face had been cleared of the blood and the smudge of flour, but nothing could be done about the bruising on the cheek and close to the eyes.

Jenny lay in her arms.

Jak had found a lace bonnet that concealed the soft, dark dent in the tiny skull. Her eyes were closed, her cheeks and hair clean, as if she'd just come from her evening bath. Ryan thought that it looked like the baby could've woken up at any moment, demanding a feeding.

Krysty had pulled the curtains halfway across the windows that faced south, leaving the bedroom in a muted, dusky light, like a cavern beneath the ocean.

Everyone stood in a circle around the bed, nobody quite knowing what to say. It was Doc who finally, hesitantly, broke the long silence.

"What next?"

Jak turned to face him. The sun was deep crimson, and it burned into the veil of his white hair, making it look like a fall of living fire.

"Next, Doc? Next we bury them. Tomorrow. Dawn. In canyon where we were today. Next we go after killers. Next we chill them all. Next after that? I don't know."

The bedroom had become still again. The evening breeze tugged at the curtains, rattling the lock on the loose-fitting rear door to the room.

"Best we go out now and leave them here together, Jak," Krysty said softly.

He nodded. "Sure. Getting dark. Light lamps. Also, cook supper. Bad at details. Christina is so good. No. Not now. She *was* so good at things. Don't know how..."

For the first time he seemed on the edge of tears and wiped angrily at his eyes, turning on his heel and leaving the bedroom and the two corpses.

The rest of them followed him out, Ryan last, closing the inner door gently behind him.

MILDRED AND J.B. COOKED some eggs and beans, with a mess of pan-fried potatoes, though it turned out that nobody felt all that hungry.

"I'll do the washing up," Dean offered.

"Give a hand," Jak said. "Something to do. Put pot on for coffee as well."

Ryan pushed his chair back from the dining table and decided on an impulse to check the bedroom, where Jak had lit two brass oil lamps, turning both of the wicks down to leave a faint, golden glow.

"You going out back?" J.B. asked.

"No. Just sort of felt like looking in on them. Mebbe sit a while."

Krysty nodded her agreement. "Think I might join you in a while, lover. Just get these supper things tidied away first."

As he stepped into the room he saw a dim shape, making him reach instantly for the holstered SIG-Sauer.

Then he saw who it was—Michael, kneeling silently on the floor like a man at prayer, resting his head and arms on the side of the large oak double bed.

Chapter Nine

Ryan's first, instinctive reaction was to think that the teenager was dead.

"Michael?" he said very quietly, so that none of the others in the adjacent room heard him.

There was no reply. But now, with his good eye adjusting to the sepulchral gloom, Ryan was able to see that the young man was alive, his broad shoulders moving in time with the slow, regular breathing.

"Michael?"

From the dining room he heard Jak's voice, whose own hearing was unnaturally sharp. "Ryan? Who you talking to?"

The figure on the floor by the bed still hadn't stirred or made a sound, causing Ryan to wonder if he was asleep.

Jak walked softly into the room, and Ryan turned to look at him, the yellowish light illuminating the narrow, lean face.

"That Michael?"

Ryan nodded. "Yeah, it is. He must've come in through the door at the back."

"He all right?"

"Can't tell. He hasn't said a thing. Just kneeling there."

Ryan turned back toward the bed. "Michael, where've you been?"

Finally the shadowy figure stirred, the white face angling toward them. The eyes were black pits in the ivory mask.

"Been in the barn."

"The barn. Which one?"

"Big one."

"Hayloft?" Jak asked, moving a couple of steps closer to Michael.

"Yeah. Under the hay."

"You injured?" Ryan also walked nearer to the teenager. "Shot or anything?"

"No." The voice was so muffled that Ryan and Jak couldn't even be sure of what he'd said.

"What?"

"No," he said, louder.

Loud enough to attract the attention of the others, who suddenly filled the doorway to the bedroom.

"Is that young Michael that I see there?" Doc asked, as a rectangle of brighter light spilled across the carpet from the dining room.

"Yeah," Ryan replied. "Michael. Get up and come in the other room, so we can talk properly."

"No."

"What?"

"No."

"Why?"

"Stay here."

Ryan laid a hand on the young man's shoulder, making him flinch as though he'd been touched by a white-hot branding iron. "You can't stay in here, Michael."

"It's all I want, Ryan."

His voice sounded like it was made from tempered steel, stretched thin and taut.

Mildred joined Ryan by the side of the teenager. "Be better if you come out. Have something to eat and drink. You must be hungry and thirsty, Michael."

"No."

"Not thirsty? Got some well water in a crystal pitcher on the table there. Frosted and cold. That sound good to you? Must be an age since you had something to drink. How long is it, Michael, since you drank?"

"Morning. No, it was lunch. Had some apple juice then. Bread and cheese."

"You'd been working in the barn, hadn't you? That's what you said when we left."

"Yeah. Went back after a meal."

"And you were there when it all happened?"

Michael nodded. Suddenly he levered himself upright by his hands on the bed, standing and looking straight at the friends with something that lay halfway between fear and defiance.

Jak moved too fast for anyone to stop him, grabbing Michael by the throat, like a terrier with a rat. It crossed Ryan's mind that Michael, normally, would have had the heightened combat reflexes to stop anyone, even someone as lightning-quick as Jak Lauren. But it was all too obvious that things weren't normal.

"What fuck happened?" Jak demanded.

His fingers were tightening, and Michael's face was suffused with blood, his eyes wide, his mouth sagging open. But he never even lifted a hand to try to protect himself from the albino's murderous attack.

"Let him go, Jak," Ryan said. "Let him go right now, or I'll have to make you."

"He knows it all." Jak relaxed his grip a fraction, allowing the other young man to draw in a shuddering breath. "Knows it all and'll tell it all."

"Not if you throttle him, Jak." Mildred spoke briskly, as though she were addressing a stubborn child. "Just let him go and we can all go into the parlor. Michael can have a good long drink of cool water, then we can sit down and let him quietly tell us what went down here." Jak let go so suddenly that Michael stumbled and would have fallen if it hadn't been for Mildred's steadying hand.

"Good, Mildred," J.B. said quietly. He'd drawn a knife ready to stop Jak from chilling Michael, but now he was able to sheathe it again.

Ryan was last out of the bedroom. He slowly eased the door shut, glancing behind him at the two figures lying motionless on the bed.

"Not all way, Ryan," Jak said. "Leave bit open."

MICHAEL DRAINED the glass of water in a single gulp, wordlessly holding it out for a refill, finishing that one off nearly as quickly.

"Want another."

J.B. shook his head. "Make you puke. Shock of cold water on an empty stomach. Wait a few minutes and let that settle."

"Sure."

The room fell silent.

Jak was sitting by a small side table, with Mildred between J.B. and Doc on the faded brocade sofa. Dean was on the floor, his back against the wall, to the right of the long window. Krysty had one of the deep, comfortable armchairs, her legs crossed. Ryan was next to her, leaning forward, his chin in his hands.

Michael was in the last of the big chairs, sitting slumped, head down, staring at the pattern on the rug.

Jak broke the quiet. "Come on. We know some what happened. Don't know who or why or when. Don't know lots, Michael. You can tell."

"Yeah. I can tell, all right."

"Then let's hear it, Michael." Ryan steepled his fingers. "From the start."

"Jenny was a bit feverish around the middle of the day. Christina gave her a bath out back in the tub. She loved that. Played with her wooden duck and the carved piglet. Cheered her up. Then, I went back to working in the hayloft and Christina put Jenny to bed in her room."

"What did Chris do then?"

"Don't know, Jak. I was hot and sweaty and covered in bits of chaff. Got everywhere. Stuck to my skin and made it itch. In my eyes and nose and mouth."

He stopped and looked at the empty glass on the floor. Dean saw the movement and scooted across to pick it up. He left the room and returned with it filled once more to the brim with the cool well water.

"Thanks." He swallowed slowly.

Ryan watched him closely. Whatever had happened during the afternoon, it had left deep scars in Michael's soul, a soul that was already spiritually challenged by all the experiences of the past few months.

The hands holding the glass were trembling, and the deep-set brown eyes skittered all around the room, looking everywhere, but studiously avoiding anyone else's face. The teenager looked thinner, with a strained, dark intensity that revealed more of his quarter-Crow background.

"Go on." Jak was like a statue, his head and body motionless, his red eyes not moving from Michael's face.

"Saw the bath of water still there in the yard. Tormented me. Like Our Savior in the wilderness for forty days and nights, when Satan came to tempt him. Tempt him away from what was right and leave him to wallow in the mire of sloth and cowardice and self-preservation."

"But Jesus resisted the temptations, didn't he, Michael?" Mildred asked.

He ignored her, sipping more of the water, some of it dribbling over his stubbled chin and down onto his black denim shirt. He sniffed and wiped his sleeve across his mouth.

"I left the barn and stripped off this shirt. Washed the dust and stuff off of me. Christina saw me from the kitchen window and came out with some lemonade. It was real good. She was baking some cherry pies."

Krysty glanced at Ryan. "They took them, as well," she said quietly.

"Gave me a pie, fresh out of the oven. It burned my fingers, but it was good. Sweet, hot and good." He leaned back and closed his eyes for a moment. "Feel weary to the bone."

"Keep going." Jak opened his mouth as if he were going to say more, then caught Ryan's eye and closed it again.

"Must rest soon."

"Be able to go to bed after you've finished telling us the story."

"Sure, Ryan. It's not truly sleep that I want. Just to rest for a while. Did I say the cherry pie burned my fingers? It did. Dipped them in the tub to cool them. I was just walking back toward the barn when I saw—"

"Saw what?" J.B. asked, leaning toward the young man.

"Dust. Two lots. One was north. A long, long way off. It was the Navaho." He looked up, seeing bewilderment on everyone's face. "Oh, I didn't know then it was them. Saw them . . . later. Yeah. Later."

"Who else did you see?" Ryan was becoming more and more concerned for Michael's mental well-being. His mind seemed to be somehow slipping sideways, making it difficult for him to focus on things, hard to stick to a coherent, chronological account of the facts.

"More dust. Closer. Lots closer. Could just about hear the engines."

"More than one engine?"

"Sure, J.B., there were two of them. Painted like in camouflage colors. Sort of small tanks."

"Big blasters? Like cannon?"

Michael shook his head. "No. Machine guns."

"Tracks or wheels?"

"They had . . . wheels."

"How many?"

"Three, I think. Or . . . no, they had four wheels. I mean, each side. Big wheels."

"Sounds like LAV-25s," J.B. said to Ryan. "Like we thought."

"They each had about a dozen men."

Jak snapped his fingers. "No. Go back some. Before they arrived. What did you do? What did Christina do?"

"Confused now." The young man buried his face in his hands. Everyone waited.

Jak half rose from his chair, but Ryan waved a warning finger at him and he sat down again.

"Take your time," Krysty said.

"Two lots of dust. Right. Remember that all right. Wondered if one of them might be you coming back from a different direction. Called out and told Christina."

"What did she do?" Ryan got no answer to his question. "What did she do, Michael?"

"Came out. Wiped her hands on a towel. There was that white mark on her cheek from the morning baking. Or, it might have been a different one. How could you tell? Nobody to ask. I think it was likely the same one."

"Doesn't fucking matter! Get on with fucking story!"

"Sorry, Jak. God, you just can't believe how sorry I am about all this. Sorry for you most of all." With a visible effort, Michael pulled himself together. "Christina saw the dust. Not sure she saw the distant one. The Navaho. It didn't worry her. She wasn't frightened or anything." His voice rose. "If she'd been scared, then it would all... I wouldn't have been... But she didn't seem at all worried. Said it was probably packmen or just travelers. Said you got folk moving west every now and again. Said it was like the old settlers."

"What did you do after you both saw the columns of dust, Michael? Did Christina tell you to do anything at all? Get blasters or anything like that?"

"No, Ryan. Nothing like that. Been different if... Spilled milk. There was milk spilled in the kitchen, I saw it. Big pool of spilled milk. I didn't cry over it."

J.B. was close to losing his struggle for self-control. The anger bit into his words. "She said not to worry. So, what did you do then?"

"I went back to the barn. I'd had a wash and the lemonade. Went back to work in the big barn."

Michael cleared his throat. "I heard trucks coming. Sounded like quite big rigs. Sometimes I saw them going past the highway below Nil-Vanity when I lived there. I didn't take much notice. That was because of what Christina said to me." He looked for the first time directly into Jak's set face. "If she hadn't said about not worrying, then—"

"Go on, Michael," Ryan urged.

"They stopped and the engines cut out. That was the first time I actually looked through the hayloft door. And I saw that something was wrong."

Now the teenager was coming to it, getting to the very core of it.

"There were men with guns."

"What kind of blaster?"

"I don't fucking know, do I, J.B.? What they call assault rifles, I think. All the same. I counted eighteen men and a couple of women. All in uniform."

"Uniform?" Mildred queried. "You mean like regular soldiers?"

"Yeah. They were real well disciplined. Oh, their uniforms were black or very dark blue. With a red stripe down the pants. Berets. Black combat boots. They fanned out immediately in a... What's the word I want?"

"Defensive perimeter," J.B. stated.

Michael nodded. "That's it. Like everyone knew what they were supposed to be doing. I thought a lot of them looked kind of like Mexicans. Mustaches and black hair. I'm sure the General was Mexican."

"The General?" Jak stood. "You telling me this was done by General?"

Ryan interrupted. "Jak, you know something we don't. Tell us about the General. Short and quick."

"Didn't believe in him. Stories. Raids on small villes. Mainly Navaho, Apache and Hopi. Came in after pueblos and took food and women. What he wanted. Like soldiers."

"Go on, Michael."

"Sure, Ryan. Not really much more to tell you. This General got out last. Loads of gold braid. Peaked cap. Tall, burly man. Looked very much in command. Christina had come out on the porch, and there was some talk. Couldn't hear it. I was too far away. She went in the house with the General and about five of the men. Rest spread out and started a search. And some of them butchered some animals. I heard the noise, but I didn't see it. I was hiding in the hay. Didn't see much else."

Ryan could visualize the scene. The disabled woman had been taken by surprise, faced with an armed military gang of renegades. She must have hoped to talk her way clear.

But it hadn't been enough.

Dean coughed. "Michael?"

"Yeah?"

"How do you know he was called the General?"

"Heard his men talking about him when they came in the barn. They weren't bothering to search too hard, like they already knew there was nothing to worry about."

Krysty was sitting forward, on the edge of the seat. "You reckon that Christina didn't tell them that you were around the place?"

"Don't think she did, or they'd have been searching properly. They didn't even come into the hayloft."

"So, you had .38 and could've gone down without being seen?"

"Sure, Jak. But I didn't have any spare ammo. Just the six rounds in the gun. And I'm not a shootist. There were twenty or more of them, with rifles and machine guns and stuff." His voice rose two octaves. "I couldn't have done a fucking thing to help them! Can't you see that?"

Jak stood, fists clenched, staring at Michael. "Can't see that. No, can't see that. See you hiding in hayloft. Christina raped and chilled. Jenny hurled against barn wall, brains everyplace. I see that!"

"Let's try and keep calm," Ryan said, also standing up and placing himself between the two teenagers. "What's happened is over and down the pike. We need to know all we can so we can decide what to do and how best to do it."

"Sure." Jak's voice was flooded with a bitter anger. "Sure. Any more to tell, Michael?"

"I hid and waited."

"Waited while—"

"Jak!" Ryan's voice cut across the room like a lash of a whip. "This isn't the way. You know it and I know it. Michael isn't a born fighter like you and me. Deathlands is a strange and deadly place to him. You know how we all feel for you. For what happened. But taking it out on Michael does nothing to change things."

"Yeah, Ryan. You told me Trader said that talk's cheap and action costs."

"Right." He sighed. "Michael, let's finish this. You see or hear anything else?"

"Nothing for a bit. Not a sound from Christina. She must've kept real quiet while... Then they found Jenny. Heard her cry. Just the once. That was when I think Christina knifed one of them. Maybe two of them. Saw a lot of blood, and I squinted through the gap in the door. Saw the soldiers carrying what looked like a body. Thought one more might've been wounded but I couldn't see properly."

"After that?" J.B. asked. "No clue about where they were going?"

"They headed south." Michael reached for his glass and found that it was empty. He glanced at Dean, who deliberately ignored him. "I saw that. Someone shouted there was horsemen coming. That was the Navaho. I think that the General must've raided an Indian camp, and that this was a revenge party, hunting them down. Couple of the men wanted to stay and fight them. Said they got massive firepower over them. Blaster advantage that would have chilled them. But the General came out of the house buttoning up his... his pants. Ordered them to withdraw."

"The Indians go into the house at all?" Mildred asked.

"No. I watched the soldiers get back in their wags with their butchered meat. Drove off fast. The horsemen came in, past the corral. Sort of rode around a couple of minutes, shouting and arguing with one another. Then they just went off, fast toward the south, after the armored trucks. And I waited and waited."

"Scared?" Jak asked with a sneer. "Too scared to come see what happened to wife and baby?"

"I figured that they were both dead."

"Sure. You figured that out and stayed in hayloft, shitting your pants."

Krysty stood. "Gaia! This is enough, Jak. Michael was alone, with a 6-shot handblaster. It doesn't matter how angry and upset you are, you have to believe that there would have been nothing that he could have done. Nobody on earth could have saved Christina and little Jenny. Nobody."

"No!" Michael's cry was torn from the deeps of his soul. "That's fucking shit, Krysty! I could have come down and chilled as many as I could of the bastards."

"And then died," Ryan said quietly.

"Better. Better than this. Better than sitting back while someone you... you cared for gets murdered. And a helpless baby! Jak's right in his contempt and his anger.'' Michael started to cry. ''It's against my being a man!''

Mildred managed to quiet the despairing teenager, even persuading him to eat a little chicken soup with some barley. But in half an hour or so, he stood and announced he was going to his own room to go to bed.

''Get some sleep,'' Krysty suggested.

''Sleep's no good,'' he replied. ''Sleep changes nothing that happened today.''

''Come on.'' She put her arm around him, but he pulled away from her. ''There isn't a thing that can change what happened today, Michael.''

''Of course. I might be a useless coward, Krysty, but I'm not a stupe.''

IN THE IMMENSE STILLNESS of the New Mexico desert, the moon rose and sailed serenely across the diamond-speckled sky. Ryan woke once, a couple of hours before dawn, and listened to the faint sound of Michael weeping.

''I can hear it, too,'' Krysty whispered. ''And I can feel his pain and loneliness. He hates himself, you know? Really loathes himself for what happened and what he did. What he didn't do. I pity him, lover.''

''So do I. But he has to see it through himself. We can help him some, but he has to live with himself.''

Chapter Ten

"I knocked on Michael's door, but he didn't answer. I thought it best to leave him."

"All right, Dean. Thanks anyway." Ryan looked at his son, aware that the young boy was considering saying something, something that he wasn't sure about. "Yeah?"

"When we go after the General and his gang, will we have to take Michael with us?"

"Why?"

He shuffled his feet, staring past his father, out through the window that faced south.

"I don't want to be with him."

Krysty was sitting next to Ryan, buttering some slices of wholewheat toast. "Because you think he behaved like a coward yesterday?"

"Guess so."

Doc sat across the table, leaning back and rubbing his fingers over the white stubble on his chin. "I should shave before we leave on this chase. If I am to meet my Maker, then I would wish to be presentable." He looked at Dean. "You think that Michael failed to show courage, do you?"

"Yeah, Doc, I do."

"Depends what you mean by courage, son."

"I mean not hiding in the straw when a woman and a baby are getting murdered, Doc."

The old man nodded. "Sure, I can see that, Dean. Of course I can. But I don't quite see how anyone would have been helped by Michael getting himself murdered as well. And, let there be no doubt that he would have been murdered within moments of appearing to these men." He looked across at J.B. and Jak. "Is that not so, gentlemen?"

The Armorer nodded, but Jak ignored the question.

"Still, a man should try or die trying, Doc." Dean wasn't convinced.

"If we had found all three dead, then there would have been no way at all for us to have learned what had happened, who the killers were. How many and how were they armed. What were the Indians doing here. So many questions and no answers to any of them. At least you should credit Michael with providing us with that information, Dean."

Mildred wiped her mouth and pushed her chair back. "Someone should go and wake Michael up. Sleep is probably good for him, but you can have too much of even a good thing. Dean, can you go and try again?"

For a moment Ryan thought that his son's unease over Michael's behavior was going to make him refuse to go. But Dean nodded and walked across the room.

They all heard him knocking, then calling out the teenager's name, knocking one more time.

"Just go in," Jak shouted. "No bolt on door."

Dean was back in a dozen beats of the heart.

"Gone," he said.

Nobody had heard the teenager leave the farmhouse, though he'd unlocked and bolted the back door. There were the marks of bare feet outside, fresh in the dew-damp earth, but they merged and blurred with the trampled trail of boots and horses and the wags, vanishing close by the trim vegetable garden.

"Perhaps he has gone into the hills from whence cometh all help," Doc suggested.

"What do you feel, lover?" Ryan asked.

Krysty closed her eyes and shook her head. "I don't feel a thing. Nothing. If he's left the spread, then he must have made good time and gone a long way off."

They split up to quarter the land around the homestead, hoping to pick up Michael's trail.

Dean and Doc stayed closer to home, thoroughly searching the house and then the outbuildings. The young boy was checking the large barn.

Doc was walking toward the smaller barn when Dean reemerged almost at once.

"In here," he called. "I found him, Doc."

Dean was crying.

Chapter Eleven

Dean ran to fetch the others. By the time they all gathered in the dusty shadows of the barn, Doc had dragged a sawhorse alongside the dangling body and managed to clamber unsteadily onto it, his sword stick drawn.

"Perhaps you can steady him while I cut through the rope," he said.

"Poor Michael." Jak sighed. "No need for this. Doesn't do no good."

Ryan and J.B. positioned themselves under the feet, ready to take the weight. There was a three-legged stool kicked to one side that Michael must have used to stand on, the rawhide rope thrown over one of the main beams. An end had been knotted to the side of a horse's stall, the other around his throat.

He must have measured it carefully before stepping off into eternity. Allowing for the stretching of the rope under his deadweight, the calculation had been about right. Michael's bare feet were less than three inches from the chaff-covered floor of the large, echoing barn.

"Broke his neck clean," J.B. said.

"Looks that way," Ryan agreed.

Mildred had been staring up into the dead youth's face with a dispassionate, professional interest. She heard their comments and nodded. "I think that's so. At least, I devoutly hope that it's so."

"By the Three Kennedys! This is like trying to slice through a bar of iron. Can you take his weight, or I fear that I'll never cut the rope."

Ryan and J.B. did as Doc asked them. There was a drying damp patch across the front of Michael's silver-threaded black jeans, where his bladder had relaxed at his passing. Ryan wrinkled his nose as he held the dead boy by the thighs, aware that he had also fouled himself.

"Ah, now it's going. Hold him . . . Now."

There was a sound like a bowstring breaking, and the full one-forty pounds that had been Michael Brother dropped into J.B.'s and Ryan's arms.

The head hung limply on the neck, the eyes milky and blank. His mouth was open, showing a tiny smear of blood across the lower lip. The rope had bitten deeply into the teenager's throat, almost invisible in the swollen flesh. Ryan noticed as they lowered the body carefully to the floor that Michael had made an efficient job of speeding his own passing from life. There was a thick double knot, positioned precisely beneath the left ear, designed to force the head to one side and snap the neck in the drop.

"Didn't have to do this," Jak repeated. "It don't do anyone any good."

Dean stood by the heavy double doors of the barn, leaning against the wall of one of the stalls, his face buried in his hands.

Doc wobbled and nearly fell as he hopped clumsily off the sawhorse, resheathing his sword stick. "The inscription on the Toledo steel says that the blade should never be sheathed without honor," he said. "I do not feel there is a great deal of honor in cutting down the stiffening body of a dear young friend who found that life was too much for him."

Mildred had dropped to her knees alongside the corpse, shaking her head sadly.

"Why like this, Michael?" she whispered. "We could have helped you. All of us."

"Was it fast?" Jak asked.

Her strong doctor's fingers were probing at Michael's neck, moving the head gently from side to side. "Can someone lend me a knife to cut the rope away?"

Ryan was the quickest, offering his slender-bladed flensing knife.

"Good." She slid the needle point beneath the cord, managing to avoid slicing into the cold waxen flesh. "The boy certainly knew what he was doing," she said, confirming what Ryan himself had already noticed.

"Would he have suffered for very long?" Doc asked. "I had a close friend who once, perforce, witnessed a hanging in some frontier township. I believe it was the sheriff of the place. Could it have been Bannock? I disremember. Though I do recall that he said it was snowing and bitterly cold. But his account of the wretched victim's choking and kicking as he slowly strangled to death over fifteen minutes or more has always remained with me. I hope it was not so."

Mildred wiped her hands on her thighs and stood. "Michael couldn't have done it any better if he'd been trained by a state executioner. Probably not so well, in fact. The fall was enough to break the neck. Dislocate the vertebrae. There is typical occlusion of the carotid artery and a almost instant cutting-off of the blood supply to the brain. The mercy of death would have come very quickly for the boy. I would think within, at the most, a handful of seconds."

"That fast?" Krysty said. "That's something to hold on to, anyway."

Mildred looked at her in the gloomy half-light. "Perhaps, at the risk of being pedantic, I should say that clinical death would probably not occur for several seconds longer, but he would have become unconscious the moment he fell. There would really have been no suffering at all."

"Sure not strangled?" Jak asked.

"I'm sure. There would have been the typical speckled marks of a hemorrhage here." She pointed to the pale skin just behind the ears. "And there are none. Other clinical signs. But, no, Jak. Michael died as he wished. Very quickly and free from pain."

"Free at last, free at last, God Almighty, he's free at last," Doc muttered.

Nobody else said anything.

IT WAS DOC who found the letter.

There was an old wooden pen with a rusted metal nib propped against a porcelain inkwell on a small bureau beneath the narrow window of the bedroom. The letter, folded twice, lay under it. On the outside was written the words: For my friends.

The old man carried it into the living room, holding it gingerly by one corner.

"The young fellow has left us a note," he said. "Who wishes to read it first?"

Ryan looked up. "Read it out loud, Doc. Best we all hear it at the same time."

"I would rather not."

"Please," Krysty said.

"Very well. If you insist. Allow me to sit down, then I shall commence."

The room fell silent. Once again, in the distance, there was the faint ticking of the clock.

Everyone was there, sitting around on the sofa and on chairs, listening.

"'My friends... For I've always thought of you as friends, perhaps the only ones I have ever had. This is to say goodbye to you all. By the time that you find this, I hope that I will have gone far away into the distant land and taken the road less traveled.'" Doc coughed. "Then there is a small aside for my benefit, where he comments that I will be surprised to learn he knew any poetry." He blew his nose. "'It's around three in the morning, and I haven't slept. I just went into the bedroom and tried to whisper to Christina and little Jenny that I was sorry I had failed them. I think they might have heard me where they are gone. It made me feel a small bit better.' "

Dean stood. "I don't think I can hear all this," he said. "Can you call me when you finished reading?"

"No." Ryan sighed. "Part of growing up is not walking away from things you don't like, Dean. Letter's for all of us. You as well. I know this is hard, but Michael would have wanted us all here. Sit down again."

Doc waited until the boy was settled before carrying on. " 'There's so many things I could say, but time passes and I have a date with a rope. My first nineteen years were spent in closed order at Nil-Vanity, and I thought then that I was happy. But I know now that I wasn't. Happiness is trying new things, new foods, new places. The day you give up on that is the day they measure you for the long wooden box. Then I was trawled here into Deathlands, a place of horrors, violence and brutality and...' Something's crossed out there. I can't read it." Doc sniffed, fumbled for his swallow's-eye kerchief and blew his nose. "Sorry. 'But I also found values that I'd never dreamed of—courage, humor and loyalty. So many, many things. Someone somewhere once said that the definition of courage was grace under pressure, didn't they? Mildred, you told me that, I think.' "

"Ernest Hemingway, Michael," she said. "Him, of all people."

Doc nodded. "'Don't aim to bore you, so Dean can relax. The last weeks seem to have been more and more difficult for me. Dark shadows at my shoulder and like a trap with no way out of it. The business with Dorothy was hard.' He underlined that last word," Doc said.

"Can I get me a glass of lemonade from the kitchen?" Dean asked.

"Not much more, dear boy," Doc replied. "'I've felt like a man trying to run through quicksand. The harder you try, the quicker you sink. Then what happened yesterday... Well, that was about the end of the line for me. Time to take what J.B. calls the last train to the coast, I guess. It wasn't that I didn't want to go and try and help Christina... I can't properly explain. Still blurred in my mind. I swear that it wasn't that I was scared. Not scared of dying. Truthfully I wasn't. I just couldn't move. Couldn't. Couldn't. Couldn't.'"

"That's a classic symptom of a serious psychosis," Mildred commented. "Clinical depression. It disrupts the way you act and think."

"The last bit of all is like a brief message to each of us. Shall I read them out as well?"

"Sure, Doc. Go ahead." Ryan settled himself in the deep armchair and looked out through the open door, across the vastness of the New Mexico desert.

"First to Dean. 'You were the nearest I ever had to a true companion, Dean. Forgive me for being such a shithead the last few days. Try and remember the old Michael. That would be the hot pipe way.'"

The boy stood and walked slowly, with dignity, out into the early-morning sunshine. Ryan did nothing to stop him.

"You next, John Barrymore," Doc said, turning to face the Armorer. "'I know how you value the skills of combat, J.B., and I feel I let you down badly. But you said that failure brought its own price. By the time you read this, I'll have paid that price. Keep your blasters oiled.'"

"Yeah." J.B. glanced sideways at Mildred, who gripped his hand.

"I am reminded of something that Rudyard Kipling once wrote," Doc said hoarsely. "He said that each man must pay the price to live with himself on his own terms. Well, I'm sure he put it better than that. But it seems to me that poor Michael has chosen to do precisely that."

"Go on, Doc," Jak said. "Time's passing and there's three graves need digging."

"Of course. Dr. Wyeth, you are the next that the lad addresses. 'You and me, Mildred, had something in common. We never thought to finish up in Deathlands. Without your wisdom and your help, I would never have made it as far as first base. Thanks and goodbye.'"

"Goodbye, Michael," she said in a clear voice.

"Krysty?"

"Go on, Doc."

"'I wish I'd been able to have the time to sit down and talk more, Krysty. About your..."seeing" and all that. I guess that there's plenty more regrets if I thought about it. Sorry if I let you down as well.' "

"No, Michael. You didn't let me down. Didn't let anyone down at all."

"Next line is for me."

"Let's hear it, Doc."

"Very well, Dr. Wyeth, very well. 'Had some laughs, didn't we, Doc? First off I thought you were a stupe old fart. Now that it's all too late, I know better. You're a wise old fart.' " The old man's voice broke, and he resorted once more to the kerchief. " 'Don't ever change, Doc. And every now and then think about your young friend from the past. What was that line you once said about forgetting and smiling?' " Doc looked apologetic. "I once reminded him of that small jewel of verse: 'Better by far you should forget and smile, then that you should remember and be sad.' Poor, poor boy."

"Anything to say to me?" Jak asked.

"Yes. Ryan is the last one in the letter, but you are next to last. 'I never knew you properly, Jak, but Ryan and the rest kept mentioning you. I know how much they all admired you and the way you've handled yourself. Certainly I liked you a lot and I guess I can say that I actually loved Christina and the baby. I know that you'll go to your grave blaming me for it. Well, I'm off to mine in a couple of minutes, and I swear that I'll die with their faces in my mind's eye. I am so sorry, Jak. If I could think that one day you might find it in your heart to forgive me... Well, it'll make eternity easier to handle.'"

Now Doc was crying, his shoulders shaking. Ryan reached out and took the crumpled note from his fingers.

Jak stood and walked to the door, following Dean. "Didn't want this to happen," he said. "Course I forgive him. But that's too late."

Ryan looked down at the neat, angular handwriting.

"'I have the feeling that you'll read this yourself, Ryan. I never met a man I respected more than you. You taught me a load of things and you saved my life again and again. But one thing I learned was that I wasn't a winner like you. And like the Trader you talk about. Fact is, I reckon I'm a bit of a loser. And losers come second, don't they? Specially in the dark hole of Deathlands. Yesterday I stood by and hid while the black hats slaughtered two good people. I couldn't help that. I really couldn't. Said that before in this letter, haven't I? But tomorrow I might do the same thing and be the cause of you, Krysty, Dean and the others getting to buy the farm. I know how you all rely on one another to the point of death. Well, you couldn't rely on me in the same way, Ryan. Now it'll never be a problem.'"

Krysty was watching him closely. "Anything wrong, lover?" she asked.

"No. Nearly done."

Rather than sorrow or pity, Ryan was feeling only a helpless anger. The deaths of Jak's wife and daughter had been unavoidable and nobody thought Michael could have done anything. Except get himself chilled. Now the boy had taken his own life, dying alone and miserable, because of his own false sense of failure. It was such a waste.

Krysty reached across and slowly took the note from Ryan's fingers, reading the last part of it out loud to Mildred, Doc and J.B.

"'It seems a pity, but I don't think that I can write any more. Truth is I'm crying while I try to finish. See the wrinkled bits on the page where my tears are falling? But you mustn't cry for me, any of you. I think that this is probably one of the best things I ever did. And it'll take me, I believe, to a far, far better place than I've ever known. So long, all of you. And try to be real careful out there.' It's just signed 'Your friend from the past, Michael Brother.'"

IT JUST SORT OF HAPPENED that everyone of the surviving friends found themselves out in the sunshine, several of them troubled with bits of grit in their eyes.

Krysty and Mildred had gone in and washed the young man's body, dressing him in a shirt and jeans that had belonged to Christina. Jak had offered his own clothes, but he'd been six inches shorter than Michael and thirty pounds lighter.

Dean had finally stopped crying and was wandering around, red-eyed, picking up pebbles and throwing them at the fence posts. Doc sat on the swing seat, eyes closed, locked into his own thoughts. Jak was walking around the spread with Ryan and J.B.

"Won't get anyone help here," he said. "Chill animals won't survive. Let others go. Might wander safe. Go chase General and chill him and men. Then come back. Mebbe."

"Sooner we get off and moving, the better." J.B. was thinking out loud. "They got wags and we'll be on horseback. If it doesn't rain, then their tracks'll be easy to follow. Catch up with them in the end." He paused. "Get trail provisions and then go."

"No," Ryan said. "One thing to do first."

"What?" the Armorer asked.

Jak answered the question. "Dig three graves."

Chapter Twelve

There was a battered rig in the smallest of the outbuildings. After an hour's intensive work on it, the flatbed wagon was in good enough condition to transport the three bodies up into the foothills to the isolated canyon, beneath the Anasazi ruins, where they were to be buried.

A couple of the older pack animals were harnessed to it with a makeshift arrangement of straps and rope. Jak drove the rig, perched on a upturned packing case, while the others walked slowly along behind.

It was a couple of hours before noon, another wonderful day, a bright sun smiling down from the unspoiled azure sky. Birds sang, and a light southerly breeze blew up from Mexico.

It was the sort of day when it felt good to be alive.

Each of the bodies had been carefully wrapped in a double layer of blankets, the shrouds tied around with lengths of whipcord. There wasn't time to think of building proper coffins for the three corpses. Jak had considered having Christina and Jenny buried together in the same grave, then decided that it wouldn't have been right.

"Long as they're side by side," he said.

Ryan had taken the albino teenager aside before they left, checking that he didn't mind having Michael interred with the other two.

"Don't mind at all, Ryan. Would say if I did. No, it's real good. Specially after the letter."

There were three shovels laid in the bed of the wagon, a couple of pickaxes and the three beechwood markers, the lettering burned into them by Doc and Dean, the old and the young working patiently together after breakfast.

Jak had rummaged in a Victorian mahogany bureau until he excavated an antique mother-of-pearl prayer book, handing it to Doc, like it was a holy relic. "Belonged to Christina's great-grandmother," he said. "She kept hid. Father would've burned if found."

The teenager drove the rig as far up the steepening trail as he could, stopping when Ryan called out to him that the bodies were beginning to slip off the wagon.

They all helped to bear the corpses the few yards to the shaded place that Jak had picked, close to the dazzling spike of a tall yucca. Between the steep walls of the canyon, the air was much cooler, carrying the scent of sagebrush from lower down the narrow trail.

The earth was soft, easy to dig.

DOC HELD THE BOOK TIGHTLY, as though it were supporting him. His voice was steady and powerful, the old phrases echoing through the sandstone vault.

"'I am the resurrection and the life, saith the Lord. He or she that believeth in me, though they were dead, they shall live. And whosoever liveth and believeth in me shall never die.' "

Everyone stood with closed eyes, except for Jak, who watched every detail of the ceremony.

" 'For a thousand years in thy sight are—' "

The albino clapped his hands together, startling the others. "Cut that, Doc."

"But the respect should—"

"Fuck that. Revenge comes first. Get to 'man born of woman' stuff."

The old man looked to Ryan for backup, but the one-eyed man merely shook his head.

"Very well. 'Man that is born of woman hath but a short time to live and is full of misery. He cometh up, and is cut down, like a flower. He fleeth as it were a shadow, and never continueth in one stay. In the midst of life we are in death.' "

Dean stepped forward first, holding out a double fistful of the dry, sandy soil, allowing it to fall gently on each of the three blanketed bodies.

" 'We therefore commit their bodies to the ground, earth to earth.' "

Mildred came next, whispering a prayer under her breath as she scattered the earth.

" 'Ashes to ashes, dust to dust.' "

J.B., dropping the dust, brushed his hands clean when he'd done.

" 'In sure and certain hope of the resurrection to eternal life, through Our Lord, Jesus Christ.' "

Krysty, her lips shaping an invocation to Gaia, spirit of the earth, stood for a few moments over each grave.

Doc resumed the prayers, looking worriedly at Jak, who was shuffling his feet with impatience.

"'Who shall change our vile bodies that they may be like unto his glorious body, according to the mighty, whereby he is able to subdue all things to himself.' "

Ryan stooped and ran his fingers through the soft, cool dirt, gathering a handful of it. He stepped first to Christina's grave, letting some of the sandy earth trickle onto the figure at the bottom of the grave, then to the baby, the bundle so tiny, finally to the last resting place of Michael Brother.

"So long," Ryan said.

"Lord, have mercy on us." Doc paused and looked around at the others. "You all have to say 'Christ have mercy on us' when I say that. I'll do it again. Ready?" Everyone nodded. "Lord have mercy on us."

A ragged chorus, led by Mildred Wyeth, repeated, "Christ have mercy on us."

Doc glanced at Jak, who hadn't moved. "Do you wish to scatter some earth in the graves, Jak?"

"Not really. But will." He bent and grabbed some dirt. Against the total pallor of his skin, it looked bright and fiery. He stepped to Christina first. "So long, love. Thanks for good times." Then to Jenny. "Goodbye," he whispered. "Really miss little one." Finally to Michael, standing on the brink of the rough rectangle of darkness, staring intently down into it. He brushed the last of the red dirt from his long fingers, hesitated then half turned away. Jak was struck by a second thought and turned back again. "Forgive you, Michael," he said. "Hear me? Forgive you."

Doc licked his dry lips. "There's some more that I could read, or I could proceed straightforward to the end of the service. What does anyone—"

"The end," Jak said.

"Very well. But first I would also like the opportunity to pay my own tribute to the dead."

Jak sighed. "Every minute passes, General and coldhearts are farther."

"I am nearly finished. Let this be done with proper respect, dear boy."

"Sure, sure."

Doc closed his eyes again, hands folded in front of him. "We now bid farewell to these our friends, gone before. In the sure and certain expectation of meeting them again, around the next bend in the road. They will not grow old, as we that are left behind will grow old. Aging will not weary them, nor the passing years condemn. At the going down of the sun, and in the morning, we will remember them all."

"Amen," said Mildred, followed by the others, Jak last of all.

There was a long moment of silence while Doc stooped slowly, knee joints cracking, and picked up his own handful of dirt, scattering a little into each of the graves. He finally straightened and peered again at the flimsy pages of the mother-of-pearl prayer book.

"The grace of our Lord Jesus Christ, and the love of God, and the fellowship of the Holy Spirit, be with us all now and evermore. Amen."

"Amen," chorused the others.

Once more Jak was the last to respond. "Amen," he said. "Now let's find fucking killers and chill them. Fill in the graves and let's go."

Chapter Thirteen

The last spadeful of earth had hardly been piled on and patted down, with a few large stones to deter the scavengers, when Jak was back at the rig, cursing at the two horses to stir them up to a faster pace on the way home. There was barely time for them all to pile on the flatbed of the rig before they were rattling off down the deeply rutted trail. Doc nearly dropped his precious sword stick, and only a frantic grab by Dean saved it.

"Slow down, in the blessed name of Phoebus, slow down, wild charioteer!" the old man yelled, but the albino ignored him, hunched over the reins, his white hair flowing out behind like a cold banner of revenge.

THE LIVESTOCK WAS released into the wilderness.

"Most'll die," Jak said, watching them go.

"Some won't." J.B. stood by the closed gate to the corral, where they'd kept the horses. There were just enough decent saddle mounts for each of the friends to have one, along with four heavily laden pack animals, including a vile-tempered mule called Judas.

Ryan and Mildred had butchered a couple of goats and one of the pigs, while Krysty worked frantically in the kitchen, aided by a sweating Dean, to get as much meat cooked as possible, ready for them to take along on their chase.

There was already a fair supply of salted and dried beef in one of the outbuildings, untouched by the marauders. Krysty also found time to do a little baking, though the bread would become stale within a day on the trail.

Doc's responsibility was to attend to the supply of water for everyone. He went to the well out back and carefully filled the canteens and bags to hang on the pack animals.

They all knew well enough that it was possible to survive for many days with nothing to eat. But to go without water in the arid Southwest in the months of summer meant survival being measured in hours.

After that the temperature control mechanism of the body began to flounder and fail. Common sense evaporated, and the brain began to boil.

Despite protestations from Jak, Ryan insisted that everyone have a good bath before they went, with all of the men taking time for a quick shave.

"Last chance we'll get for who knows how long. Trader used to say a person who felt good fought good."

While he waited for Krysty to finish drying her dazzling hair, Ryan walked around the back of the house, where all of the doors stood open, and found Jak busily filling some old green bottles with lamp oil.

"What's this?" he asked.

"What look like, Ryan?"

"Looks like someone aiming to end their past in a mountain of fire."

The young man nodded. "Be about right."

"Not the way."

"Who says?"

"Me."

Jak half smiled. "Forgot how sure you always was that you was always right, Ryan."

"I am this time."

"Your house?"

"No."

"Whose house, Ryan?"

"Yeah. Your house. But that doesn't make it right, Jak."

"Couldn't care less. Don't give fart in tornado for this place no more."

"It's a fine building. You and Christina made it yours, after the other troubles you had. Filled with memories, good and bad. It isn't right to set fire to it all. Not now, Jak. And certainly not like this."

"Think I'll come back?"

"Sure."

"To stay?"

Ryan hesitated. "I can't guess at that, can I? But it's possible. While it's possible, then you don't burn it all away. I tell you the truth, Jak. I reckon that's an insult to the memory of Christina."

Just for a heart-stopping moment, Ryan thought that the red-eyed youth was going to attack him. His right hand reached behind him, where at least one of his throwing knives was hidden, and he'd dropped into a combat crouch. Ryan had actually started to go for the SIG-Sauer on his hip, when Jak straightened and smiled, smiled properly for the first time since yesterday, when they'd found the bodies.

"Stupe," he said.

"Me?"

"No, Ryan. Not you. Me. Got to go on. For their sakes. Fighting with you's stupe."

"All I'm saying is that you might want to come back here when all this is over and done. Mebbe not, but it doesn't seem like a good idea to burn the whole place down."

"No," Jak agreed.

"YOU AREN'T LOCKING the doors or anything, Jak?" Mildred asked, surprised.

"No point."

"Suppose someone comes?"

Ryan laughed. "Mildred! Anyone comes by and finds the spread empty, you think a lock and a bolt would stop them getting in? Course not."

"No, I suppose..."

"Left note," Jak said, pointing to a white rectangle that fluttered from the center of the front door, in the shelter of the porch.

"What's it say?" Krysty asked, dismounting to adjust the length of her stirrups.

"Says I'm gone and I'll come back."

"That enough?"

"Sure, Krysty. Local folks and Indies who know me won't do no harm. Others don't matter."

They set off heading south, with the late-afternoon sun sinking to their right, casting long shadows away to the east. There was very little wind, and the tracks of the eight-wheeled war wags and the pursuing Navaho were clearly visible.

They were less than an hour out from the ranch, with sufficient sun to keep going for a while, when they found the corpse.

It had been dumped into an overgrown drainage ditch to the right of the narrow highway. The only clue to its presence was the cloud of blowflies that rose humming into the air from their luxurious feeding.

And the smell.

If you'd asked Ryan just what death smelled like, he would probably have found it a difficult question to answer. Like asking someone from the predark United States just what a rush-hour urban freeway smelled like. Everyone would recognize it, but it was so common that it was real tough to try to put a description into words.

So it was with the scent of decayed and corrupted human flesh in Deathlands.

"Sweet and sickly and sour, all at the same time" had been an attempt by Krysty.

But the great truth about the odor of mortality was that you could never imagine that it might be anything else. Once you'd smelled a putrefying corpse, you would never again mistake it for anything else.

Ryan, Jak and J.B. all swung down from horseback and went to investigate.

The body was male. It had been stripped completely naked and was around five and a half feet tall, looking like it had once weighed in around the one-eighty mark. There was a straggling mustache, and the hair was black and had once been sleek, but was now matted with blood and dust.

"General's man that Christina chilled," Jak said, squatting on his heels and peering at the body.

"He look Mex?" Dean called. "Michael said a lot of them looked Mex."

"Don't look nothing," Ryan replied.

"Doesn't look anything, lover," Krysty corrected.

"Yeah," he said.

Assuming that it was what Jak had guessed, then the man had been dead for somewhere around thirty-six hours. He'd probably died very soon after the woman had stabbed him and had been dumped by the marauding gang of killers as soon as the wags were far enough away from the spread.

Thirty-six hours in the heat of a New Mexico summer and a lot of people would find it hard to identify their own ever-loving mothers.

Soft tissues like the eyes, lips and genitals went first. Though it had been hidden in sagebrush, the predators had found the corpse easily enough. The stomach was grossly distended with the rotting intestinal gases it contained, and the man's skin was all a gleaming black, like highly polished leather. Hundreds of glittering golden ants were scampering busily around the tops of the spread, lolling thighs.

The knife wound was clearly visible, a pale-lipped bloodless gash, five or six inches in length, running sideways a handbreadth above the groin.

"She did him good," J.B. observed, shooing away the insistent flies.

"Quick with a knife, Christina," Jak said softly. "Very quick."

Ryan wrinkled his nose as the evening breeze carried a fresh wave of the foul stench to his nostrils. "Yeah," he said. "She did good."

He and J.B. climbed back into their saddles, rejoining the others. But Jak stood still, looking down at the stinking corpse.

"I understood that time was of the essence in pursuing this matter," Doc said.

"One moment," the white-haired teenager replied. "Just one moment."

He drew his massive Cold Python from its holster and thumbed back the hammer, leveling the six-inch barrel down into the ditch.

"Waste of a round," J.B. commented.

"Not to me."

The gun boomed, sending a flock of wild turkeys bursting wildly from concealment fifty yards down the trail. From the height of the gray stallion he rode, Ryan was able to see the predictable effect of the .357 round.

At almost point-blank range it struck the dead man through the center of the blackened face, smashing away part of the nose and exiting into the dirt behind the skull. There was no blood, just a thin trickle of a glutinous yellowish liquid from the entry hole below the missing right eye.

Jak holstered the blaster and walked to where Dean was holding the reins of the teenager's horse. He vaulted into the saddle with an effortless acrobatic skill.

"Feel better?" Mildred asked.

"Just a little," he replied. "One down and plenty to go. Good beginning."

At Jak's insistence they rode on well past dusk, until Ryan pointed out to him that they could easily miss a fork in the trail by pushing too hard in the dark.

So they camped.

Chapter Fourteen

They were on the move again before dawn.

Breakfast was a hasty few mouthfuls of jerky and bread, washed down with plain water. They were all agreed that a fire wouldn't be a good idea. It would take too much time and announce their presence to anyone within fifty miles.

While they ate, there was a brief combat meeting. Despite the invaluable information from Michael, their knowledge was extremely limited. The enemy was a couple dozen well-armed and well-trained men and women in two armored war wags, led by someone who called himself the General. It could be that they had their origins close to the old Grandee border with Mexico. Or below it.

There was also a number of mounted Native Americans, quite probably Navaho, following the pair of wags southward for their own reasons.

"Likely they've got the same motives for pursuing this General as we do," J.B. said, his sallow face a pale blur in the predawn gloom.

Ryan nodded. "Agreed. What we know points to raiding on pueblos and isolated communities and homesteads. Steer away from the big villes and the powerful barons with their sec armies. If he hit a village in the last week, seems likely there could be a hunting party out after him."

Jak's hair blazed like a beacon in the darkness. "Been good friends with Indians around here. We get together and have more chance."

Doc had been suffering from the jolting gait of his roan gelding. He lay flat out while he nibbled on the last of Krysty's fresh-baked bread. "How far do you think we'll need to ride to catch these runagates?"

"To the big river," J.B. suggested.

"Through jaws of hell," Jak vowed.

NONE OF THEM KNEW the region of what was once southern New Mexico all that well. Ryan and J.B. had ridden that way with the Trader a few times, but neither had particularly clear memories of those occasions.

"There are some big caves," Ryan said, as they moved their horses along at a brisk walk.

"Right. Millions of bats. Trader was triple worried about rabies. We had to keep the wags locked down sec tight. Nearly suffocated." The Armorer took off his glasses and squinted at the midmorning sun through them, wiping away a smear on the sleeve of his coat.

"Yeah. It was Abe, wasn't it?"

"Went out for a shit. Found himself smack in the middle of a bat storm."

"And fell down that hole. Turned out to be the remains of someone's liquor cellar."

J.B. grinned. "Ace on the memory line, Ryan. Trader wouldn't let anyone go out after him for nearly an hour. Thought that it might be an Apache trap. And when we found him he'd gotten pissed out of his skull on two quarts of ancient Thunderbird."

"Are there any villes toward the Grandee?" Krysty asked, heeling her Appaloosa forward to join the two men. "Could the General be heading for one?"

Ryan shook his head. "Doubt that, lover. Word seems to be he keeps off the red trails. Sticks to the blue back roads. More likely got a base down south."

"There's El Paso and Juarez across the bridge." J.B. looked behind. "Doc's falling off the pace some. Want me to go hurry him up?"

"No. Not yet. I'll ride back with him and sort of ease him along. Old man's got pride. You mentioned Juarez, the Mex ville. Remember that Easter?"

"Sure. Cohn was duty nav. Had us a thunderstorm. Rain so thick you could've cut it with a knife. Just on the edge of Juarez and he got us lost."

"Took us right through the middle of an Apache camp. Rain was so heavy that they never saw us and we never saw them. Not until we were driving slowly out the other side. Nobody ever let Cohn forget it."

Krysty looked ahead of them, where Jak was sticking out at point. "Is the kid all right?"

Ryan smiled. "Sure. Best way of coping with grief is figuring on paying the person gave you that grief."

THE DAY PASSED without any sort of incident.

Jak set the pace, though Ryan twice warned him against tiring the horses.

"Better to take a half day longer to get there than not get there at all," he pointed out.

The morning had broken with a beautiful sunrise. The sky shaded from pale gold in the far west to a deep orange in the east, around the rising sun. Off to the northwest there was a tall bank of clouds, their flanks tinted by the brilliant dawn light.

"Beautiful," said Doc, leaning back in the saddle to appreciate the enchanted vista.

"Storms." J.B. delivered the single word with a terse flatness.

"Is that your opinion, John Barrymore? A scene that would have brought tears to the eyes of Tiepolo or Turner and you simply say it means there will be a storm."

The Armorer looked puzzled. "Don't catch your drift, Doc. You saying you think it won't storm?"

"Course it will," Ryan added. "Be a serious chem storm. That's what those clouds mean."

"But the beauty of them, gentlemen! Do none of you have eyes for that?"

"Rain, lightning, flash floods. That's all." Jak heeled his horse on ahead.

Doc turned toward Mildred and sighed. "Sadly, my dear, we are surrounded by true Renaissance princes, are we not?"

"Frankly, Doc, I don't give a damn."

THE STORM SKIRTED AROUND to the west, never approaching within twenty miles of them, though that was still close enough for them to appreciate its grandeur.

The skies darkened and huge banks of purple-black clouds rose into space. Every now and again there would be dazzling flashes of chem lightning, the deep thunder rolling across the vastness of the surrounding deserts.

Later in the afternoon the clouds lifted, revealing a pale strip of blue beneath them. But that was frequently darkened by a gray misty curtain of falling rain.

"You mentioned flash floods, Jak," Dean said. "What's that mean?"

The albino glanced sideways at the boy. "Means shit-lot rain in shit-short time."

"What sort of floods?"

"Big. Camp in steep-sided canyon. Storm higher up. Bad. Foot of rain in couple hours. Wake up and twenty-foot wave on top of you. Can happen."

"Wow. Hot pipe!"

"No. Cold pipe."

THE ONLY MINOR DRAMA came in the late evening, when they'd finally stopped to camp.

Jak had taken them to a small water hole, that turned into a shallow, snaking stream, under the looming bulk of a shattered highway bridge.

"Getting to edge of places I know," he said. "Take all water we can."

The horses were quickly unsaddled and Dean led them to the muddy pool, watching them carefully to make sure they didn't gorge themselves.

Doc undertook the job of filling all of the bottles and skins for the group, going to remove some of them from the packs carried by Judas, the mule.

"Come on, boy," he said, sidling up nervously to the animal.

Judas turned its long, demonic skull in the direction of the old man, one bloodshot eye rolling in its deep socket. A pendulous lip curled back off ferocious teeth, and it suddenly snapped out at Doc.

There was the ripping of material and Doc showed remarkable reflexes in hopping out of the way of the savage bite. A shred of broadcloth, torn from the shoulder of his frock coat, dangled from the mule's jaws.

"By the Three Kennedys!" He looked around in the dusk, seeing that everyone else in the party had observed the incident. Most were laughing. "It is not a matter for humor," he snorted. "The brute needs a lesson."

"Punch it, Doc," Jak called, his teeth white in a broad grin. "Good left hook."

"I shall not demean myself to sink to the level of this vicious and cunning animal," Doc replied, struggling to repair his tattered dignity.

"Try befriending it," Mildred suggested, trying and failing to check her own amusement. "Sure you two must have a lot in common you could talk about."

"Were I not a gentleman and you most certainly no lady, then I would be delighted to call you out, madam."

The black woman threw back her head and hooted with merriment. "Pistols for two at dawn and breakfast for one. You silly old fool, Doc. I could put a bullet through your third waistcoat button and still have time to take a leak."

"Not if Doc used the Le Mat," Ryan said, busily unrolling his blanket for the night. "The scattergun barrel would make a mess of the best shootist in Deathlands."

Mildred nodded. Doc carried on trying to remove the water bags from the mule, and the camp was established.

"THERE ANY HUNTING farther south?" J.B. asked, picking at his teeth with a saguaro spine, trying to get rid of a stubborn shred of gristle lodged between two of his front teeth. "This jerky won't last forever."

"Come to some low hills soon." Jak was already wrapped in his bedroll, eager to get to sleep in order to make an even earlier start the next morning.

"I seem to recall that there was a biggish forest in these parts. When we passed through here with Trader." Ryan looked toward the darker shape in the night that he knew was J.B. "You remember it?"

"Can't be certain. Fact is, the older I get, the more one tree starts to look just like the one before it. And like all the other trees."

"Yeah. Trees. Came out week's hunting. Before Jenny was birthed. Lotsa deer. Mainly pines. Scrub oaks. Long ridge, with Grandee other side."

"Think we're closing in on them, lover?" Krysty was also inside her bedroll, just alongside Ryan.

"Tracks show it. I figure that we're probably traveling for a lot longer hours. The wags'll have the edge over the horsemen, providing they got plenty of gas."

"Reckon they'll know that they're being followed, Dad? By the Indians?"

"Likely. From what Michael told us, it seems certain that they took off from the homestead as soon as they saw riders' dust coming their way. So the Navaho'll be pushing them as hard as they can, without blowing their ponies. And the General's trying to keep a distance and still save fuel."

"Just like Trader would've done," J.B. added.

Ryan nodded. "Yeah."

Doc yawned, very audibly. "I confess that this outdoor life might well be manna for the poor soul, but I have aches where I didn't even know I had muscles to ache. I shall be retiring now and bid a fond farewell to all my friends. And goodnight to Mrs. Calabash, wherever she may be."

RYAN WOKE INSTANTLY, his hand going for the butt of the SIG-Sauer under his rolled-up jacket. He was immediately aware that J.B. was also awake.

"What is it?" he whispered.

"Gunfire," the Armorer replied. "There's some handmades and some semiauto."

The rest of the group slept on, undisturbed by the faint crackle of shooting, far, far off in the arid wasteland to the south of their camp.

The noise was barely audible, muted and muffled by distance, but it had been sufficient to jerk both men from sleep.

There came a booming sound, louder than the others. Krysty stirred and muttered something, but didn't wake.

"Mortar," Ryan said quietly. "Has to be the General and his men."

"Attacking or being attacked?" J.B. considered his own question. "Probably being attacked. Navaho could mebbe have come up on them in the darkness."

"Worth us going to take a look?"

His eye had become accustomed to the night, and Ryan could actually see his oldest friend, sitting straight up, his glasses glinting in the sliver of moonlight that lurked behind some high cloud.

"No. Must be fifteen or so miles away. Wind's from the south. Firefight could be even farther off. Make a good start in the morning. Should find out what's going on in the first couple of hours. Around full dawn."

As was generally the case when it came to anything to do with blasters, J.B. had an ace on the line.

Chapter Fifteen

They told the others about the distant firefight as they broke their fast with some of the remaining jerky, washed down with the cool, muddy water from under the highway.

"South?" Jak queried.

"Yeah," Ryan said. "Fifteen or twenty miles was about our guess."

J.B. nodded. "Automatic blasters and some single shots. Could likely have been a gren launcher being fired as well. Has to be the General."

"We're getting closer," Dean said excitedly.

"Right," his father agreed.

"Then we need to get started."

"Sure, Jak. But we aren't just going to gallop in and ask the General to suck on our blasters." Ryan glanced to the east, where there was just the faintest hint of a watery glow. "Saddle up and we can move on out. Getting closer."

As J.B. HAD PREDICTED, they came across the scene of the previous night's battle a little after full dawn.

Ryan had chosen to ride at point, pushing the gray stallion on at a brisk walk. The ground was still damp from the cool night's dew, and it was safe to ride fast with no risk of columns of swirling dust betraying their presence.

Also, the sun was still below the horizon to their left so they would throw no shadows for any watchers to pick up.

After just over an hour's ride, Ryan held up a hand, stopping the others, calling quietly for J.B. and Jak to join him.

"There's a pair of low mesas about a half mile ahead, and a ravine running between them. Be a good place to try and stage an ambush. There's an arroyo across the trail a hundred yards in front. Leave the horses there and the three of us can go and recce on foot. Find what we can find."

J.B. PICKED HIS WAY around the site of the firefight, sniffling the air like a hound dog, frequently stopping to examine the trampled dirt. Gradually he pieced together a picture of what had happened here in the early hours of the morning.

Ryan and Jak kept to the edges of the battle scene, trying to work out their own interpretations. After about a half hour, the Armorer rejoined them.

"Clear enough," he said.

The two wags had been parked on top of the right-hand mesa, around fifty feet high. It was a sound defensive position, with a good view on all sides. The General had placed four sentries, obviously aware of the proximity of the pursuing Navaho. The dead man had been one of those guards.

"Indians came up blind side. Circled right around and into the ravine."

"How many?"

"Dozen or so. If we looked, we'd likely find a place over to the west where they left their ponies. Came up the steep rocky wall and took the guard from behind. Knocked him out and rolled him down the slope onto the trail. They must've collected him on their way out after the attack failed."

"The graves are their dead?" Jak asked.

"Certainly. No other possibility." J.B. shook his head. "Can't really have had much chance of success. Looks as if the General made his people sleep inside the wags. Navaho wouldn't have had a real chance, even if they took out all the tires."

One of the other sentries must have heard the scuffle and raised the alarm.

"From that moment the Navaho lost it. Light was poor last night, otherwise they'd have been totally wiped away. Took three fatalities."

It seemed that the wags had collected the surviving sentries and rolled away, still heading south, leaving the shattered war party to bury their dead.

And deal with their prisoner.

THE ASHES OF THEIR FIRE were still warm.

"Defeat must've shocked them," Jak said. "Looks like they stayed here couple hours before going after General. Chilling him helped being beat."

They had all experienced the skill of the Native Americans of the Southwest in making the passing of an enemy a slow and endlessly agonizing experience.

"Still smell the burned meat," Krysty said, as she and the others came to rejoin Ryan, J.B. and Jak.

In the cold, clear light of morning, the details of what had been done to the prisoner were all too obvious.

Mildred looked at the raggled corpse with a professional interest. "Top surgeon would have been proud to have kept breath in the poor bastard's body as long as they did." She shook her head. "Know their human physiology, don't they? Where the main blood vessels lie, so as not to cut them by accident and let the spirit fly free. See where they've cauterized some of the cuts, like those around the groin, to make sure he didn't bleed to death too quickly and spoil the game."

"Not game," Jak said, already losing interest and turning toward the horses again.

"Upon my soul!" Doc had gone pale as he stared at the tortured body, noting the missing eyes, the sockets filled with the ashes of fire.

The nose had been sliced away, and more splinters of charred wood filled the gaping hole. The lips had been cut off, the teeth clubbed out of both jaws. A lump of wood had been jammed in place to hold the mouth wide open, giving the captors a number of options in sustaining their revenge.

"Broke every joint in the body," Dean said with awe. "Every one."

"No, that's not true," Mildred argued. "A lot of them, but not all." She ticked them off, one by one. "Shoulders dislocated and then a sharp knife used to cut through the tendons and ligaments there. Elbows smashed. Wrists. All the fingers. Some toes. Ankles. Both knees pounded to a bloody pulp. Lot of ribs splintered as well. Cuts behind the knee and at the top of the thighs."

"Why's there blood on his ears?" the eleven-year-old asked. "They shoot him there?"

"No." Mildred bent down. "They hammered a whittled spike of wood into each ear."

Doc had walked a few paces away. "How can you be so damnably calm, madam, at this... this desecration of the temple of the human body?"

She turned to him. "Doc, like you, I wasn't born in Deathlands. But I saw sights nearly as bad as this when I did an internship in the casualty department of a big hospital in... Doesn't much matter where. Call it Gotham City or Metropolis, if you like. I saw druggies taught a lesson by dealers. Babies taught a lesson by parents to stop them crying. Little girls—and boys—young as four, taught a lesson in satisfying male sexual aggression." Her voice was stretched tight like wire and she was nearly crying. "Jesus, Doc, there's always been cruelty and there always will be. Best you can do is try not to let it touch you."

"But this was gloating and deliberate. Surely inexcusable. The men who did this sought only suffering and pain for this naked wretch."

"Naked wretch fucked and chilled my wife, Doc," Jak said.

THE WEATHER STARTED to deteriorate almost immediately after they left the pair of mesas behind and began to canter southward again.

The storm clouds that had been skirting them the previous day now gathered on every point of the horizon, closing in over their heads, squeezing away the last section of blue.

The temperature dropped and the wind began to rise, swirling up savage dust devils and making all of the animals skittish. Judas in particular was difficult. He was an iron-jawed stubborn brute at the best of times, trying to bite or kick anyone who came near him. Now, with a storm threatening, he was even less eager to keep up with the rest of the group.

Jak rode his gelding alongside the mule and kicked out at it with his combat boots. "Worst comes to it, I'll blast him and we can cook and eat him."

"Sure could do with some decent food," Mildred said. "Those the hills ahead of us that you were talking about, Jak, for some hunting?"

"Yeah."

Visibility was closing in fast.

Already the wind carried small spots of chilly rain, dashing into their faces.

"Knew we'd forget something," Ryan shouted, struggling to be heard above the gathering storm.

"What?" J.B. had already taken off the well-worn fedora and stuffed it down the front of his jacket, holding his head bowed to try to keep the rain off his glasses.

"Slickers. Weather was so good, I never thought to add any waterproofs to the load."

"Me, neither. Still, we get wet, we get wet. Nobody died from just being wet."

"Trader say that?"

J.B. shook his head at Ryan. "No. I did."

FOR THE FIRST TIME since they left the Lauren spread, they were starting to see some signs of civilization. Though it was predark civilization.

The rain was falling steadily as Jak led them across the ruins of a big highway. The pavement was cracked and corroded by a hundred years of unattended frosts, winds and sunshine, with all kinds of rank weeds and shrubs pushing up through the surface.

"Where did this go?" Dean asked.

Jak shrugged, pointing a finger to the east. "From there—" he pointed again to the west "—all the way to there. And back again."

Ryan had noticed that the albino teenager was beginning to show a few small signs that he was moving out from under the weight of the two murders.

There was the ruins of a gas station on their left, the blackened stumps of the old pumps standing like the corpses of burned martyrs.

The foothills were now only five miles or so ahead of the group, but they'd vanished in the sweeping bands of rain that drove into their faces.

Ryan heeled the gray alongside J.B. "Goin' to lose the tracks," he said.

"The wheels of the wags are digging real deep. And there's enough of the Navaho horsemen to leave a good trail. I reckon we can keep a watch on it, unless the storm goes on and on. But they've been heading right on south all the time."

It was true. The double set of wheels and the pursuing hooves had hardly deviated more than ten degrees from due south during the whole journey.

The rain was intermittent throughout the long afternoon. At times it became so heavy that the wooded hills ahead of them vanished completely, wiped away behind the banks of swirling cloud. Several times there were peals of thunder, rolling flatly across the desert, spooking some of the animals.

"HORSES ARE GETTING exhausted, Jak."

"Plenty daylight left, Ryan."

They'd halted a little after five o'clock. The rain had eased, but the ground was a soft quagmire, with pools in the hollows. The track was fetlock-deep in mud, slowing their progress, making it hard going.

"No point driving them into the ground."

Jak had slipped from his saddle, reaching down to tighten the girth. His white hair was stained by the red mud, flattened to his angular skull with the rain.

"No point stopping."

J.B. coughed, leaning forward over the pommel. "That's crap, Jak."

"What?"

"Total and utter crap."

The albino teenager turned away from his horse, staring at the Armorer. In the gray light, his eyes burned like tiny chips of ruby laser.

"I say we go on."

J.B. wasn't a man to back down. "Tracks show they're still around four hours ahead of us. Been riding all day, since before dawn. Like Ryan says, the horses are bushed. I'm bushed. Truth is, Jak, that you're bushed as well."

"Bushed fails to communicate properly the full extent of my bushedness," Doc said, his voice creaking with fatigue. "If we do not cease this hard traveling quite soon, I shall not be answerable for the consequences to my health."

"Then fall off and stay here," Jak snapped.

"That's enough." Ryan dismounted, aware of the stiffness that yelped out from his tired muscles.

"Suppose I go on and you stay?" Jak was facing him, his body language aggressive and combative.

"Then you likely get chilled and we get there a few hours later and try to avenge you as well as Christina and Jenny." He waved a finger at Jak. "But it means that you don't share the vengeance, and it means you get to be dead for nothing. That what you want?"

Jak didn't answer his question, rubbing a hand absently down the neck of the gelding. They were on the flank of a ridge, the broad valley below still invisible as the storm clouds moved away across it.

He finally said something, but so softly that none of them could catch the words.

"What?" Ryan wasn't going to let it lie. In the days that Jak Lauren had ridden with them, there'd been times of conflict between them. Now things were different.

And the same.

"Don't tell me what to do, Ryan."

"Now why the fuck not?"

"Not father!"

"Course not. Way things are, we all have to live on the trust of each other. You've been there, and you know it's true. No change now. I can't stop you from going on alone without sending you to buy the last bullet, and I won't. Because it won't make any difference at all to the rest of us. But listen to me good, Jak. If I thought you behaving like a triple stupe might endanger all of us, then I'd chill you myself and not lose a moment's sleep over it. You understand me?"

Jak nodded. "Brains says you're right. Heart says you're double wrong."

Krysty was standing in her stirrups, watching the rain clearing away ahead of them. "Looks like the ruins of a ville down there," she said.

"Be a good place to spend the night." Ryan hesitated a moment, checking that he wasn't about to get a leaf-bladed throwing knife between the fourth and fifth ribs. Then he climbed back in the saddle. "Let's go see."

Chapter Sixteen

The township had been called Opium Wells. The yellow metal sign leaned to the left, as though it were frozen in the act of toppling over. The main lettering was still just readable, though the altitude and population details were long faded away.

There were two skeletons wired together beneath the sign. One was the whitened bones of a sheep, shreds of wool still blowing in the light breeze. The other was clearly human, even if the leering skull had broken off the neck and lay in the dark sand a few paces away. The way that the skeleton had been joined in an ossuary tableau made it clear that the man was supposed to be copulating with the sheep.

"Welcome to Opium Wells," Doc said, looking at the grisly spectacle. "Xenophobia capital of Deathlands. Friendliest little town in the west."

"The General?" Jak asked.

"No." Ryan shook his head dismissively. "Look at it. Those bones have been lying out there for a real long while. Weeks. Mebbe months."

It was Jak's turn to shake his head. "No! Not now. I know that. But might be got his base not far off. In the caves? Could be? They did this last time passed by."

"Right. Sorry, kid. Only teasing you, Jak. Could be right, I guess. Someone with a sick sense of humor."

"I think it's funny, Dad."

Ryan smiled at the boy. "Like I said, Dean. Someone with a sick sense of humor."

The place was completely derelict. None of the buildings still had four walls and a roof, and most of them showed the obvious blackening of gasoline fires.

"Someone went to some trouble to take this place off the map," J.B. commented.

They had dismounted, tethering their animals together to the sawed-off remains of what might once have been street lamps. The rain had been so heavy that there were pools of water everywhere, including several right where the horses were tied, giving them all the chance to slake their thirst. Once again, Doc led the way to top up their own shrunken supplies of sweet drinking water.

"Big storm coming up out of the north," Mildred said, huddling her shoulders under her quilted denim jacket. "Real cold feel."

The sky was gray all around, except where she pointed, where a bank of clouds swooped toward them, as black as the underside of a raven's wing, laced with the silvery pink of chem lightning.

"Best find the best shelter we can," Ryan said, looking around the desolate ruins of the township.

At its height it looked like Opium Wells had around thirty houses, a couple of stores and a church. The only building that seemed as though it might offer them any sort of cover was the church. It had been white-framed, but wind and sand had stripped it to bare wood. The windows were gone, mostly boarded over. The bell tower was missing, ending in a jagged stump at about the level of the second story.

Three of the walls still stood, but the back wall was completely gone, the timbers on either side charred and buckled. But it still looked their best bet.

Jak spit in the dirt. "That chem storm can fuck things. Best bring animals inside with us. Bad thunder, close, and all them bolt."

Ryan glanced at J.B., who nodded his agreement. "Right. We got a half hour before it reaches us. Looks like there's part of the roof left on the church. We'll all try to get some wood and start a fire. Be sheltered so nobody'll see it. Give us some warmth and protection. Finish the jerky. I'll go check out the church, while the rest of you scavenge some wood for a night's fire. And keep your eyes open for snakes."

A sheet of rusting corrugated iron was flapping back and forth, torn loose from a row of jagged nails around what had once been the side entrance to the church.

Ryan drew the SIG-Sauer. The ingrained habit had kept him alive as long as it had. "Man who walks in a strange building without a cocked blaster in his fist will likely come out on his back." Trader knew things like that.

He paused in the doorway, allowing his eye to adjust to the semidarkness.

The hairs at his nape began to prickle with that certainty that someone was hiding in the shadows.

Moving very carefully, Ryan backed out of the church, looking around for J.B. He waved a hand to him, using the old signal that meant danger. The Armorer immediately readied the Uzi and walked quickly and silently across the old main street, dodging a rolling ball of tumbleweed, to join him.

"Someone in there?" he whispered.

Ryan nodded. "Can't see anyone, but you can feel it."

There was no need for either man to question or doubt the instincts of the other. They'd both been around far too long for that.

"How do you want to tackle it, Ryan?"

"Both go in. Me left, you right. Flat against the wall. Play it as it lays."

"Not likely to be the General's men," J.B. breathed. "More likely Navaho. Wounded men."

They paused a moment outside the ruined church. Ryan nodded, and a heartbeat later they were both inside, eyes straining to penetrate the gloom.

The interior was stripped, with a few broken benches piled in one corner, and the general air of destruction that typified abandoned buildings throughout Deathlands. There were rusting cans and plastic rubbish. A brown rat, skin dappled with a cancerous growth, moved in front of them, left to right, unhurried and unafraid.

There was a ramshackle staircase hanging from one wall that probably once led up to the vanished bell tower. Lances of gray light probed through the corners of the broken and boarded windows.

J.B. pointed with the snub nozzle of the Uzi toward the heaped pews in the corner. Unless there was someone lurking in the blackness of the ravaged second story, it was the only possible place for anyone to be hiding.

Ryan nodded, leveled the SIG-Sauer and squeezed the trigger once.

In the confined space, the powerful handblaster boomed out like the wrath of the gods, the bullet tearing through the wall a couple of feet above the benches, leaving a splintered hole through which a rod of watery light came peeking.

"Come out or get dead," he shouted, his voice riding over the echoes of the shot.

For a few tense moments there was no reaction to the 9 mm bullet. He leveled the blaster again, this time aiming into the center of the broken furniture.

"Last chance," J.B. called.

They heard a rustling sound, like a scorpion behind an arras. Ryan glanced sideways at J.B., both men ready to open fire at the first sign of a threat. Behind them, Ryan was aware that the rest of the friends were waiting just outside, drawn by the gunfire. Nobody moved.

"Don't shoot us, mister. We're fucking nearly dead anyway from no food."

"Come out. Slow and easy and keep your hands where we can see them. One wrong move and we take you out."

Ryan's finger had already taken up first pressure on the trigger of the SIG-Sauer. The voice had sounded genuinely frail and terrified.

He'd lost friends, though, chilled by people who were genuinely frail and terrified.

The discarded pews moved and toppled in a splintering heap, sending up a choking cloud of dust. Both Ryan and J.B. dropped into a crouch.

"Coming out, mister. Don't shoot, please."

The figure in the gloom was tall and skinny, hands held high, followed by a second person.

"Stand still," Ryan shouted. "There just the two of you? Nobody else?"

"I'm Jerry Park from West Texas. This is my woman, Gemma. Should we come closer?"

"Sure. But keep those hands up."

Ryan turned to J.B. "Check out there's just the two of them. I'll cover you."

But they'd been telling the truth.

RYAN AND HIS COMPANIONS had very little spare food, banking on some successful hunting the following day. But they shared what they had with the young couple, all of them huddled together in a protected corner of the old church. The horses were hobbled in the far corner of the stuccoed building, beneath a faded fresco of the Blessed Saint Beubo among the lepers.

The threatened storm had arrived even more quickly than they'd expected, bringing endless peals of thunder and sheets of vivid chem lightning that turned the dusk to brilliant day. Rain pounded on the remnants of the roof, dripping ceaselessly from broken iron guttering.

They'd scavenged enough wood to keep a bright fire going, providing a cheerful center as the storm raged violently all around them.

Jerry Park had a hooked nose that had once been badly broken and never properly set. His eyes were brown, so dark they seemed almost black. He was around twenty and close to six feet tall, but so emaciated that Ryan doubted that he would have bothered the scales much beyond eighty pounds. There was an empty holster at his hip and an ancient sheath knife with a broken blade stuck in his frayed belt.

Gemma was also painfully thin. She wore torn cotton pants and a hand-dyed woolen shirt. Her bleached blond hair was tied back in a raggedy ponytail.

Both of them were barefoot.

Nobody questioned the couple until they'd demolished most of the remaining stock of jerky and swilled down a bellyful of good water.

Then predictably, it was Dean who began. "Where you going?"

Jerry answered. "Got a cousin with a spread this side the Grandee. Place called Agua Verde. Heard of it?"

Nobody said anything, letting him talk. "Me and Gemma come from West Texas. I told you that, didn't I? Little ville. Three houses and a privy, my old man used to say. Called Eagle's Fork. Damned sure you won't have heard of it. Nothing to do there. Dirt farmers. Me and Gemma decided to head out and find my cousin, Paulie."

"You know where this Agua Verde place is?" J.B. asked, the firelight glittering red and gold off the twin lenses of his glasses.

Gemma answered. She had a thin reedy voice, like a little girl's, and she constantly watched Jerry as though she were scared about saying the wrong thing.

"Thought we did. Jerry's pa gave us a sort of a map. Done good for the first few days. Like familiar places, y'all know. Then it kinda went shitty on us. Showed a river that wasn't there. Couple roads that like vanished."

"Worst was the wells and water places," the young man said bitterly. "He said— Say, you wouldn't have any more of that jerky, would you, folks?"

"No, sorry," Krysty replied. "But we figure on hunting tomorrow. You'd be welcome to come that far with us. Ride bareback on the pack animals."

Ryan nodded. "We can make some good kills and you're welcome to some meat. Stock up on water in the foothills. And that'll set you on your way again."

"Thanks, mister," Jerry said. "Noise you keep hearing's my belly rubbin' on my backbone. Can't remember the last time we ate proper."

"You see anyone passing by?" Dean asked, glancing at his father to make sure he wasn't putting his foot in it.

"Yeah, we did," Gemma replied. "Must've been about noon, wouldn't you say, honey?"

"Yeah."

"We hid. Like when you all come in, didn't we?"

"Sure did. There was some noise earlier on. Couple wags. Mebbe three or four. Couldn't be sure. Never seen them. Just heard the engines. Going south."

"So, who were the people came by in the middle of the day?" Ryan asked, fairly certain what the answer would be.

"Indians," Gemma replied. "Lots on horses. They stopped around a quarter hour."

"Near a half hour," Jerry corrected. "Ate some food. Smelled like cornbread fritters. Near died smelling it. And some refried beans."

"They pissed in here," Gemma said. "Heard it."

"Smelled it, too, honey."

"Didn't hear what was said? Where they was going? Nothing like that?"

The couple swiveled and stared at Jak, not answering his questions.

He tried again. "You hear them talk?"

"Sure. They spoke their language. Couldn't make a word of it." Jerry continued to stare at Jak. "Mind if I ask you something, kid?"

"Don't call me 'kid.'"

"Sure thing, buddy. Just that I figure you gotta be some kinda mutie. That right?"

"No." The single snapped word should have been enough of a warning.

But it wasn't.

Jerry was insistent. "That white hair and you got triple-odd eyes. Red, ain't they?"

"Red with blood of enemies I chilled," Jak said. "Bit out throats and sucked all blood."

"Holy Jesus in the desert!" Gemma exclaimed. "That surely ain't true, is it?"

Dean giggled, giving it away.

Ryan looked past the couple, out through the dark, empty doorway. "Storm might be passing away," he said. "Be worth us trying to get some sleep, good and early. Get moving then, before first light."

So the party of nine wrapped themselves in blankets and settled down by the smoldering embers of the fire.

Well before dawn, two of them would be dead.

Chapter Seventeen

Trader stirred and muttered to himself, trapped deep in midnight sleep.

It had been a long time before the warm darkness had finally spun its web over his brain. Every week that crept past, it seemed that his sleep pattern was more and more disturbed. He was either sitting up at three in the morning, locked into the dark night of his soul, staring into the smoldering embers of their fire, or he was crashing out, with the evening sun hardly dipped over to the west, beyond the Cific.

Even while his eyes closed, the battle was nowhere near finished for him.

The Trader had always prided himself on being a man who never ever dreamed, or never had any dream that caused him a moment's concern.

"Dreams are weakness," he used to say, when he ran the two large war wags into every corner of Deathlands, when even the most powerful baron would hesitate to alienate the Trader.

Everyone knew that if you crossed any of Trader's men or women, then you were crossing the grizzled leader as well. And he'd come looking for you, with his famous battered Armalite in his arms, like the avenging Angel of Death Incarnate.

He used to boast that he had no enemies. At least, he had no enemies still living.

At his side, deeply asleep, Abe twitched and rolled onto his back, hands cupped protectively around his groin.

Trader was sliding helplessly into the same dream that had been plaguing him for several weeks now. More or less since his ex-gunner had tracked him down in the far Northwest, bringing back memories of one-eyed Cawdor and the pale and laconic Dix, memories that he'd really believed were buried forever.

The memories had formed the backdrop for the repetitive dream that was now composing itself from the broken shards of the tranquil mirror of sleep—a primitive landscape, barren and wild. Volcanic rocks had been twisted and sheared into myriad bizarre, glass-edged shapes. Walking was extremely difficult. Driving was impossible.

The two wags had been left behind. Trader couldn't quite recall where they were.

In the darkness of their campsite, Trader's lips moved, the words hardly disturbing the night air. "Deathlands is my land," he said.

He was wearing steel-toed combat boots, but the razored rocks had cut them apart. His feet were hot, sore, blistered. The sky was a dome of beaten copper, with the sun like molten gold, hanging at its center.

Trader knew that Ryan and J.B. were with him, following close behind, letting him break the trail for them. They rode on his back, sucking at his power, trying to drain him of his life force, so that they could usurp his authority and leave him to die in the shimmering oven.

He paused and stared around. There was a glistening expanse of cracked salt flats a quarter mile ahead of him. The heat distorted everything, but Trader thought that he could make out some mountains, their jagged peaks tipped with snow. How far away? Ten miles? Hundred miles?

Ryan and J.B. were behind him.

Trader turned.

Salt flats. And snow-topped mountains, an eternity away from him.

No sign of Ryan and J.B.

Trader completed the circle.

It was the same every which way he looked.

"Why don't you boys come alongside?" he said. But his throat was dry, his blackened tongue swollen like an old piece of sunbaked harness. He tried to swallow, but his spittle had become fine red dust.

Trader reached a hesitant hand toward his face, feeling the tug of the Armalite strung over his shoulder. There was stubble across his chin, and the puckered heads of old blisters. The corners of his mouth were cracked and so tender that he jumped in his sleep and nearly awoke at the fiery agony.

There was a temptation to lie down and rest, but the honed boulders would have slashed his desiccated flesh back to the bare bones.

At his feet was a small pool of cloudy water, less than a yard across. In its shallows there were shadowy fish moving, tails waving sluggishly. Trader knelt and dipped a hand into the warm liquid, brought his fingers to his mouth and licked them. He spit it out, his mouth puckered at the dreadful alkaline bitterness. It was bitterly undrinkable.

Thirst was overpowering. Trader would have done anything for a mouthful of crystal water. If it had meant pressing his mother's face down into white-hot charcoal, then he'd have done it without a moment's hesitation.

Without a pang of conscience.

That was one of the great hidden truths about the mysterious and solitary man called the Trader. He didn't have anything approaching a normal conscience. Guilt never plagued him. If he had to do something, then he did it. Slit a baby's throat. Gun down a helpless old man. Burn a ville to ashes. Anything.

Betray a friend?

"No."

Chill a friend?

"Yeah."

A friend betrayed was a permanent threat. One day, in some frontier pesthole, there'd be a voice out of the shadows telling you not to turn around. And there'd be the blazing pain of a full-metal jacket bursting your heart and lungs.

A dead friend was no threat to anyone.

While he'd been thinking about that, the landscape had changed around Trader.

Changed from the salt flats.

Now Trader was among the distant peaks. There was no sensation of time or distance passing, but now he could look back and see Ryan and J.B. and... No.

"No!"

The desert was far below and far, far behind.

Right at the farthest edge of seeing, Trader thought he saw something moving fast across the cracked, white surface, a tiny body and immensely long legs, scuttling with gigantic steps. But he blinked, and when he'd rubbed his eyes, the thing had disappeared from sight.

If it had ever been there.

Now the repeated dream was starting to gather its familiar momentum. Trader had started to perspire and his eyes, beneath the closed lids, were flickering from side to side in jerky, involuntary movements.

He was alone.

Betrayed and abandoned by all of his friends. Friends? Men and women who worked for him. Rode with him.

Chilled for him.

The air was a little cooler up in the mountains, away from the baking heat of the lifeless desert. A light breeze was coming from the north, rustling the long meadow grass, blowing at the delicate asphodels.

Trader felt younger, more free.

Despite the pleasant surroundings, the Trader was conscious of an uneasy feeling of apprehension. Somehow it seemed like he'd been there before, almost knew what was going to happen and knew it wasn't good.

The path was winding downhill into a steep-sided valley, cool among graceful pines. Somewhere in the background Trader would hear a dim roaring, muffled and far away.

Now the trail went up a steady incline, among purple rolling hills.

"Ryan? You here? I can hear you, J.B., close by me. Come out where I can see you, friends."

The sound became louder, more distinct.

Under his blanket, Trader clenched both fists, the thumbs tucked into the palms, a classic signal of uncertainty and a seeking for security.

The ridge of granite was dappled with streaks of silver quartz, the colors dulled by the leaden sky. The gorge dropped away in front of Trader, less than a quarter mile off, the rainbow mist from its colossal fall already visible.

The Indian was sitting on a large boulder to the right of the trail, holding up a hand in greeting to Trader. And to Ryan and to J.B., who were walking with him.

"It is a good day, brothers," he said.

Trader nodded. "A good day."

"The walking woman has not passed this way. Have you seen her on your travels?"

Trader looked to see if either of his two oldest companions knew what was being said. But they were both staring toward the invisible waterfall.

He answered the braided Navaho himself. "We have seen no man and no woman walking this way. No animal and no fish and no bird and no creeping snake."

"I am Walks Without Fire and you are Man With Fire in Belly. You are dead."

"No. No, I'm not."

"It is true. You have had much suffering and lonely pain, and that will soon end."

Trader rocked back and forth in his sleep. Tears bunched at the corners of his closed eyes and seeped over his cheeks. The night was passing.

"Am I dying, Ryan? John Dix? Come on, guys, you can tell me. I'm the Trader. You know me."

But the two men were no longer standing with him. Trader had a vague memory of Ryan saying he had to go to do something up in old Seattle.

And the skinny Navaho had vanished.

The scenery had changed once more, bringing him closer to the brink of the drop into the boiling caldron at the base of the falls.

The path had become agonizingly narrow, with a sheer drop to dragon's-teeth rocks, thousands of feet below him. Only forward. Onward and up. A tattered well of ice-cold mist draped around his head and shoulders.

Trader could hear voices, whispering behind him, invisible in the thickening fog. It was a legion of susurrating voices, and he knew them all.

Knew none of them.

"Stay fucking dead," Trader breathed, as he lay in an uneasy sleep.

They were pushing him onward, fingers that feathered at his spine, edging him higher and closer to the slick rocks at the top of the falls.

Now his feet trembled, hanging into the singing space. He glanced reluctantly into the mighty chasm and the toppling torrent of diamond water.

"Please," he said.

It wasn't a word that came easily to the Trader, not a word he'd used all that often in his life. Certainly not for the past twenty years or more.

It was just like all the other times.

No moment of transition. No actual act of tripping or stumbling or being propelled outward.

Just the falling.

Trader started to scream.

He knew that this was just a dream. A scary kind of dream, like lots of ordinary people had. Maybe they had them every night. But Trader didn't.

So there was no need to scream.

Not in a dream, a dream where glistening slabs of rock moved past with a surreal slowness. Where water, cold as eternal death, soaked through your clothes and ran into your eyes and nose and mouth. Making it hard to...

Scream.

Trader couldn't squint through the cascade and see what awaited him at the bottom—the circling maelstrom of grinning green foam, lips parted, ready to suck him inside its maw.

He fell into its heart, at what felt like one-hundredth real speed.

And sank, his lungs bursting.

He fell and began to rise again. A tiny flickering green sun, far above him, drew him out into light and safety. In Trader's mind, the dream had always ended in a bowel-churning terror, not in this quiet ascending toward life.

But something was going to go wrong.

He was near the surface, with a cupful of air remaining in his chest.

"A living man," he whispered through a rising crescendo of bubbles.

When something from the darkness gripped him tightly.

ABE JERKED AWAKE, certain that a gang of stickies had come on them in the night and he was now going to die a hideous death. His ears were filled with a scream so brimming with terror that he very nearly lost control of his own bladder with the contagion of true fear.

Then sense and awareness eased itself back and he won control over himself, kicking out of his blanket and crawling cautiously across toward Trader.

Cautiously because this nocturnal horror had struck at Trader for five out of the past six nights. Each time Abe had shaken him awake. On the previous night, the older man had gripped him by the neck and tried to strangle him. But Trader had become tangled in his own blankets and Abe had been able to break free.

"Wake up, Trader," he said. A part of him worried that the screams might have attracted night prowlers.

"I'm awake." The voice was trembling, an old man's voice. "What the fuck do you want, Abe?"

"Nothing, Trader. Just I thought you might've been having a bad dream, or something."

"Me? A dream, Abe? Come on, man, what the fuck're you saying? Trader doesn't dream."

"Sure, sorry. Course. Sorry."

But Trader was already asleep again.

Chapter Eighteen

Ryan's eye blinked open. Three heartbeats later he was gripping his 9 mm SIG-Sauer.

The ruined church was relatively silent. The only noise was the shuffling of the horses and the mule, their shifting shapes just visible in the moonlight that seeped through the doorway.

It had stopped raining in the last few minutes, as Ryan could still hear water trickling from the damaged gutters. The rest of Opium Wells seemed quiet.

But something had triggered his combat reflex.

Something out of the ordinary.

He lay still. The worst thing a person could do in a suspicious situation was to make a hasty, ill-planned move.

Very slowly Ryan looked around the building, counting bodies under blankets. Unless there was something they didn't know, they were the pursuers and not the pursued. So everyone was taking a needed rest.

Krysty lay next to him, and Dean on the other side. The boy sleeping on his back, snoring softly and rhythmically in the darkness.

Then came J.B. and Mildred, very close together, with Doc last in line, beyond them. Jak was the easiest of the seven to spot, on Dean's left, his hair blazing like a warning flare.

And the two starving young people they'd saved, Jerry Park and Gemma from Eagle's Fork, in West Texas. They'd been sleeping wrapped in each other's arms, over where a corner of the old altar still stood, jagged, close by the end of the nave.

Ryan narrowed his eye, straining to be sure.

"Fireblast," he said, so quietly that he never even heard it himself.

The couple had moved.

Ryan's first gut reaction was to wake everyone, search for them together.

But until he knew where Jerry and Gemma were, that could be close to suicide.

He faked sleep, sighing a little and rolling over onto one side, desperately scanning the place for some clue. But Ryan still couldn't see either of them.

Which left two possibilities.

They were aware he'd awakened and were watching him from the blackness. Jerry had claimed he had no blaster, and the holster had been empty. But Ryan recalled that same holster had been well-worn. It wouldn't have been that difficult, once they spotted the riders coming in, for them to have hidden weapons anywhere inside the church.

Or outside.

That was the second possibility.

Ryan waited, steadying his breathing, his finger still on the trigger of the SIG-Sauer.

The two choices really came down to only one.

The longer he stayed still beneath the blankets, the more vulnerable they all were. People didn't sneak away together in the middle of the night unless they meant evil.

He crawled out of the bedroll, waiting for the flash of fire and the boom of the blaster.

Nothing happened.

Two voices spoke from either side of him.

"Trouble?" J.B. queried.

"Outside?" Jak asked.

Both questions were asked in the faintest whisper, both men pulled out of shallow sleep by Ryan's movement.

If Jerry and Gemma had been in the building, they'd likely have been pressured into making some sort of play by now. But there was still nothing.

There was no need for any more talk between the three old friends.

Ryan went first, his blaster reaching out into the darkness ahead of him, pausing at the doorway. There was no sign of life outside.

J.B. was holding the scattergun at his hip, Jak just behind him, gripping the Colt Python.

Ryan crouched and peered out, keeping perfectly still, listening and looking. He heard a faint sound, like someone digging in soft sand, nearby, around to the left. He gestured in that direction, ghosting through the door in a fighter's crouch. The Armorer and the albino teenager covered him from the shadows.

There had been a heavy dew and the ground was soft, making it possible for Ryan to move around the side of the church in total silence.

Now the sound was clearer, ahead of him, just around the corner where a part of the tumbled roof was still piled against the eastern flank of the building.

Ryan looked behind him and made a circling motion with his free hand, sending J.B. and Jak around the church in the opposite direction, ready to cover any attempt to run for it from the young couple.

They vanished into the blackness and he continued creeping forward, reaching the angle of the walls, looking around it.

The moonlight was thin and diluted, filtered through a bank of low clouds, but it still gave enough light for him to make out Gemma and Jerry.

They had their backs to him, the man kneeling by a pile of tumbled adobe and stone, burrowing away, throwing dirt between his legs like a hyperactive prairie dog. Gemma stood watching him.

Ryan could see the glint of dull metal in her hands, which looked like a .22.

He began to edge closer.

Jerry was talking quietly, panting with the effort of the digging.

"They'd chill us if they could."

Ryan wasn't too sure of the stress in the words. Had the young man said, "They'd chill *us* if they could."

Either way, it didn't make much difference.

"Got it." Jerry pulled out something wrapped in oilcloth, which he uncovered. It was another handblaster, a .357.

Over the years, Ryan had seen some speckled lengths of old vids, played on hand-generated viewers. Some of them—most of them—had involved various ways of chilling. One of the things he'd often noticed and puzzled at was how people seemed to always shout warnings to their enemies that they were about to begin shooting at them.

Stupes.

He leveled the SIG-Sauer and drilled the woman between the shoulder blades. The light hadn't been good enough for a safe head shot.

The 9 mm bullet, exited through the splintered remnants of Gemma's sternum, slicing through her lungs and heart, killing her instantly.

Ryan fired a second time, aiming at the kneeling man. But the woman's corpse staggered a few disconnected steps, arms flailing, and dropped the blaster. She fell into the line of fire, and his shot hit her under the left arm as she toppled, the full-metal jacket tumbling and distorting, ripping through the ribs and chest cavity, angling upward and bursting out through the top of her left shoulder.

For a starving man, Jerry Park was fast in his reflexes and faster on his feet.

He dived away, rolling behind the fallen debris from the church roof and wall, managing to snap a shot off in the general direction of his attacker. The bullet whined fifteen feet past Ryan's face, making him throw himself flat.

The woman was dying noisily, thrashing around, moaning and weeping, pink frothing blood choking her as it erupted from her open mouth.

"Bastard!" the young man screamed, firing twice more, the shots going high and wide.

Ryan lay still and said nothing, knowing that J.B. and Jak would be closing in from the other side.

"Ryan!"

"Stay where you are, Krysty. Everyone keep inside. It'll soon be over."

Another shot whistled by, closer this time, aimed at the sound of his voice.

J.B. and Jak still hadn't showed their hands. Ryan stared into the darkness where he expected to see them appear.

"Come out, son," Ryan called. "Got no chance. Throw down the blaster and just walk away. Keep walking."

"No food and water. And you butchered Gemma, you shithead bastard!"

"You were aiming to chill us, boy."

"Wanted to steal some food and a couple of horses. That was all."

There was the familiar note of self-pity that Ryan had heard in dozens of voices, the voices of men who knew they were soon going to die.

"Come out, Jerry."

"You'll chill me. Don't trust you."

Ryan half smiled. The young man was right. If he'd come out and thrown down his blaster, Ryan would have shot him down without a moment's compunction.

It wasn't a game.

For several long seconds, nobody spoke. The woman had died, lying sprawled near the small pit where the blasters had been concealed.

Ryan caught a glimpse of something white at the far angle of the church's wall. Jak's hair. That meant J.B. would be there, as well.

If they all opened fire, the young man would have no chance. But it meant wasting a lot of ammo. And ammo in Deathlands was more valuable than a handful of jack. Be like dropping a brick of gold to crush a rat.

"Give you a count of five, Jerry," Ryan called. "Then it's finished. One, two, three..."

Though he must have realized his position was totally helpless, the skinny young man made a try for it. He came out firing, jinking to left and right, then sprinting straight toward where Ryan was lying in the dirt.

He stretched out the SIG-Sauer, holding his right wrist in his left hand for extra steadiness and accuracy. Jerry was around fifty feet away from him, his own blaster blazing.

Ryan put two spaced bullets into the young man, one into the stomach, just above the belt, the second a hand-span higher.

The first shot would have killed Jerry Park. Slowly.

The second one did the job a whole lot faster.

His handblaster went flying into the night sky, landing thirty yards behind him. It seemed like Jerry's feet had broken away from him, moving under their own control, sending him staggering to his left, arms flailing, mouth open. A scream rose from his chest into his throat, never quite making it as far as his mouth. The blood that flowed from the two mortal wounds was as black as jet in the threads of moonlight.

"Done for," Jak said, stepping out into the open at the far angle of the church's walls.

"Why?" Mildred asked, emerging with the others from the doorway.

"Guns. Horses," Ryan replied.

"You had no choice? You had to kill both those distressed and hungry young people?"

Ryan holstered the SIG-Sauer. "No, Mildred, I didn't have to chill them both. I could easy have let them chill us."

He turned away from her and walked back into the adobe building.

Chapter Nineteen

Dean Cawdor was the first of them to go out, with the earliest light of morning still an hour away. The air was fresh and cool, and the land lay under a pale pinkish glow.

Inside the Opium Wells church, the rest of the party was readying itself and all the animals for another hard day's riding.

The boy picked his way outside, pausing to listen. His father had warned everyone that the carrion lying by the church wall could attract the desert scavengers. But there was no hint of the presence of coyotes.

Dean unzipped his dark blue pants and readied himself to urinate. He'd just started, hearing the powerful stream as it hissed into the sand, when a hard hand clamped itself over his nose and mouth and he felt the hot pain of a knife point, pressing in beneath his right ear. A ruby of warm blood inched down his neck, vanishing into the collar of his shirt.

"Still, little one," a voice breathed. "Very, very still and those dark ones, the night winds, might not visit you for many years."

Dean considered trying to get at his own turquoise-hilted knife, but he had enough sense to realize the utter futility of the idea.

The hand smelled of horses and was extremely strong, and there was the odor of male sweat and bear grease.

"We might not wish you harm, child. But we must know who is inside and where they go. I will slowly take away my hand, and you will answer my questions. Or you will sleep forever in the long blackness. Do you understand me?"

Dean nodded, ready to try to bite the hand, kick backward, scream like a banshee and run like hell.

The voice was calm, not unfriendly. Dean's guess was that one of the band of Navaho had been back-tracking, maybe heard the sound of the two shots from the SIG-Sauer and returned to scout out what was happening.

"My knife will drink deep if you even begin to think of a stupe plan. Now my hand is moving."

Dean took a deep breath, filling his lungs for a warning cry to his father and the others. Then he hesitated. If the man was a Navaho, then they might even have a commonality of interest against the General.

"Won't shout," he whispered, pulling an embarrassed face as his voice went all high and squeaky on him.

"It is good. How many of you?"

"Plenty."

"Blasters?"

"Plenty."

Dean heard something that might have been a stifled laugh. "This is good to hear."

At the side, Dean was aware suddenly of movement and a second, whispering voice, meaning that it could be the whole hunting party around him.

The man holding the knife to his throat spoke again. "There was shooting, boy. We would know what happened. And we would know what you do out here in our lands above the Grandee."

Dean took a calculated risk, drawing in another breath. But, before he could speak, the hand was back over his mouth.

"Death is long, boy."

The hand moved away once more. Dean licked his lips. "My Dad didn't raise me to be a triple stupe, mister."

"So, what do you do here?"

"We aim to chill the General and every one of his cocksucking gang of bloody murderers."

Dean heard the gasps of surprise from all about him.

"You chase the General?"

"Yeah. And you're the band of Navaho that we know's been chasing the fuckers as well."

"This is true."

"Woman we know and her little baby—" he hesitated for a moment "—and another real good friend all got chilled by the General."

Someone else spoke at Dean's back, in the guttural tongue of the Native Americans. Others in the band were talking excitedly. Finally the man holding him leaned closer and whispered into his ear.

"The small ranch beneath the hills?"

"Yeah."

"Ah. We passed by it but we did not stop. We were also hurt much by this General and his murderers. If we had known there were those hurt, then we—"

"Wouldn't have done nothing," Dean said. "Already way too late for them."

Unconsciously he had been speaking just a little louder than before.

The point of the knife had moved away from his neck and the tension had eased.

"We had best speak with—"

Out of the cool blackness, Ryan's voice interrupted him.

"Got six blasters on you, mister."

The hand was jammed across Dean's mouth again, the edge of the blade laid across the front of his throat. The man holding him was so powerful that he effortlessly held the lad off the ground, his feet flailing helplessly.

"Boy dies," the Navaho growled.

"We all will."

"You can't see us."

Jak's voice said, "I see all nine of you. Big man holding Dean got check shirt and long hair tied at back with ribbon. Want to know more?"

Something was muttered in Navaho, drawing a swift, angry reply from the man who gripped Dean.

Ryan spoke again. "You think this is a standoff, but it's not. Worst happens to us is that you slit the throat of my son. That'd be a bad thing, but I guess that one day I'd manage to get over it. Do that and every one of you dies. Make sure the bodies get mutilated and blinded. Give you all a triple-bad time to crawl throughout eternity."

"Boy says you after General. Tell me."

Dean kept still, knowing that there was nothing he could do to help his father and the others. The only consolation he was able to find was the fact that not many people actually wanted to get themselves chilled.

Ryan was calm, his voice unhurried. "Friend of ours—the one sees in the night—had a spread up north. Fine wife and baby there. Another young man was staying with them while the rest of us went hunting."

"What is the name of the young one who can see so well in the dark?"

"Apaches called me Eyes Of Wolf," Jak replied. "I nearly married Steps Lightly Moon." He paused. "Name among Anglos is Jak Lauren."

The Navaho hesitated a few moments. "You are the one with the hair like snow?"

"Yeah."

"My people know about you. A friend to us. It is said that your woman and baby and friend were all sent into the beyond by the General."

Ryan answered him. "That's right. We figured that you and your people might also have a grudge. Be chasing him. Might even know where the cold-heart son of a bitch has his headquarters. Could be we could ride together on this."

"Let me speak awhile with my brothers on this. What is your name?"

"Ryan Cawdor. Apaches called me One Eye Chills. Let the boy go before you start talking."

"He is our only card."

Dean could almost see his father's grim, lopsided smile. "Not even the two of clubs, mister. Not when we got a fistful of aces back here."

The Navaho let go of Dean's mouth. "How many? The truth? How many of them?"

"Six. Got scatterguns and an Uzi automatic. Steyr rifle with a night scope. True what Dad says. You can chill me and nobody could stop you. But then..."

"A threat from a child." The Navaho laughed and repeated what Dean had said to the others.

"Not a threat. It's a promise," Dean insisted. "Best you believe me."

The knife disappeared, and he was pushed firmly in the direction of his father.

"They let Dean go," Jak called, the albino's excellent night vision helping again.

"Here," Ryan said.

The boy's eyes had adjusted to the darkness and he could make out the group of six friends, standing or kneeling in a loose semicircle, about thirty paces away from the whispering Indians.

The brightest point of light came glowing from Jak's hair.

Behind him, they could all hear the Navaho in deep conversation, their voices rising.

"It sounds as though our putative allies are a little undecided," Doc said. "Which reminds me of the time I stood astride the Continental Divide, on one of my camping trips of yesteryear. There was a sign that said that it was the place for the undecided raindrop."

"How's that again, Doc?" Krysty asked, fascinated with the old man's peculiar story, despite the dangerous tenseness of the moment.

"Well, my dear madam, it is simple. It was one of the points in the old United States where a drop of rain might be carried either to the east or the west. To the Pacific or to the Atlantic Ocean or the Gulf."

"What if it fell—" Dean began, but a shout from the leader of the Navaho interrupted him.

"We have spoken."

"And?"

"We will come and talk more."

"That's good," Ryan said.

THE GENERAL WAS better known among the isolated communities of the Native Americans than among the flea-pit villes of the Anglos.

The leader of the Navaho, whose name was Sleeps In Day, told Ryan and the rest of the group about the attacks by the heavily armed band of killers.

"General is not a stupe. He knows that to tackle any baron in the Southwest could lead to defeat. Though he has two wags—once he had three—and twenty or so men and women, he would lose against sec forces."

"So he picks on ranches and the hunting camps of your people?" Ryan asked.

"It is so. We have blasters, but not many. They are old and much repaired. Few repeating rifles. No grens."

"How did the General come to lose his third wag?" J.B. asked.

The powerfully built Navaho smiled, his teeth white in the dawn that was now creeping fast across the land. "A number of the young men of the Comanche were clever. And lucky. The wag was trapped in soft sand crossing a river. There was much driftwood and dried branches close by."

One of the other Navaho said something, and the whole party laughed.

"What did he say?" Dean asked.

"Two Dogs Fighting said that the evil men were like rabbits in a cooking oven. Their cries made our Comanche brothers smile for many long minutes."

"They burned them?" Mildred queried.

"Yes. Piled the brushwood around under cover of night. Kept them trapped in their useless wag with arrows, then set them on fire."

"What did the General do? How come he didn't try and save his wag?"

Sleeps In Day looked at Ryan. "The General is not a man with a heart of bravery. Only the coldest of meltwater trickles through his body. He saved himself and abandoned his followers to the dreadful death they deserved."

"What did General do to make you chase?"

The Navaho looked across impassively at the albino teenager, pausing before answering the question.

"What they did to your woman . . . the one who was kind and walked crookedly. And to the baby. The General did that to our women. To our little ones."

One of the others said something, a harsh, angry, monosyllabic sound.

Mildred nodded. "I still remember enough of the language from my college minor. He said that nine of their people had been murdered."

"Nine!" Krysty shook her head, the long hair seeming to discharge a shower of bright sparks into the cool morning air. "Gaia! We owe it to the land to carry out a cleansing of this man, don't we, lover?"

Ryan nodded. "Yeah."

To the Navaho, he said, "You have any idea where the General holes up?"

Sleeps In Day nodded slowly. "They have their home camp in the place where there is always night."

"Caves," J.B. said.

"Yes. There are many bats in the caves. Creatures of the dark. It is right for the General."

"Then we best go pay him a visit," Ryan said. "And soon."

Chapter Twenty

After the first brightness of the dawn, the sky darkened once more, as though time were being reversed and night was looming over the far horizon.

Ryan hunched his shoulders against the cold norther that was blowing across the foothills. "Some serious rain going to be falling," he said.

"It drops upon the General." Sleeps In Day smiled grimly. "The gods are with us, brothers."

J.B. had heeled his gelding alongside Ryan. "Those wags can get through most kinds of weather, but a flash flood would slow them down some."

The sky to the south was as black as pitch.

Even as they all looked in that direction, there was a dazzling bolt of purple chem lightning, cutting from land to sky. Dean counted off the time until they heard the distant rumble of the thunder. "Twelve to fifteen miles," he reported.

"How far to the caves?" Ryan asked.

The Navaho passed the question to his comrades, all sitting silently on their stocky ponies. The one called Two Dogs Fighting answered him.

Sleeps In Day translated. "It is half a day at a fast ride. A full day if we go more slowly and more carefully."

"Other side of these hills?" J.B. was standing in the stirrups, looking as far ahead as he could.

The Indian nodded. "There is an old blacktop that we will cross. The camp of the General is hidden beneath the land, very deep."

"Any your people made inside?" Jak rubbed his white hands together, feeling the morning cold more than the rest of them.

"No. Not to return alive."

Ryan whistled between his teeth. "Time's wasting," he said. "Let's go."

But the leader of the Navaho held up a hand. "A moment, so that we are all sure of what is happening."

"How do you mean?"

"We ride together against the General."

"Sure." Ryan puzzled at what the check-shirted Navaho was leading up to.

"If we win?"

"Then he gets chilled and we all go home."

"Who chills him? Who will count coup on this shadow from the dead world?"

"Me," Jak said. "Anyone does it... me."

"We have lost more. Every man has lost a wife or a sister or a child."

The teenager's bloodless lips peeled back off his sharp teeth, in a feral, dangerous smile. "Then we see.

Man gets there first gets to do it." He pointed to himself. Me."

THE TRACKS WERE EASY to follow, eight big wheels on each wag, driving their relentless way south. The General didn't seem to be in too much of a hurry, probably unaware that he was still being followed. J.B. was a good tracker, but he was happy to give best to the Native Americans.

The youngest of the Navaho, called Man Sees Behind Sun, was the finest. He led the way on a spirited pinto, occasionally vaulting from the blanket across the animal's back, stopping and running his fingers across the furrows, feeling the temperature and the moisture of the hatched marks.

He told Sleeps In Day that they were closing in on the wags. "He says that we are only about four or five hours behind them."

"Could be that they're just taking it easy to try and economize on gas," J.B. suggested. "Probably their HQ got a good store of it."

They reached the edge of the threatening storm a short time later. The air had the bitter flavor of ozone from the lightning that had strafed the mountainside, spooking the animals, making them skittish and difficult. Judas, in particular, was even more stubborn than usual, taking a bloody chunk out of the thigh of one of the Navaho who made the foolish mistake of riding in too close to the mule.

A number of small streams flowed down toward the arid plain, all of them filled to overflowing, bubbling and racing over the quartz-lined rocks.

The gradient had become more steep, and the tracks of the wags showed that the hill had been a problem. At one point, with a steep drop to the right, there were clear skid marks, going to the brink of the fall.

"Slowing them down," J.B. called to Ryan.

"Yeah. Not helping us any."

"Storm's riding ahead of us. We're on its tail. They're in its heart."

DOC FOUND HIMSELF at the head of the procession, perched on the big barrel-chested roan gelding, leading the first of the trio of pack horses on a strong rawhide line tied to his own pommel.

The trail was narrower, less than twenty feet across. To the left was a rock face, craggy and irregular, streaming with muddied water. To the right the trail vanished into singing space. There had been a metal fence bordering the old road, back in the times of the long winters, but it had long gone, leaving only occasional rotted iron posts.

As he rounded a sharp bend, half-turned in the saddle to call something out to Mildred, who was next in line, the old man barely registered the mutie cougar.

The creature was poised to spring, on a spur of wet, gray rock a dozen feet above him.

"By the..." he began. His hand fumbled for the butt of the commemoration Le Mat in his belt, but Doc knew in his heart that he was going to be too slow.

Way, way too slow.

The animal screamed as it leaped, a throat-tearing cry of crimson hatred and hunger.

It hadn't eaten for three days. In fact, the tiny, injured bat that had provided its last meal had upset it, given it a tearing illness that raced through its body, making breathing difficult, distorting its sight so that it missed three separate kills of deer within the hour, that very morning, before the storm had hit.

Now the cougar knew it was seriously sick.

A band of pain pulsed across the wedge of cranial bone above the eyes, and it had a feverish desire to move. The storm had left water everywhere, further enraging the mutie animal. The sore on its lips where the dying bat had nipped it with its needle teeth was throbbing with a sucking agony.

It wouldn't go near the puddles, despite a raging thirst. Clots of thick greenish-white foam dangled in ropes from its tender, aching jaws.

It had heard the sound of hooves moving along the overgrown blacktop, where it waited, crouching patiently among a glade of stunted lodgepole pines. There had been food passing along the track earlier, but it had been sealed in noisy, shiny boxes, impossible to enter.

The cougar measured a good twelve feet from its nose to the root of its yard-long tail, and stood nearly four feet tall at the shoulder.

As it leaped down at the snow-haired human on the dappled gray-white horse, it was consumed with a blind lust to rend, crush and kill.

Its normal caution and hunting cunning were long gone, abandoned in the orange mist of the virulent strain of rabies that was destroying it.

As it jumped, its thrusting rear paws slipped in the mud that coated the rock, throwing it slightly off its aim, which momentarily saved the life of Dr. Theophilus Tanner, of South Strafford, Vermont.

The cougar had aimed its spring at the throat of the man, but it fell short, its honed claws raking across the chest of the gelding, its weight knocking the horse sideways—sideways toward the drop into the ravine on the right of the trail.

Doc clung to the horse's neck as the animal, spooked out of its skull, reared and kicked out, whinnying in terror at the apparition from hell.

Mildred was riding second, behind the string of pack animals, with Judas on a lead rein just behind her. The mule was so vicious that it would have been madness to try to attach it to the other three horses.

J.B. was third, with the rest of the party strung out behind him. The Navaho had chosen to ride as a rearguard, all nine of them together.

Only Mildred, on the crown of the bend in the track, saw what had happened.

What was happening.

The enormous buff-colored animal, its heaving flanks streaked with gray-orange mud, its jaws flecked with foam, eyes staring blindly, landed awkwardly in the rutted highway. It spun and snapped for a moment at its own hind legs, then powered up from a crouch, snarling, straight at the belly of Doc's own mount.

The dainty little bay mare that Mildred rode was also spooked by the attack of the raging carnivore. She took a dozen rapid, pecking steps backward, making Judas bare its teeth at her. The mule then kicked out behind it at J.B.'s gelding, starting a chain reaction of utter confusion, with those farther down the line having no idea what was going on up at the front.

Doc had his sword stick jammed into his own saddlebag, and he made a desperate grab for it. But the cougar was beneath him, disemboweling his horse with a single raking blow, opening it from chest to groin, spilling the doomed animal's intestines in greasy loops into the mud.

The three pack animals had totally lost all control, rearing and screaming and edging one another toward the sheer drop over the cliff.

Mildred drew her pistol, gripping the ZKR 551 in her right hand, struggling to control her terrified mare with her left hand. But she was no great horsewoman and found it impossible to take a shot at the mutie creature. The only chance of using her skill as a shootist was to slip from the saddle of her mount, but it was rearing and kicking so wildly that it was hopeless.

It was a scene of wild chaos, in which things still seemed to be happening with a fearsome slow motion.

As Mildred watched, Doc's horse started to fall sideways, dying from the ferocious attack. The cougar had slithered away a few yards, sliding on its stomach through the slimy mud, its eyes locked on the white-haired old man. And one of the pack animals was teetering on the brink of the cliff, hooves scrabbling for grip.

Despite the odds, Mildred fired twice, feeling the .38 buck in her hand, but she had no idea where the bullets went. All she knew for certain was that neither of them struck the crouching cougar.

Then Ryan arrived, a wild, whooping figure. His big gray stallion brushed past Mildred, the SIG-Sauer drawn in his right hand, his heels kicking into the flanks of his horse to urge it on.

"Jump, Doc!" he yelled. "Jump now!"

The last of the string of pack animals was going over, head thrown back, spine arched like a bent bow, its weight dragging the other two after it. The tautened line attached to Doc's saddle began to pull at his dying gelding.

"Jump!" Ryan screamed, fighting against his own animal's terror, trying to draw a bead on the snarling cougar that was flattened against the streaming rocks, less than ten paces away from him.

Doc half leaped and half tumbled from the saddle, managing to snatch at the lion's-head hilt of the sword stick as he toppled off, on the side away from the ravine.

On the same side as the rabid carnivore.

Mildred could only watch helplessly, aware of the mule behind her, braying at the top of its lungs. And J.B. and the others jostling together to try to find out what was happening around the gooseneck bend in the trail.

Ryan fired twice, the heavy handblaster booming out above the bedlam of sound. Both rounds missed by a yard or more. Normally that alone would have deterred a cougar, but this one was different, too far gone along the road of diseased madness to be checked in its purpose.

Its corded muscles tensed as it readied itself to drive in at the helpless figure of Doc, rolling in a disorganized tangle of arms and legs in the dirt.

Ryan knew in that instant that he was going to be too late to save his old friend. One blow from either of the cougar's front paws would be enough to take Doc's skull off his shoulders.

Mildred saw the damnedest thing she'd ever seen in her life.

The mountain lion was in midair, when Ryan threw himself from the high saddle, straight at the animal, swinging the heavy blaster at the cougar's head.

There was the satisfying clunk as the barrel of the P-226 smashed into the creature's jaw, splintering one of its front teeth, knocking it off balance, so that it rolled sideways in a spitting bundle of blind fury. Blood trickled from its open mouth, mixing with the sticky froth.

Ryan came up into a combat crouch, the double-action blaster steady in his hand, drilling toward the mutie animal.

Doc was scrabbling on hands and knees, trying to locate the butt of his Le Mat.

"Bastard," Ryan hissed.

The cougar's brain had vanished into a whirling madness. It knew that it had leaped at the helpless two-legs, and should by now be savoring the hot salt taste of spilled blood, feeling bones crunch and crack with their delicious inner sweetness.

But something had gone wrong.

Now it crouched again, only the tip of its tail twitching, conscious of a new pain in its mouth, breathing thickly, swallowing with difficulty.

The thirst redoubled.

And there was another of the stinking humans, kneeling submissively before it, ready to receive the swift benison of its wrath.

Ryan squeezed the SIG-Sauer's trigger, aiming carefully at the center of the animal's face, drilling the bullet through its clogged nostrils, past the soft tissue, into the boiling chamber of its brain.

For the cougar there was a devastating impact that rocked its head on its heavily muscled neck. Darkness descended over its eyes, and there was a strange chill feeling at the rear of its angular skull.

"Again," J.B. called from somewhere behind Ryan. "One more."

The mortally wounded cougar had somehow struggled up to its feet, standing unsteadily, growling deep in its throat. Blood and brain tissue were trickling from the shattered back of its head, and more bright arterial blood dripped steadily into the dull watery mud below it.

Ryan shot it through the chest, a little to the right, splintering ribs and ripping the irregularly pounding heart to shreds of torn muscle.

The cougar toppled on its side, its legs carrying on for several seconds with a strained, walking motion, as though it didn't realize that it was dead.

Its breath leaked out in a curiously human sigh, and then it was still.

Ryan was aware of a cacophony of noise all around him.

The three pack horses had vanished over the drop, and were about to pull Doc's roan after them. The old man had risen shakily to his feet, taking a hesitant step toward the doomed animal, stopping at a shout of warning from Ryan.

"Leave it, Doc. Too late."

The saddle horse disappeared with a high, thin scream of agony and terror. There was a moment of relative silence, then they all heard the sickening crash of the four animals striking the jagged rocks three hundred and fifty feet below.

"I fear that I needs must rely on my own legs for transport," Doc said a little shakily.

"Not necessarily." Mildred grinned, pulling at the leading rein. "There's Judas here, ready and able. But not very willing."

"I would rather die, madam, than trust myself to that spavined brute."

Ryan was already reloading the SIG-Sauer, looking back at the watching faces of his friends and the Navaho. He turned to Doc. "Could be death to try and make it that way," he said.

"Still to be preferred to that devil's walking parody of all four-footed things."

Judas was standing, splay-legged, glaring at the angry old man. Sensing it was at the center of the discussion, it threw back its head and brayed noisily.

"There, Doc." Dean sniggered. "Can't wait to get to be better friends with you."

"If you are that eager, you spawn of Satan, then why don't you ride the donkey and I'll take over your pony?"

The boy grinned again. "Thanks a lot, Doc. Thanks, but no thanks."

Ryan grabbed at the bridle of his own horse and swung himself back into the saddle. "Time's wasting, Doc. Looks to me like Judas or nothing."

"Then I fear that it will have to be nothing."

"That your last word, Doc?"

The old man folded his arms across his scrawny chest and nodded. "Indeed. That is my last word."

Chapter Twenty-One

"Looks like a fish trying to ride a bicycle," Mildred commented, heeling her mount alongside Krysty.

"More like a goat astride an alligator," the flame-haired woman suggested.

"Oh, yes," Doc snorted. "Merriment and what-not! You cackling harpies! You two would have been most admirably sitted to suit... I mean suited to sit, knitting beneath the shadow of Madame La Guillotine, and jeering at the tumble of every aristocratic pate that rolled into the blood-sodden straw."

"Temper, temper, Doc," Mildred warned, wagging a reproving finger at the red-faced old man, perched uncomfortably on the back of Judas.

"I confess most freely that I had no idea what temper meant until I attempted to ride this misbegotten son of a sea cook. My dear and saintly mother once hired an Irish cook. Flaming red hair, begging your pardon, Krysty, my dear. No connection, I am most certain." The mule stopped suddenly, nearly tipping Doc over its head. He responded by giving it a clout around the side of the jaw with a clenched fist, and it immediately resumed its halting gait forward.

"You have a wonderful way with animals," Sleeps In Day said solemnly.

"Runs in the blood," Doc replied.

"How about this Irish cook?" Mildred asked.

"What's 'Irish' mean?" Dean asked.

"It would take me far too long to answer that," Doc said. "But I tell you she had... What was her name? Mary? Marie? That was the name of the latest flame."

"What are you talking about, Doc?" Krysty asked. "Try and stick to the point, will you?"

"Mary, it was. Hair like... Anyway. She had the most ferocious temper I ever knew. I would only have been about nine or ten, and I took pleasure in teasing the poor woman. I knew her rages and that gave a spice of true terror to the teasing. But she taught me a lesson one day. Sadly my mother dismissed her on the spot, but I still remember it."

"What did you do, Doc?" Mildred swatted midges away from her face. After reaching the edge of the storm, the dark clouds had raced ahead of them, leaving a sultry, leaden calm. A heavy sky lowered upon the sixteen riders.

Nearly three hours had slipped by since the sudden attack from the mutie cougar, and they were moving along, southward, still following the blurred tracks of the two wags.

"A simple matter of changing over the sugar and the salt as Mary was preparing the luncheon. The potatoes and the stew were peculiarly sweet while the lemon mousse—her pride and joy—was oddly bitter." Doc lifted a hand to his mouth, but failed to smother a mean little snigger.

"That's really shitty, Doc." Mildred eased herself in the saddle. "Be glad when we can finally rest some," she said. "Anyway, what did this redheaded cook do to punish you? Hope that it was nothing trivial."

"The woman came from a long line of powerful giants," Doc replied. "She took advantage of my relative weakness to strip me of my knickerbockers and my drawers."

"What?" Dean said.

"Took off his pants," explained J.B., who had fallen back to hear the story.

"Then what?" Krysty asked.

"Covered my... the... all of... in molasses."

Everyone laughed at the expression of remembered distaste on the old man's wrinkled face.

"All over your cock and balls?"

"Yes, my dear young Dean. Precisely as you so explicitly put it. And, indeed, all over my rectal orifice. That was not so uncomfortable in itself, but the removal was... To recall it still brings tears to my eyes."

"And your mother fired her?" Mildred tutted. "Shame on her and shame on you. Still..."

"Still, what, madam?"

"Explains a lot about you, Doc."

He would have pursued the matter further, but Judas chose that moment to sit down like a ton of bricks, making the old man slide backward over his rump, finishing in the mud.

"Sure right." Ryan grinned at Sleeps In Day. "Doc has a wonderful way with animals. Or do they have a wonderful way with him?"

MAN SEES BEHIND SUN, the youngest of the Native Americans, spotted a steep-sided, narrow arroyo a couple of hundred of yards ahead of them, not far from the crest of one of the rolling, sagebrush-covered hills. He called their attention and led them quickly to it.

"Why we going there, dad?" Dean asked, as they walked their mounts in a long line, with the first spots of rain already beginning to patter heavily around them.

"In a chem storm, the higher you are and the more exposed you are, the more dangerous it is."

"I know that. But we're going up the slope."

"Navaho says we can get inside that arroyo. Protect us from chem lightning."

"What about a flash flood? Always thought you should never shelter in a small valley in a storm."

Ryan nodded. "True again, Dean. That's why we go up so's we can go down. No risk of getting trapped in a flash flood if you're close to the top of a rise."

And so it proved.

RYAN SAT HUNCHED OVER, his back against the steep slope of the arroyo, his mind numbed by the ceaseless pounding of the rain on the top of his head and nape.

It was as bad as anything he could remember.

Trader had once said that the only thing rain did to a healthy man or woman was make them wet.

But Ryan could recall a near tragedy when Trader's saying had been proved false.

There had been an engineer on War Wag Two. His name was Lek, a fat guy with only one eyebrow and a silver streak through his dark hair, the result of a knife scar in a pesthole on an island near Ell Ay. He'd always been unbalanced, and the Trader had warned him a couple of times about his behavior.

One day in the Apps, they'd been camped in the middle of a torrential downpour. The rain slanted against the sec-steel roofs and walls of the two ponderous wags, making conversation almost impossible.

There'd been an argument...Ryan couldn't remember the details. In the close confines of the war wags, it was all too easy to have a major row about a minor disagreement.

Lek had freaked out. Ryan had always been suspicious that the engineer was secretly into jolt. But Trader was strict on drug users and abusers. At least Lek had been clever enough not to get caught.

Now he started screaming about being locked in. Going "clostro" was what it was called.

The man had darted to one of the side doors and started to open the sec bolts. Trader had given the order to leave him be, not wanting to risk a fight inside the wag.

Ryan could still remember the way the noise of the storm grew suddenly much louder as the vanadium-steel door swung open, hastily pulled shut by someone.

"Okie," he remembered. The water was streaming between his boots, tinted a grayish brown by the dirt it was washing away from the top of the arroyo.

Everyone had crowded to the ob ports along the side of the war wag, and a voice had come crackling over the intercom, warning that someone was out in the rain. Nobody answered the voice.

Ryan closed his eye, recalling what he'd seen through that smeared armaglass.

Lek stood with his arms straight down at his sides, hanging limp, as if someone had simultaneously dislocated both of his shoulders. His legs were apart, as if he were braced against the enormous weight of water tumbling onto him. His shaved head was bowed, his uniform instantly soaked through.

Trader used the external mike. "Come in and stop fucking around," he boomed.

Lek seemed to ignore the voice. Then he turned slowly toward the wag, his face splitting into a madman's smile, very gentle and very homicidal.

Ryan remembered Trader's immediate order to seal the wag and not allow the deranged man back inside.

The silver streak in the mat of sodden hair glistened like a mag flare, and the streaming face shone like a polished melon as Lek slowly lifted his head to stare directly upward, opening his mouth wide.

Hunaker had been pressed against Ryan, squinting through the same circular window.

"Fuckhead's goin' to drown himself," she hissed. "Shit for brains!"

Hun wasn't that often wrong.

Lek was almost invisible, the tumbling shroud of rain masking his outline, so that he looked like a vaguely humanoid statue, veiled in solid water.

Ryan rubbed at the condensation that misted the window, trying to see more clearly what was happening.

Lek seemed almost to be melting, sinking to his knees, his mouth open, filling with the solid rain, his staring eyes pits of frothing liquid.

"Want me to go out and bring him in, Trader?" Ryan called. "I could deck him first."

"No." The single flat syllable was unarguable.

"Down," Hunaker whispered, her breath warm against the side of Ryan's stubbled cheek.

The madman had slithered onto his back, chest heaving, hands now lifted toward the merciless heavens. But he had still made no attempt to save himself by turning onto his stomach, keeping his face out of the downpour.

Hunched down in the arroyo, Ryan was breathing slowly through his half-open mouth, trying to avoid sucking in water from the storm. Lightning had rocked the ground, striking less than a hundred yards away, outside the walls of the gully. The bitter stench of the chem storm flooded his nostrils and the thunder pounded at his brain.

It addled his mind, making it difficult to remember what he'd been remembering.

Lek.

Down and dying and drowning.

As the rain tumbled into Lek's open mouth, flooding his nostrils, the man had suddenly begun to thrash around, as though he'd realized too late what was happening to him, sensing his own dreadful, choking doom.

The New Mexico rain now felt as though it were gathering momentum and power. It bounced back off the ground, filling the air with a fine spray of tiny droplets. For a moment there was a scintilla of panic, fluttering at the back of Ryan's mind, the fear that he would no longer be able to breathe properly without inhaling the invasive liquid into his strained lungs.

And end like Lek.

"Going into spasm," someone had said near the navigation deck of the war wag.

The man was thrashing from side to side, his fingers knotting above his head, though he was still making no obvious effort to try to keep the torrent from pouring into his nose and mouth. His chest was heaving as he coughed and retched, yellowish water bubbling from between his gaping jaws.

Suddenly Lek's back arched and stiffened, so that the only points of contact between his body and the streaming earth were his heels and the crown of his head. A moment later everything relaxed as all the cords were cut.

"Heart failure." The voice from the starboard machine-gun port was J.B.'s.

Ryan could still recall the way the raindrops bounced off the blind, staring eyes.

He also remembered that Trader had refused to have the body buried, regarding it as a total waste of time and energy.

IT WAS LATE AFTERNOON when one of the Navaho glimpsed the two small wags, cresting a rise about three miles ahead of them. The pursuers were closing in.

Chapter Twenty-Two

The food was gone, tipped into the abyss with the four dead animals.

Ryan had considered the suggestion of Sleeps In Day to go down after the animals and butcher some meat, but it would have taken them hours and lost vital pursuit time. So they'd snatched the chance of pressing on with no supplies and very little water, hoping to take what they needed when they finally caught up with the General and his killers.

The sight of the struggling wags, laboring to reach the top of a steep incline through deep mud, encouraged everyone in the pursuing group.

"Could take them," Jak said.

"They are near to their home." The leader of the Navaho brushed back an errant strand of sleek black hair from his dark eyes. "Night will come well before we catch up with them. And they will be safe."

Ryan shook his head, moving in the saddle to face the Indian. "No. They might be in their base, but it doesn't mean they'll be safe. No."

"Is there anything between here and there?" J.B. asked. "Shelter? Any sort of ville? Pesthole?"

Sleeps In Day turned to his companions, repeating the question in their own tongue. There was a shrugging of shoulders and shaking of heads.

But Ryan noticed that the oldest of the group of warriors was looking as though he were nearly going to speak.

"What about him?" he said, pointing at the long-haired, heavily built man.

"Who? You mean Thomas Firemaker?"

"Yeah. Ask him again."

Sleeps In Day did as Ryan asked. The older man looked embarrassed at finding himself the center of attention, and he didn't reply for several long seconds. Then he muttered something, pointing a little way to the east of the trail that they had been following south.

"What?" Ryan said.

"Thomas says he remembers coming this way, hunting with his father." More speech from the other Navaho. "His father... No, the father of his father was dying of rad sickness at the time and they looked for a place for him to die."

At the mention of rad sickness, both Ryan and J.B. glanced instinctively down at the tiny rad counters each wore on his lapel.

Both had moved from the safe green into the slightly more dangerous yellow. But it was still a good distance from the threat of orange and the serious menace of red. They both knew that the southwestern area of Deathlands was one of the worst for hot spots of residual nuke radiation from the days of skydark, partly because of the number of secret missile installations that had been seeded throughout the region.

"And what did they find?" Krysty asked, taking a cautious sip of water from her canteen. At least the storm earlier had given them all the opportunity to top up their drinking supplies.

Thomas Firemaker spit out a short sentence and then heeled his mount away from the others.

"What's wrong with him?" Dean pulled on the reins as his mount started to follow the other pinto pony.

Sleeps In Day answered. "The General murdered the mother of his mother and his own mother and the sister of his mother and the sister of his wife and the brother of his sister's wife as well as the son of—"

Dean held up a hand. "I get the picture. Yeah, I see."

"What did Thomas tell you about this place where he took the dying man?" Mildred rubbed at her eyes, showing the exhaustion that all of them were feeling.

"He says it was unspoiled, behind where the land had once jumped and slipped. A place where in the ghost times the Anglos would stop to eat."

"Diner," Mildred said. "By God, but he means there's an old diner."

FROM THE OUTSIDE, Mom's Place was still in amazingly good condition.

On the way to the diner, following the grudging leadership of Thomas Firemaker, they had passed a place where there had obviously been a massive earth slide, blocking off the highway. But some time in the past couple of years the rains had eroded the blockage away, reopening the side trail, revealing the single-story diner for the first time in a century or so.

It had originally been covered in a thick layer of stucco, painted to resemble genuine adobe. But the hundred years of extreme weather had cracked and fissured it, reducing it to an indeterminate pallid gray brown.

"All the windows are still there," Dean said. "Hardly ever seen anyplace predark like that."

His father eased himself, stiffly, from the saddle, throwing the reins over the stallion's head and looping them around a rusted metal fence that had probably once marked the edge of the parking lot of the isolated eatery.

"Place is sheltered here," he said to Dean. "I'd figure that about ninety percent of the damage done to buildings in the old times gotten done by man. Or muties."

"Make that ninety-nine percent, Ryan," J.B. said, hissing through his teeth as he straightened his back. "Dark night! I'm not cut out to ride on four legs. Sooner we can catch the General, the better. Mebbe even steal both of his wags to ride back home again."

The wind was rising as the day crawled to its ending. A six-foot ball of tumbleweed rolled down from higher up the hills, brushing past the wall of the diner, spooking Judas just as Doc was in the process of clambering off its back.

"By the Three Kennedys!" Doc managed to keep his balance, and quickly knotted the reins around the fence. "I have traveled many a country mile with you, Ryan Cawdor, but I have seldom taken less pleasure in the journeying. I am very much a man of peace, as you will all bear witness, yet I shall be more than happy to speed this General and his thuggish gang into the blackness of an afterlife. Anything to avoid having my buttocks separated by this jolting creature. After half an hour it becomes uncommonly like sitting astride a circular saw."

The Navahos hadn't dismounted, sitting together in a tight bunch.

Ryan glanced back at them. "What's the problem, Sleeps In Day?" he called.

"We will not enter."

"Why?"

The other warriors muttered among themselves. The burly leader nodded to them. "We all say we will not enter."

"Sure. I hear that. But you have to say why."

"No."

"Look. It's going to be one hell of a storm some time in the next hour or so. We need shelter. We need rest. This time tomorrow there'll have been a shitload of chilling done. Not all of us might make it home. So, we all have to be at our best. Come on, we're together in this."

The Navaho shook his head, stubbornly refusing to say anything to Ryan.

It was Doc who broke the silence. "My dear Cawdor, perhaps I might offer a solution?"

"Sure. Go ahead."

The old man stalked across the damp sand to stand close to the huddled group of Native Americans. He addressed his remarks to Thomas Firemaker.

"You mentioned that you had been here, in this place, some time ago."

The oldest of the group nodded slowly. Sleeps In Day answered for him. "It is so."

"When the diner was sealed off by that earth slip? Of course it was then. You must have stumbled upon this by accident, while out hunting. And you had an elderly and sick man with you. Am I correct so far?"

The Navaho leader looked impassively at him. "There is no magic in this," he said.

"Of course not, my dear man. I have no pretence to be some sort of shaman. I have no wisdom." Mildred coughed loudly to show her feelings, but Doc ignored her. "But I believe I understand the reasons for your obvious reluctance to enter Mom's Place. Should I continue?"

Sleeps In Day didn't reply, but Ryan called across. "Carry on, Doc."

"The old man died, did he not? He died here, in this isolated relic of a forgotten past. Ended his days in the haunted catacomb of long-gone white men. Thomas Firemaker, is this not the truth of what happened?"

Sleeps In Day started to speak in his own tongue, translating Doc's words. But the long-haired old warrior replied himself. His English was slow and halting from a long lack of use, like a farm gate in need of oiling.

"You speak right. It was a hard passing, with snow lying thick. In there—" he pointed with a long forefinger "—I see things as they were. It is like..." He struggled for the word, finally whispering to his leader.

"He says that the diner is like a water hole of time, still and held forever."

Doc nodded. "An oasis, by God! A time capsule. I've seen that sort of thing before in Deathlands. Like a fly trapped for all eternity in a glistening bead of amber, unchanged and unchanging. And now you fear that the spirit of your father's father lies in wait for you in there. That is it, is it not?"

His voice rose at the last few words, and he triumphantly rapped the ferrule of his sword stick against a small rounded boulder at his feet.

"Been watching too many reruns of *Perry Mason,* Doc," Mildred called.

But everyone was concentrating on the face of the oldest of the Navaho, seeing the struggle written clearly there. "It is as you say. The passing from here to the other side was long and painful. In the ending it fell to me to help him cross. There was much pain and he cursed as he died."

"Cursed you?" Doc asked.

"Cursed my father. Me. This place. Said his spirit would never leave it."

Krysty had dismounted and walked to stand alongside Doc. "I have the skill of 'seeing,'" she said. "I can feel if there is evil anywhere. It's something I inherited from my mother, Sonja, when I was a child in the ville of Harmony."

The Navaho looked at her, no sign of emotion on any of their faces. Sleeps In Day hawked and spit in the dirt. "Words are chains of silver. They bind us. How do we know you speak the truth about this?"

Her emerald eyes flashed like green fire in the gloom of evening. "You don't. No way I can prove this. But in your hearts I think you can tell the difference between truth and lies. And you know which I deal in." She waved a hand at the others behind her. "What we all deal in."

Thomas Firemaker spoke. "You feel bad things here?"

Krysty shook her head, her bright hair seeming like sparks of living fire around her face. "No. I would tell you if I did. To risk danger when there is no need is without any point. I say we should go in and be safe against the night."

It wasn't quite that simple.

The Indians argued among themselves for several minutes. Surprisingly Thomas Firemaker appeared to be strongest in favor of using the diner for shelter. It was one of the others, Young Pony Runs, who seemed loudest in opposing the idea. He was in his early twenties, with a massive scar across his forehead, barely healed. It was caused, so Sleeps In Day had told them, by the butt end of a rifle from one of the General's men. He was yet another in the party with a special reason for chilling the General personally.

"Why can't we go in, anyway, Dad?" Dean asked. "Let them do what they want."

"No." Ryan was adamant. "This isn't an easy alliance, Dean. I'm not going to try and push them one way or the other."

At that moment, Sleeps In Day swung his leg over his horse and vaulted athletically to the ground, followed by the rest of the party. Young Pony Runs was the last to move.

Mildred went first, standing by the doorway, ready to push it open. "Welcome to Mom's Place," she said.

As she touched the outer door, there was the crashing of breaking glass.

Chapter Twenty-Three

"Termites," she said. "Wood's rotted and it only took a touch for the whole front pane of glass to fall in." She grinned. "You can all put away the blasters."

As she scuffed away the piled shards with her boot, the rest of them relaxed, holstering pistols and uncocking rifles.

"Mebbe the whole place is likely to fall on our heads," J.B. commented, staring anxiously up at the flat roof. "Walls have some cracks in them."

"Stood for a hundred years." Ryan grinned at his old friend. "And I guess it'll stand for another ten hours or so. Let's find out."

The window glass at the front was dulled by the scouring winds of the region, flyblown and covered with thick dust and the ghostly veils of myriad spiderwebs.

A sign hung crookedly, with the single word Closed.

"I'll go first," Ryan said, the SIG-Sauer P-226 tight in his right hand.

He took a couple of careful steps, feeling the boards creaking under his feet. Then he stopped, paralyzed by the sight that met his eyes.

Ryan had seen a number of flickering, and rarely complete, predark vids over the years, often showed on soiled bed sheets with someone panting away over a pedal-operated power generator. He had always found such films totally fascinating, giving a peephole into the past.

It was surprising how often these vids seemed to show characters sitting in diners, eating and drinking and using the setting to carry on the plot lines. In fact, it had sometimes seemed to Ryan that people in the sunny times before the long winters had spent most of their time in diners.

Now, in Mom's Place, in the wilderness that was southern New Mexico, Ryan found himself in precisely such an eatery, perfectly preserved, like some magical hologram.

"Fireblast," he breathed.

The building was about eighty feet long and twenty-five feet wide, with a counter running along most of one side, a flyspecked mirror behind it. Along the other wall, by the front window, were a number of small booths, with plastic tables bolted to the floor, two swivel seats on each side.

On each table was a chrome box of what looked like loose sheets of faded and brittle paper, and what Ryan knew from the vids were salt and pepper shakers.

At the back was a pair of single doors. One had a sign that read Does and the other one Bucks. He had a vague idea that these must be men's and women's crappers.

One by one they walked inside, standing in a huddle by the broken door.

"Think there'll be some food?" Dean asked, but nobody answered him.

J.B. catfooted around the end of the counter and cautiously pushed at a swing door that opened into a small kitchen area. "Nobody," he said over his shoulder. "Not a sign there's been anyone here for years."

Krysty stood with a hand on Ryan's arm. "Gaia! Like some sort of museum."

Doc sneezed. "Sorry, my friends, but I fear the powdered rocks of ages have infiltrated my poor old sinuses and given them a severe working over." He stared around him. "I have never..." he began. "This is like...like some of the more atmospheric paintings of Edward Hopper. I can hardly believe it."

The nine Native Americans had followed more slowly, not one of them actually setting a moccasined foot over the dusty threshold of the diner. They peered around with something that seemed very close to fear.

"Seems safe," Ryan said. "Anyone wants to look around can do so."

KRYSTY LAUGHED as she stood arm in arm with Ryan, reading the faded, hand-lettered notices pinned up all along behind the counter. "Friendliest little diner in the whole damned world," she said.

Ryan nodded.

No long hairs . . . girls not counted.

Truckers do it all night long.

The NRA Never Rejects America.

Prices do not include tips.

If'n you don't like it, then get the fuck out of here.

"Wouldn't have cared too much to have met Mom," Ryan commented. "Don't think I'd have cared too much for eating in her diner, either."

"They used to call me Greaseball Tanner, in my fancy dining days—though I never got fat," Doc said. "Just look at the menu. I have not seen so much potential heavy grease since the last time I went to mud wrestling."

"French fries with everything" was the proud boast at the top of the menu.

"Wouldn't mind buffalo burger, onion rings, bacon, two eggs your style and fries," Jak said. "Wouldn't care how had cooked."

"How about their all-day breakfast?" J.B. asked. "Could do a job on that right now."

"Choice from ham, link sausages, patties, eggs, mushrooms, steak, tomatoes, hash browns, corn, okra, bread, coffee. No add-ons for set price."

The dish of the day was catfish and boiled potatoes, and at the bottom of the board was the selection of desserts.

Mildred had picked up one of the printed menus from a table, which gave amplified details of the dishes available on the blackboard. "Gets better and better," she said. "Listen to this description of their chicken special dinner." She took a breath and started to read. "A boneless breast of chicken has been personally selected for your dining pleasure. Our cook has coddled and cared for it, covering it in a secret blend of herbs and spices, and left to marinate for up to thirty minutes."

"One of the all-time *cordon bleu* marinades by the sound of it," Doc said sourly.

She pulled a face at him. "Miserypuss! Where was I? Yeah." Mildred continued to read from the stained menu. "It's served on a bed of fluffy rice with a selection of vegetables, hand-picked at dawn and prepared with... Can't read it. Buried under a seal of ancient ketchup."

"Never mind, Mildred." Krysty laughed. "Sounds just about good enough to read, but not good enough to eat. Reckon I'm glad that Mom's Place is permanently closed."

Dean had gone through into the kitchen, calling out to his father. "Looks like they just left!"

Ryan joined the boy, smiling ruefully. "Something sad about this sort of thing. You're right."

At a superficial glance, it really did seem that the people who'd run the diner, a hundred years ago, had just walked out for a breath of the darkening late-afternoon air, leaving everything just as it had been.

There were cups and dishes in the steel sink, the crusted food thoroughly fossilized by the passing time.

The greasy water had long, long drained away, leaving a coating of whitish scum on the dull metal.

The chopping board had been in use, though the vegetables had disappeared into a dry, multicolored smudge on the hacked wood. Knives and spoons were all around, where the dead hands had laid them down in that moment of panic that had brought word of death from the skies. Death had probably been borne on the polished wings of neutron missiles, death that had taken away the soul of every living creature and left the buildings standing.

The eight-ring stove had several pots and pans on it, all filled with a rotted powder where there had once been stews, refried beans and potatoes.

"There's cans of food on the shelves," Dean said, pointing to the long wall of the kitchen. "Oh, but it looks like they've all blown."

They had. Every one.

Now all of the Anglos were in the room, while their Navaho colleagues stayed in the outer part of the diner, unable to conceal their unease.

Mildred and Doc were looking in the cupboards, while Jak had picked up the biggest of the serrated meat knives and was balancing it on his palm, as if he were considering adding it to his armory. "Nice," he said, dropping it back onto one of the work surfaces.

Krysty was taking off the last orders from the spike and trying to read them. "Too far gone. Don't seem many, like business was bad that day."

A calendar was tacked to the inside of the outer door, showing scenes of beautiful New Mexico. It was for the year 2001, a year that was barely started when it was over.

When it was all over.

"Some brandy here," Doc called. "Better part of two-thirds full."

He handed it to Ryan, who glanced at it. The label was torn, but he could still read the words Emperor Maximilian. The back door was unbolted and Ryan opened it and threw the bottle into the scrub, hearing the crash as it fell.

"Why did you do that?" Sleeps In Day asked. "It is that you think we cannot be trusted with liquor."

"No. Not that at all," Ryan replied.

"Then what?"

"That was a hundred years old. I once got triple sick from something that old. Might taste all right, but I still figure it's better to pass on it. We're a small force, Sleeps In Day, and we can't afford not to have everyone fit and well for tomorrow. You agree?"

The Navaho stared at him, then took a slow, long breath. "Yeah."

"ONE OF THEM'S GONE," J.B. said, beside Ryan as the one-eyed man started to unroll his blanket.

"Who?"

"Kid."

"Man Sees Behind Sun?"

"Yeah. One that was so good at reading the trail. I noticed he's gone."

The two old friends kept their voices pitched low, not drawing attention to their conversation. They could easily have been discussing the rate of fire of a Mannlicher Model L against a Steyr SL.

There was no sign in the body language of either man that the news of the missing Navaho could be terminally disastrous for all of them.

Ryan glanced around the diner. The rest of the Native Americans were gathered at the end two tables, sitting and talking quietly. "They know?"

"Must do." The Armorer shook his head, sucking air between his front teeth with a faint whistling sound.

"Gone to tell the General where we are?"

"Could be."

"Then we chill the others right now." Ryan stood. "Use the Uzi on them. I'll pick up the spares with the SIG-Sauer. Not worth taking a chance."

"You sound like Trader," J.B. said, grinning. "If in doubt, fill the graveyard."

"Trader kept himself alive a long time thinking like that, didn't he?"

"Sure. Might still be this side of the black river for all we know."

"So?"

J.B. shook his head at Ryan. "Doesn't make sense. Think about it. They want to betray us, then they wait until we sleep and try to take us all out. No point going to tell the General where we are. No advantage in that."

Unheard by either of them, Jak had ghosted up behind the two men. "Agree with J.B.," he said. "No point."

"So, where's he gone?" Ryan asked, feeling vaguely annoyed with himself for overreacting the way he had.

The light outside had quickly faded close to darkness. The albino teenager called across to the Navaho. "Sleeps In Day?"

"What?"

"Where's Man Sees Behind Sun gone?"

The Indian didn't answer immediately, and Ryan felt the familiar faint prickling at his nape. Then it passed with the chief's reply. "We think that the wags could have trouble on last part of journey home with the weight of rain."

"And boy's gone look?"

"Correct. He will be back before the middle of the night to tell us."

Ryan was suddenly angry. He slammed a fist on the nearest table, making it shake and rattle. "What the fuck do you think this is? Some bastard sun-dance game with a white buffalo and all your mystic shit?"

All of the Navaho were on their feet, gripping weapons. The Anglos had stopped what they were doing and stood frozen, hands on blasters.

The only exception was Doc, who was out in the kitchen, oblivious to the tension, singing loudly to himself.

"It is wise what he has done," Sleeps In Day protested. "You know that."

"I don't know shit!" He was aware of a vein pulsing across his temple, the livid scar flaring from the chillingly pale blue eye, down to the right corner of his thin-lipped mouth. "We fight together or we split up, now. The kid might get caught and betray us all. Could be they'll see him and follow him back here. Then we all get to be fucking dead. You should have stopped him. You're the leader!"

Krysty was staring at him, mouth half open, as if she were going to say something but didn't know what.

Sleeps In Day sighed. "No. Your ways are not the ways of the people. True, I am leader of this hunting party of warriors. But I do not command and order my brother to do anything. We all do what we wish. After the slaughter of our sisters and brothers by the General, we all wish his death. We see that we are stronger with you Anglos. That is all."

Ryan licked his lips, passingly surprised at just how dry they'd suddenly become. He blinked and rubbed the back of his hand across his eye, feeling the tension ebbing from him, the red mist lifting his mind.

"I'm tired," he said. "Best keep a watch. Your men want to share it with us?"

Sleeps In Day translated the suggestion to the rest of his group, and all seven nodded agreement. "Yes," he said. "We will wait and watch together."

At that moment, Doc pushed through the swing door, singing the last lines of the song. He stopped, sensing that there had been a tension in the diner in his absence. "Have I been missing something? Is something wrong?"

Ryan grinned. "No, Doc. Not a thing."

Chapter Twenty-Four

Man Sees Behind Sun reappeared between midnight and one o'clock in the morning.

Ryan himself had been on watch, along with Two Dogs Fighting, patrolling the area of scrub around the building. There was a clump of saltwater cedars at the edge of what had been the parking lot, and Ryan spotted the blur of movement that was the returning young Navaho.

The Steyr SSG-70 was ready in Ryan's hands, and he brought it slowly to his shoulder, knowing how easily a sudden movement could be detected in darkness. The Starlite night scope fixed to the bolt-action rifle, with its laser image enhancer, showed the details among the shadows of the bosk with a shimmering clarity, picking out the crouched figure of the warrior working his way cautiously toward the diner.

"Come ahead," Ryan called, having checked to make sure that nobody else was close by.

"How you know he there?" Two Dogs Fighting asked, appearing from the blackness behind Ryan, who had realized some time ago that all of the Navaho spoke English to some degree.

"Blaster sees behind night," Ryan replied.

DESPITE HIS PROTESTS, Dean was awakened and sent out on watch with Young Pony Runs, while everyone else gathered in the dining section of the time-trapped eatery to listen to the report from Man Sees Behind Sun.

Doc, sleepy-eyed, was trying to fold the fragile paper napkins into an infinitely complex shape that would result in a perfect chrysanthemum, but the great age of the material kept defeating him.

Krysty had asked Ryan whether he intended to take the young warrior to task for creeping off without letting them know where he was going, but he'd already decided there was no point in pursuing the matter. Better by far to simply accept what had happened and let the matter drop.

Trader always used to say that wasted words were as much good as pebbles dropped down a dry well.

The pretence of incomprehension was gone, and Man Sees Behind Sun spoke in his own words, not bothering to let Sleeps In Day translate for him.

"The rain was bad and I thought, when we saw the wags at a distance, that there might be trouble in climbing the hills. They are steep ahead."

Doc crumpled up another failed piece of origami and threw it on the floor.

"I went through the night, following where I was able. There was enough of the moon to see the trail of the wags. It was as I thought. One had gone. The other had not."

"What do you mean?" J.B. asked, leaning forward. "You mean there's a stranded wag out there?"

"Yes. It is so."

"Where?"

"South."

The Armorer clenched his fists in irritation. "We know it's south. We don't know how far."

"Between one and two hours."

Ryan caught J.B.'s eye and nodded to him. "Call it around seven miles. That would tie in with what we saw there."

He turned again to the Navaho. "You have a chance to see if the men were with it? Or whether the General's taken the crew along with him, back to their base?"

The thin-faced teenager took his time in answering. "I cannot be sure," he finally said.

"But?"

"But I think some had gone and some had not. I crawled close to where they were buried above the... What is the word for the rod between the wheels?"

"Axle," Jak said.

"Yes. The mud was thick, completely above the axles of the wag, and it will take much digging to free it. As it starts to dry, so it will harden."

Ryan tapped with his fingers on the plastic tabletop. "How many men?"

"Four or five. One is a woman."

"You heard her?" Krysty asked.

The young Navaho hesitated a moment, seeming to be embarrassed at the question.

His own chieftain pressed him. "You heard the voice of a woman, Man Sees Behind Sun?"

"I saw her."

"How?" Mildred asked.

"She climbed out and made water close to where I was hiding. Very close."

Jak grinned. "Means she pissed on you?"

"It is not good to ask that," Sleeps In Day said sternly. "Not good."

The albino stared at him, holding the eyes of the older man with his own ruby gaze.

Ryan broke the moment. "Four or five and one a woman. That's all we need to know."

"Why didn't chill her?" Jak asked. "That close."

"It would have raised an alarm," Sleeps In Day replied. "He did right."

"Guess so."

Jak looked at Ryan. "Start vengeance tonight."

THEY WERE READY TO MOVE in less than fifteen minutes. The only thing that held them up was an argument over the animals. The Navaho wanted to take their ponies with them, while the Anglos preferred leaving them behind at the diner.

"They'll raise the alarm," J.B. said. "Specially the damned mule."

"Then leave them. But our ponies are trained in war. They will not betray us."

Everyone was up on their feet, except for Doc, still struggling with his paper-folding. At the very beginning of the discussion he'd made clear his preference.

"I'd walk barefoot across the hot plate of Hades rather than have to willingly climb aboard that razor-backed, whoreson creature again" had been his comment.

But the Native Americans were united in their decision. In the end, Ryan decided that there was no point in sustaining the division. Time was passing, and it would be a meaningful victory if they could destroy one of the General's wags and take out some of his force before dawn. But to delay their combat plans by even a half hour more could jeopardize the entire deal. First light comes early in the Southwest.

"All right," he said. "We'll go with you and ride. But I say we stop a half mile off and tether the horses. You agree?"

"I agree," Sleeps In Day replied.

"Excellent," Doc said loudly, turning every head in his direction.

"Thought you didn't want to have to climb onto Judas again," Mildred said.

"What, madam? Oh, that! Well, that is true, but look at this." He proudly held up a tiny paper model of a Chinese junk, fully rigged.

Dean opened the front door, creating a ripple of wind across the diner, enough to destroy the fragile little vessel in the old man's hands.

"Sorry, Doc," the boy said.

"Everything passes." Doc sighed. "If I have to endure further torture on the back of that mule, then let us begin. Soonest started, soonest finished is my motto."

THE NUKE STORMS of the past day or so had made the trail more difficult. At one point they had to detour a half mile to the east to avoid a narrow defile where the gray-orange mud lay churned and thick.

There was a brief flurry of further rain, driving in on the teeth of a cold norther.

The visibility was very poor, and Ryan had to keep resorting to the Starlite night scope.

For some time they were riding in silence, along a narrow diagonal valley, with sparse clumps of stunted live oaks standing among the sagebrush. But the trail finally began to wind upward again and, at last, Ryan held up a hand, calling softly for the others to halt.

"I can see it," he said. "Best tether the horses here and go ahead on foot."

As he dismounted, Ryan noticed that two or three of the Navaho were fumbling with small leather pouches that they wore around their necks. He knew they contained a mixture of magical, shamanic symbols, different for each man—a pinch of sand or a pebble or a bone or the tip of an arrow.

Sleeps In Day caught him watching. "It will be a good day to die, brother," he said.

"SOMEONE HAS TO STAY with the horses."

"Why me?"

"Because I say so, Dean."

"Why not the youngest of the Indians?"

They were around six hundred yards from the stalled war wag, in the middle of a grove of elders.

Ryan bent down so that he didn't need to raise his voice to his son. "You do it, Dean, just because I tell you to do it. Now, if you don't like that, then get right on your pinto and ride away from me."

"Dad!" Dean sounded shocked.

"I mean it. You know I mean it. There isn't time to discuss what's wrong and what's right, son. This is the razor-edge between living and not living. I can't risk one of the General's people circling us and taking out our mounts. That happens and we don't get to win."

"Oh. So, if someone comes, I chill him?"

"With the blaster. That 9 mm Browning cannon of yours. Don't wait until it's too late. Better you shoot too soon and miss and warn us than holding fire and not giving us time to get back here. All right?"

"Sure, Dad."

Ryan patted his son on the shoulder. "Good, Dean. That's real good."

THE WIND HAD FRESHENED, driving away the banks of sullen clouds that had been veiling the moon. The land was bathed in a silver light, making the approach to the bogged-down wag a deal more dangerous.

Man Sees Behind Sun led the way, with the rest of them strung out in a ragged line. Ryan would have felt more comfortable with a proper skirmish approach, pausing now and again for the pointman to go on recce.

But this attack wasn't in any sense under his command, and he had to force patience on himself.

Krysty was at his side when he voiced his doubts. "Just hope they don't go whooping in without any warning or word," he said. "Get us all a slice of the farm if they do."

"You sound like Trader when you say things like that, lover. A real lack of trust of anyone except yourself and those closest to you."

"Guess that's likely true enough," he admitted. "Is that bad or good?"

She shook her head, her fiery hair almost invisible in the darkness. "Can't say. Just have to wait and see which way the cards fall."

"You feel anything?"

"No. You know that a firefight can't be read like that. Mebbe a doomie could guess at what might happen. Not my skill. Just have to wait."

Chapter Twenty-Five

It was an LAV-25. Originally built to take a crew of three, it had probably had a lot of its useless comm equipment stripped out to enable it to carry more men.

Just as the young Navaho had said, the vehicle had slipped sideways off the muddy trail, halfway up a fairly steep incline, and slithered down into a quagmire, where the axles had vanished.

It was in no danger, and a digging detail would have shifted it within three or four hours.

"No guard," Ryan whispered, having checked the surrounding area with the night scope.

"Must figure they're safe enough, this close to their home base." J.B. studied the stranded vehicle. "We got two choices."

"Get them out and chill them. Or leave them in and chill them." Ryan looked sideways to Sleeps In Day. "You got a preference for how we do it?"

"Preference? That is a word that I do not know."

"Means having to pick between two ways."

"I would like to have them outside. It would be good to try and have prisoners to let us take some revenge."

"Not really time for that," the Armorer argued. "Just how far off is the General's HQ?"

"Close. The main entrance to caverns is beyond the next hill."

"So they could hear shooting?"

The Native American put his head to one side, considering. "I think they would not. The wind comes up to us from the Grandee. It would carry noise away north from here."

"Shame we got no grens," J.B. said. "Open the lid and drop one in and watch 'em cook."

Ryan nodded. "Agreed. But we don't."

"We could do what has been done before."

Ryan looked at the Navaho. "What?"

"Set a fire around them."

It was an option, but Ryan didn't like it. "I reckon they must be aware there's some risk. Might be one of them on watch from the ob slits or inside the turret. Can't see clearly enough to be certain of that."

"Four or five inside." Krysty looked toward the horizon. "Dawn'll soon be on the way."

Young Pony Runs coughed to draw attention to himself. "I will crawl close. Then knock on the walls of the wag. They come out and shoot me. I fall and they look to see if I am dead. You hide close by and shoot them all."

Ryan blinked his good eye. "I don't... You mean to stand there and let them chill you?"

"Yes."

He considered the idea, deciding that it wasn't a good combat option, with the likelihood that the defenders of the war wag would choose to stay snug inside.

"No. I can't let you sacrifice your life just like that. Death in a firefight's one thing, but not this."

"You cannot stop him," Sleeps In Day said.

"Sure. But I won't support it. There has to be a better plan than that."

IT CAME from Jak.

"No need big fire," he said suddenly.

"How do you mean, Jak?"

The teenager nodded toward Ryan. "Important thing is make think fire."

J.B. slapped his hands together. "Dark night! Kid's got it. Sorry, Jak. Slipped out."

Doc had been tracing invisible patterns in the sand with the ferrule of his sword stick. "Forgive me, ladies and gentlemen, but I fear that the young man's runic comments have quite flown o'er my head."

Ryan explained. "Jak's right. A big fire wouldn't work. Take too long and the risk of it being seen at the base. But if we lit a real small fire..."

The old man grinned, his perfect set of teeth floating like a row of ghostly ivory in the darkness. "A little smoke and they will believe we intend to burn them out. The frightening thought of remaining inside a potential oven will work wonders on their depraved minds and—"

"Rats from holes," Two Dogs Fighting concluded.

"Precisely," Ryan said.

He chose Jak and Man Sees Behind Sun to go with him, leaving J.B. and the others to follow close and pick positions where they could move in support.

Once everyone knew what they were to do, everything clicked quickly into place.

Ryan had emphasized that the day would be lost if anyone opened fire too soon. "Seems like four or five, and we know one of them's a woman. So, be triple patient. Make sure that they're all out in the open."

Trader had used to say, in that sort of situation, that a man who pulled the trigger too hastily could reckon on chilling some of his friends with the bullet.

RYAN CHECKED his wrist chron, knowing that J.B. would be doing the same, somewhere in the surrounding blackness, taking up the agreed positions in a loose circle around the LAV-25.

Ryan had the only night sight and had handed over the Steyr rifle to Mildred as the finest shot among them, a move that attracted some surprised looks from the Navaho at the idea of a woman having skill with a blaster.

She should be able to pick off some of their enemies as they scrambled from the turret on the wag, while Ryan, with Man Sees Behind Sun and Jak, should be close enough to take out the others.

That was the idea.

DESPITE THE RECENT RAINS, it wasn't hard to find sun-dried branches of sagebrush and mesquite and, best of all, a cluster of creosote bushes.

Moving with infinite care, Ryan and his companions dragged the clumps of vegetation along with them, closing in on the stalled vehicle. As they got near, Ryan sniffed the air. Jak was right at his side.

"Gas?" the teenager whispered.

"Yeah. Must have a small leak. Could help us."

It was only a dribble of crude gasoline, running into the sand between the rear wheels, but it would be helpful to get their fire going.

They'd all been out in the night long enough for their eyes to have become reasonably accustomed to the darkness. When they got within a dozen yards of the bulk of the wag, they all kept still, watching intently, trying to decide if the General's people had anyone on watch. But there was no sign of movement around the turret.

Ryan had figured that their chances were good, even if someone was watching from inside the wag. The big 25 mm Bushmaster cannon would be far too clumsy to hit them at close range. And they would hear if anyone started to move the M-240 coaxial machine gun to open fire on them. The only serious risk that he considered was someone with a small-caliber handblaster firing from one of the ports on the side.

But there was nothing.

"Asleep," the young Navaho whispered.

Ryan knew that there were two exits available on the LAV-25—one directly from the turret, and the other nearer the front. If the plan worked, then those inside were likely to come out either or both.

"Probably both," Ryan muttered.

"Who lights fire?" the young Indian asked.

"You. I'll take the top of the wag, and Jak can cover the front. But nobody does any chilling until we think everyone's out. That way we should get them all. Don't want anyone left safe and snug inside, able to start firing the cannon and warning the General that he's under attack."

"I have ignites to begin the flames," the Navaho said. "Take all of the brush to near gas leak."

Ryan nodded. "Sure. Let's get everything in place for the fire. Others should be where they should be by now."

THE ARMAMETAL WAS COOL to the touch. Ryan climbed up, using the foot- and handholds, taking the greatest care not to let his combat boots scrape on the hull of the wag. He knew from years of personal experience that any slight sound would be magnified to those inside.

He stood for a moment, steadying himself on the top of the turret, looking out toward the horizon and seeing the pale glow of the false dawn. Time was moving too fast. Ryan gently tested the handle on the hatch, but wasn't surprised to find it bolted shut from within.

There was a flicker of movement ahead of him as the albino swung himself up over the protruding front of the wag.

Everything was ready.

Time seemed to stop as Ryan sat down and waited for the action to begin. He'd readied himself mentally, steadying his breathing and slowing his heartbeat. There would be blood on his hands in the next five minutes, as there had been a hundred times before.

Perhaps his own blood.

His sensitive hearing caught the tiny scratching sound of a self-light. Almost instantly his nostrils detected the scent of fire, the arid bitterness of desert smoke, overlaid with gasoline and the odor of the sagebrush.

"Now," Jak breathed, a scant eight feet ahead of him.

A tiny flame became visible between the tops of the bogged-down tires, under the vehicle, growing stronger, the smoke now visible in the darkness.

Ryan saw the Navaho move out from the fire that he'd lighted, jogging a few yards and crouching behind a boulder, becoming instantly invisible.

Now the tension was rising.

Fifteen years ago he'd sat with Trader, both men leaning against a tree near the crest of a hill, the older man with his Armalite while Ryan had been holding a pump-action Remington 870 scattergun.

They'd been hunting somewhere up around the Cascades when they realized that they had become trapped between two bunches of stickies. They didn't know how many there were in either party, but they knew the muties were closing in on them like the jaws of a nutcracker.

So all they could do was sit and wait.

Trader had picked a daisy from a clump near his boots and was gently plucking it apart, petal by petal, peering at it, as though he were admiring the wonders of Nature.

Ryan had never forgotten that moment.

Now, with the wisdom of age, he realized that Trader had been doing it partly for his benefit, demonstrating just how calm and unworried he was by the imminent threat from the wolf's-head bands of muties.

As the first of the stickies breasted the rise, unaware of the presence of the two norms, Trader had dropped what remained of the flower and dusted his hands clean before ripping the muties apart with a burst from the Armalite. Ryan had never even touched the trigger on his shotgun.

Now he was waiting once more to spill the lifeblood of enemies.

The fire was growing, the flames crackling and the smoke thickening around the stranded wag. It could only be a matter of seconds before someone inside smelled the danger through the vent ports.

"What de fuck!"

The voice was thick with sleep, puzzled.

"Hey, there's a fucking fire someplace."

"Outside or in here?"

"¿Quien es?" a woman asked.

"Get your foot outta my fuckin' face, will ya!"

Ryan had the SIG-Sauer cocked in his right hand, balancing himself and waiting.

Jak wore his satin-finish Colt Python in its holster, but Ryan guessed that he might choose to rely on the assortment of leaf-bladed throwing knives that he kept concealed on his person.

Man Sees Behind Sun had been carrying a sawed-down shotgun of indeterminate age and make.

The smoke was thicker, wreathing up, almost white in the darkness of early morning.

Now the voices that Ryan could hear from inside the trapped war wag were rising, overlapping, showing the first signs of serious panic. It had become almost impossible to catch what was being said, or shouted, just an occasional word. "Burned! Indians! Alive. Hatches."

Ryan stifled a cough. He heard the sound of a sec bolt snapping back and readied the powerful handblaster, flattening himself down behind the turret where a quick glance wouldn't be likely to spot him in the smoke and blackness. He figured the General's troops weren't likely to take too much time and care looking around before getting out of what must seem like a death trap.

The main hatch to the wag crashed open.

Chapter Twenty-Six

The only person, out of more than twenty involved in the brief skirmish, who was able to see what was happening was Dr. Mildred Wyeth.

She had found a good prone shooting position, and rested the barrel of the Steyr between two large sandstone boulders, the polished walnut stock cradled against her shoulder. A 7.62 mm round was already under the pin, and her right eye was pressed to the rubber-edged sight.

She'd seen Ryan climb slowly onto the rectangular bulk of the war wag and hunker behind the turret, in back of the big gun.

Jak moved into her range of vision like a snake, his white hair as bright as a magnesium flare with the Starlite enhancer, sitting cross-legged, just at the back of the forward hatch. As far as Mildred could make out, the teenager wasn't holding any sort of weapon.

And the Navaho was crouched near the bundles of brush that all three men had dragged to the wag. The scope didn't give anything like full daylight clarity, with the figures slightly fogged and blurred, but it was still a hundred times better than the darkness that Mildred saw every time she removed her eyes from the sight.

The flame was extremely bright, making her blink, the fire spreading quickly, bands of smoke uncoiling like clouds of white chiffon.

She moved her focus slightly, whispering a warning to J.B. on her right and Doc on her left. "Get ready. Any moment now." She heard the words passed along the line by Dean and Krysty to the patient Navaho.

The front hatch clattered back, heard by everyone around, followed only a half second later by the main entrance to the wag, on the turret.

Mildred's index finger curled around the narrow trigger, taking up the first pressure. She drew in a deep breath and held it. At the level of pistol shooting where she'd represented the old United States, in the Miami Olympics of 1996—which were the last ever—everyone knew that you spaced your shots to coincide with the momentary gaps between the beats of the heart.

This kind of shooting didn't need that sort of hairbreadth accuracy. The range was less than fifty yards, and the targets were all close to six feet high.

A man was out of the front, sliding down and looking around. He held a rifle of some sort. The first person who emerged from the turret was also a man, followed by a short, naked person that Mildred guessed was male, though she couldn't be sure.

"Three out," she announced.

The last of them had stooped to peer under the wag, shouting something to the others. But the words were inaudible. Mildred guessed he was trying to warn them that it was a false alarm, but the first couple was already sprinting, heads back, arms pumping, toward a bosk of live oaks, about a hundred yards away, near the skyline.

Mildred drew a bead on the first of them, centering the sight on the pale shirt the man wore, conscious at the same moment that a woman with very long hair was just clambering out of the turret, right beside Ryan.

The one-eyed warrior kept count. One left from the turret and a pair from the front. That left one or two, depending on the count of Man Sees Behind Sun.

The odor of smoke and the stink of rancid sweat wafted up to him from the open hatch. Human bodies, packed together, smelled rank and feral.

Just as he heard the cold snap of the Steyr, and a muffled scream, the woman surged up from the hatch. There was just enough light for Ryan to see that she was completely naked, her back to him.

Mildred saw her target go down, arms thrown up in the air like some famous old black-and-white photo she remembered. From the Spanish Civil War?

As she shifted her aim, there was some sort of a scuffle on top of the wag. The short nude man was looking toward her, raising a blaster. Jak was up on his feet, steadying himself against the cannon, like an avenger from a comic book, his mouth open, hair blowing in the night wind. Steel flickered in his right hand and the short man dropped his rifle, hands going to clutch at the knife in his throat.

Mildred fired a second round from the concealed Steyr, the sound reaching Ryan as he readied himself to kill the woman. But some sixth sense must have told her that he was behind her, and she flailed back with her right arm, catching him across the wrist, sending the SIG-Sauer spinning into the blackness.

"Fireblast!"

Mildred saw her own clean kill through the scope sight. The bullet had hit the running man through the head, an inch behind his right ear, blowing away most of the left side of his face and emptying his skull of brains and blood.

Despite the neural control room being destroyed, the message didn't seem to have reached the man's legs, which carried on sprinting for safety. Arterial blood jetted from the gaping hole, black in the moonlight.

"Like a headless chicken," J.B. whispered at Mildred's elbow.

It was several seconds before the corpse dropped to the ground like a bundle of dirty rags.

Mildred turned the sight from left to right, seeing that the three men from the wag were all down and dead, but that Ryan seemed to be having trouble with the naked woman.

He'd been ready for a simple execution, and her silent frenzy had taken him by surprise. Her body glistened with sweat, and his nostrils were flooded with the rutting smell of recent sex. There was enough light for him to make out something of her features—thick lips, spittle dribbling between them, a narrow nose and heavy, dark eyebrows.

Her mouth was wide open, and she was hissing in what might have been anger, hatred or terror.

She was braced, the lower part of her body still inside the turret, keeping herself in place on the ladder, clawing at Ryan with long, strong fingers. He was far less steady, perched on top of the wag, the metal slippery with dew, and her attack was difficult to repel.

One hand raked across his face, nearly snagging the patch off his missing eye. It was one of the dark night horrors for Ryan, that something sharp might gouge at the raw socket. He jerked back from her and managed a short clubbing right to the side of her jaw. But the punch wasn't delivered with full force and had little effect. The woman spit in his face and hit at Ryan with the edge of her left hand, catching him a glancing blow on the side of the neck. An inch or two farther back and a little harder, and he'd have been rolling off into the dirt with his mind turned dark.

An elbow, aimed at his groin, narrowly missed its target as he half turned and took it on the thigh.

"Want help, Ryan?"

He was too busy to take a breath to answer Jak. It should have been easy. The muzzle pushed into the angle of the jaw, with the crackling of the cartilage, the jolt running up his arm as he squeezed the trigger and the woman's body going slack and empty.

It was so simple, he could hardly believe that it hadn't happened.

"Fuckin' scum!" the woman roared.

Ryan brought his left hand around, smashing the forearm into her open mouth, wincing as her teeth opened up a gash just below the elbow.

"Again!" The voice out of the gloom belonged to Mildred.

But Ryan had a better idea. The blow had briefly stunned the woman and given him a moment to reach for the hilt of the big panga. He drew the eighteen-inch blade from the greased leather sheath, using it as a dagger rather than an ax. The one-eyed warrior stabbed it into the woman's body, below her pendulous breasts, feeling the ease with which the needle point penetrated the flesh of her stomach, like a hot knife through a slab of butter. Blood gushed out, hot across his wrist and arm.

She sighed once, a sound that was almost sexual in its languor. Her head swayed back away from Ryan, and he could taste the bitterness of her bile, wrapped around her last evening meal of chilies, pork and onions.

With a great effort, the wounded woman managed to heave herself out of the turret, flopping forward, where Jak bent over and slit her throat open, from ear to ear. He pushed the twitching corpse into the damp earth below the wag.

"That it?" J.B. asked from the sudden stillness.

"Guess so."

The small fire was almost out, the smoke blowing toward the east. Ryan rubbed at the scraped wound on his arm, deciding that it wasn't worth binding up.

In the last minutes, the light from the eastern sky seemed to have grown much stronger. He could make out the figures of J.B., Krysty and the others, coming slowly from cover.

The young Navaho warrior, Man Sees Behind Sun, bounded toward the wag and vaulted lightly onto it. He slapped hands with Ryan, ignoring the congealing blood on the Anglo's fingers. Jak had dropped down and was retrieving his throwing knife from the neck of the dead man.

"Lady gave you some trouble, partner," J.B. called, unable to keep the grin out of his voice.

"You can do the business next time. She knocked my blaster out of my hand. Can you get it for me?"

"Sure."

Man Sees Behind Sun was kneeling by the open hatch. "Smells of wickedness," he said.

"Not what I'd have called it." Ryan grinned. "Plenty of other things."

"We could free this wag."

It had crossed Ryan's mind, but time was too much against them. "No. Too late."

"I will look inside. There might be blasters or food we could eat."

Ryan reached out and took the SIG-Sauer out of the Armorer's hand, nodding at the expected warning about making sure he fieldstripped and cleaned it thoroughly, after it had been dropped in the dirt.

The Navaho leaned down and peered into the darkness inside the wag. "I will go in."

"Tell him to watch out," J.B. called. "Could be grens or anything in there."

But the warrior was already climbing down, feeling with his feet on the steel ladder.

"Tell my brothers I count the first coup," he said. Now only his head and shoulders were visible. "This is a good day to—"

With a startling violence, the young man disappeared, cut off in midsentence.

"Fireblast!" Ryan cocked the SIG-Sauer and stared into the dark interior of the war wag, helpless to do anything to save the young man from whatever had seized him.

"What's happened?" Krysty shouted.

Jak had turned and was already running back toward the wag, the steel gleaming cold in his hand.

But all of it was too late to help Man Sees Behind Sun.

Out of the stillness, floating up to the listeners, came a bubbling laugh, gentle and loathsome.

"Nice trick, you 'pache bastard! Suck on this."

They heard a cry of pain and bodies moving against each other.

The voice of the warrior sounded thin and strained. "He's got a gren. Pulled pin!"

Life was suddenly measured in tiny splinters of time.

Chapter Twenty-Seven

A deaf man wandering by would have been amazed at the scene, wondering what could possibly be happening to trigger such terminal chaos.

Jak reacted fastest, turning and sprinting toward a dip in the ground about fifteen yards away, throwing himself into it in a perfect racing dive.

The others all moved with varying degrees of speed, most hurling themselves straight onto the ground, curling up, hands over ears.

Ryan was stranded.

He knew that one of the General's men had played it double cunning, sitting tight and still in the fetid blackness of the wag, hearing the confusion and the killing of his companions, taking out Man Sees Behind Sun by dragging him down the cockpit and chilling him there.

But he'd done more.

The dying cry of warning from the Navaho told them that the man had pulled the pin on a grenade.

Grens came in all shapes, sizes and colors. A scarlet and blue band around the dull top would mean that it was an implode. But it might be a burner, a frag, a high-ex, a shrap, a stun or a smoke.

All of that raced through Ryan's mind when he heard the shout from the warrior.

Since he was—literally—sitting on top of the bomb, it didn't much matter to him what kind it was.

It mattered what sort of a fuse. Normally they had a delay of between five and eight seconds, assuming they worked properly. Many of the grens around Deathlands were, amazingly, from before the long winters. Hundred-year-old pieces of weaponry weren't always that reliable.

"Pulled pin!"

Combat reflexes took over.

Ryan kicked out at the open hatch, seeing it start to fall in agonizingly slow motion.

But he was already moving.

Dropping the SIG-Sauer for a second time, he started to roll backward, jolting himself as he came off the turret, keeping going in a clumsy somersault.

It was only about four feet from the rear of the LAV-25 to the furrowed earth, but it felt like forty feet. The breath was driven from his body as he landed awkwardly.

A clock was ticking in his brain.

Three and half seconds gone.

Part of his mind screamed for him to get up and run like smoke for cover, but the cool, considered part knew that might be the best way to buy the farm.

If the gren was high-ex, then the effect in the confined space of the wag's interior could be catastrophic. The force of the explosion would come close to destroying the vehicle, the burst going up and outward.

Ryan burrowed down, keeping his body as flat as he could, head away from the war wag. He cupped his ears with his hands, closing his eye, letting his mouth sag open, knowing from years of experience that this was the best chance of avoiding terminal injury when the gren exploded.

Six and a half seconds gone.

Seven seconds...

The ground trembled with the power of what sounded to him very much like an implode. They had been invented in great secrecy, using antimatter, in the last years before the nuke holocaust. When an implode was detonated, everything around was sucked instantly into its heart, as though a sudden, immensely violent vacuum had been created.

The wag behind him vibrated in the enfolding mud, and the hatch of the turret flipped backward with a dull clang. There was a hissing of air and the bitter scent of the gren as it destroyed the interior of the LAV-25. Overlaying it was the never-forgotten stench of burned meat.

Ryan's ears were ringing from the implosion. He touched them and found that he was bleeding a little, with still more blood dribbling from his open mouth. He realized that he must have blacked out.

"All right?"

The voice was familiar, but it had a weird metallic ring, as though it had been electronically reprocessed, the words echoing again and again. Ryan wondered whether it might be the man called the Armorer.

Someone held him by the left shoulder, shaking him hard as though they imagined him to be locked deep in sleep. "Come on, lover."

"Awake," he tried to say. But a thief had somehow stolen his tongue from his mouth and replaced it with a large, moist feather pillow.

"Stunned," J.B. said.

"Awake," he said again, this time relieved that his tongue had been replaced.

"He's coming around." It wasn't a voice he recognized at all, sounding slightly guttural, as though English might not have been the man's first language.

"He trapped Man Sees Behind Sun inside the wag."

"No." Ryan knew that wasn't true. Well, it had a kind of partial truth to it, which he could easily explain if they gave him a chance.

He opened his eye, finding that he was lying on his back, about eighty yards from the burning wreck of a small war wag. There was plenty of smoke filtering from every orifice in the military carcass, but very little flame. The sky was still dark, with the first pallid fingers of dawn light barely visible away to the east.

"Implode," he muttered.

"What, lover?" He could smell Krysty, close by him, the familiar scent of her body rising over the permeating miasma of oil, rubber and gasoline. And scorched flesh.

"It was an implode gren."

"Yeah, we know. We all heard it. Are you feeling all right, lover?"

"Bruised and scratched but nothing bad."

"You shut the door on our brother." The accusation came from a dark figure to Ryan's right, one of a group of eight men, the surviving Navaho.

"There was another of the General's killers left inside. When Man Sees Behind Sun went on the recce and counted them..." He coughed and cleared his throat. "He counted wrong. The man was hiding, and he pulled the kid down and was chilling him in the command center of the wag."

"Who released the gren?" Now he knew the voice was that of Sleeps In Day.

"Don't know. Could easily have been the enemy. Think it was. Kid shouted to warn me."

"Why did you not help him?"

This time the words came from Thomas Firemaker. Ryan could hear the pain and the anger in his voice.

"How?"

"Pull him free."

Ryan sat up, wiping grit from his face, feeling his own anger swelling, the scar on his cheek throbbing. "He told me the pin was pulled. I'm sitting right on top of the oven. The gren went off about seven seconds after that. I nearly got my fucking head blown off as it was, you triple stupe! What the fuck could I have done?"

"Simmer down, lover." Krysty patted him on the arm. "It's over."

"Our brother died," Thomas Firemaker insisted. "And you closed the door where he might have escaped."

"Sure I did. If I hadn't, then the noise would have been heard by everyone from the Lakes to the Grandee and all the fucking way back again!"

"But our brother died," Thomas repeated, as though Ryan hadn't bothered with an explanation.

"Sure. So did all the men and women we set out after. Not a bad deal. One life for their lives."

"Bastard!"

Ryan was on his feet, shrugging off Krysty's restraining hand. "Nobody, but nobody—"

The leader of the Native Americans, Sleeps In Day, stepped between Ryan and Thomas. "This is not the time and not the place."

"I'll fight him now." The skirmish hadn't gone well. The violence from the woman, then the unexpected death of the teenage Navaho and the destruction of the wag had all taken a toll on Ryan's nerves. He was more than ready to take on Thomas right there and then.

"Let it lie, Ryan," J.B. cautioned. "We got a job to do."

"Fuck the job."

He was aware that the Navaho had all gone into a huddle and Sleeps In Day was holding Thomas by the arm, whispering urgently to him.

"Dad."

"What?" Ryan moderated his own seething rage at the sight of the slight figure of his son, right at his side. "What do you want, Dean?"

"Not worth fighting, Dad, is it? We gotta get on to revenge Christina and Jenny and Michael."

He closed his eye and turned away. "I guess that's so, son. All right."

He raised his voice to the Native Americans. "I'm truly sorry the boy died. He died real bravely, and his warning saved a lot of lives."

There was a long silence. Then the entire group turned toward him, the rising sun throwing their faces into deeper shadow.

Thomas whispered something and several of them nodded. But it was Sleeps In Day who answered for them all, clearing his throat.

"I think you speak the truth to us, Ryan Cawdor. Perhaps our brother was doomed anyway. It was his day to die, as we say. But you locked the door on him and made his death certain."

"His death was certain the moment the bastard inside that wag pulled the pin on the implode," J.B. said, his voice tight and angry.

"A man does not turn his back on a friend."

"Bullshit!"

It was Ryan's turn to try to act as the peacemaker, touching J.B. on the shoulder. "This isn't helping," he said, looking at the Native Americans. "No way of deciding this. Just the one question. Do we go on after the General or do we stop now? Or split up and each try to chill them on our own? Which way do you want to play it, Sleeps In Day?"

"We go on together. After all is finished, we may talk of this again."

Ryan nodded. "Sure. Fine with me. Now, time's wasting and the sun's rising fast."

IT SEEMED LIKELY that the General would send out a relief party to dig the trapped war wag clear, probably soon after first light. They'd find the destruction and the bodies, and would know that there was a serious threat close by their camp. And would send word back to the General.

The attempt to infiltrate the underground headquarters would be far more difficult.

It was a simple problem, and Ryan knew that there was a simple solution.

Chapter Twenty-Eight

The J. C. Wright Caverns.

From the appearance of the sign, it somehow looked like it had been battered and faded, even when it was new, which was around a hundred years ago.

Better than Carlsbad. That was the main boast on the huge billboard. One of the main supports had rusted through and tumbled, leaving the sign leaning at a drunken angle toward the left, part of it buried in the gray sand.

"'Not so big and not so many bats, but beautiful and cozy.' That is, I believe, about the only totally honest advertisement I have ever encountered," Doc commented, slapping Judas across the top of the head as the mule tried to sidle sideways and brush him off onto a big saguaro.

Everyone had reined in, stopping to look at the sign, which teetered on the side of an ancient blacktop. The marks of the surviving wag passed within a hundred yards of the sign, turning to follow the sand-covered highway south.

"How far?" Krysty asked.

"Sign says it's only a few minutes ahead," Mildred replied. "Could mean anything between five and fifty. Probably nearer the latter."

Ryan looked behind them. The smoke from the burning wag was almost extinguished, but there was still a menacing pillar rising vertically for two or three hundred feet into the dark sky, until the light breeze tugged it out of shape. If the General had men out on watch, then it seemed an even chance that one of them might have spotted it.

Dawn was less than an hour back.

"Reckon we should think about getting ready to meet their patrol," he said.

"To repair the wag?" Sleeps In Day asked.

"Yeah. Could cross our path in a few minutes."

"Ruins of gas station there." Jak pointed to the right with a long, bloodless finger, where there seemed to be a dirt road cutting in from the west, and the dust-covered foundations of a few buildings.

"Be good," Ryan agreed.

"Let us go and hide there," Two Dogs Fighting suggested. "You stay here with your good blasters. Any you miss will fall onto our spears."

If they'd all sat around and argued for half a day, Ryan doubted whether they'd have been able to come up with any better plan.

All it needed was a little checking of the nuts and bolts of the idea.

HE AND J.B. AGREED that the rescue and repair party wasn't likely to consist of more than seven or eight. At the outside. The General was only a spit away from his home base, in territory that he knew well. Though he might suspect there was some threat, he would probably only look for it to come from a handful of poorly armed savages on ill-fed pinto ponies.

Dean and Doc, along with Young Pony Runs, were delegated to take all of the animals, including the protesting Judas, and lead them into an arroyo that ran behind the gas station. The mule had made its feelings known with spectacularly vicious braying and kicking out.

"You keep it real quiet or you slit its throat, Doc," Ryan warned.

"Mayhap I might gently open a large artery anyway, Ryan, my dear fellow."

"Just keep it quiet."

Sleeps In Day led Two Dogs Fighting, Thomas Firemaker and the other four warriors to form a ring around the scattered remnants of the tiny ville. In less than five minutes they had each scraped out a shallow trench, quickly piling the loose earth over themselves.

Ryan stared at where he knew they were hiding, but couldn't see any trace of them.

"Hope they can use those old blasters they got as well as they can camouflage themselves." He sniffed the air. "Wind's veering and freshening. Could be there's plenty more double-heavy rain on the way."

J.B., along with Jak and Krysty, picked hiding places for themselves along the side of the blacktop, using the shattered remains of a storm drain as cover.

But the bulk of the responsibility for the firefight was going to fall on the shoulders of Mildred and Ryan, the best shots in the group, she with her Czech target pistol and he with the Steyr hunting rifle.

"COMING." The voice was Jak's. The full light of the day hadn't yet flowered over the hills, and the albino's sight was still excellent.

"Ready, Mildred?"

"As I'll ever be."

J. B. Dix had stood up briefly, clenching his fist and opening it five times.

"There's five of them," Ryan said. "Remember who they are and what they did, Mildred. Christina and the little baby. Michael Brother. I need you. Take them out clean and fast. Head shots if you figure you can make them good. But they have to be all aces on the line."

"Sure. And so we bid a fond farewell to the good old Olympic spirit. Today's event for Mildred Wyeth is the free pistol massacre. I'll go for gold, Ryan."

THE FIVE MEN RODE donkeys and wore the uniform that Ryan knew belonged to the followers of the man called the General—black shirts and pants, with a red stripe down the leg, black berets and black boots. They were still a couple of hundred yards away, but Ryan could already make out that four of the five sported mustaches.

There was no sign that they were aware of being watched or of any potential threat. They rode slow and easy, legs out straight, laughing and joking with one another. Ryan noticed that they carried picks and shovels strapped to their saddles, ready to dig out the wag.

"Lambs to the slaughter," Mildred breathed, wiping the palm of her right hand down the side of her reinforced military jeans. "Lord forgive us for what we are about to do."

"Amen," Ryan whispered.

The range had now dropped to below a hundred yards. The group had ridden past where the seven Navaho warriors lurked amid the ruins of the gas station, looking neither to one side nor to the other.

"I'll start with the tall one on the left," he said.

"Fine."

"Wait as long as you can," Ryan warned.

Where they waited, among a nest of boulders, the ground was slightly higher than the trail ridden by the General's men, which made for more difficult shooting.

Sixty yards.

Ryan still hadn't brought the rifle to his shoulder, waiting as long as possible. The wind was now fresh to strong, blowing directly up from the south, reducing the chances of anyone at the General's caverns hearing the shots. Also, the five men were now in a shallow dip in the land, which would also tend to trap the sound of the blasters.

Ryan glimpsed Jak, flat on his belly, crawling through the stubbly grass toward the riders. The sun, peeking through a belt of low clouds, glinted off something metallic held in the teenager's right hand.

Thirty yards.

"Now?" Mildred asked quietly.

Ryan lifted the SSG-70 and pressed his eyes against the Starlite scope. "Now," he agreed.

He had time for only a single shot, seeing through the cross hairs of the sight that his man was kicked backward off the donkey, arms wide, the left side of his face vanishing in a mist of blood and splintered bone.

It took only a moment to work the bolt action on the Steyr, but by then Mildred had fired three times.

The six-shot revolver had been chambered to take a big .38 round. Mildred's hours of dry practice paid off. She used the short-fall thumb-cocking hammer in a blur of movement, the echoes of the three rounds blurring together so that they sounded like a single shot.

She had fired from a standing position, just as though she'd been in the butts at the Games, right arm extended, left hand gripping the other wrist, sighting along the barrel, with both eyes open. Cock, aim and fire. Cock, aim and fire. Cock, aim and fire.

Each shot was aimed with lethal precision. If the center of each man's nose had been the target bull, all three .38s would have been top-scoring aces on the line.

The men went down as though they'd been felled by a sweeping sword of divine retribution. The first of them hadn't even collapsed off his donkey, a corpse in the dirt, before the fourth was clinically dead.

The fifth man had the luck that his animal reared and threw him onto his hands and knees, behind the braying, rearing animals, briefly covering him from the devastating fire of the rifle and the revolver.

Ryan had him in the sights for a moment, but he hesitated, not sure of a clean kill. But he knew that there was no way that the dismounted man would be able to escape from the rest of the waiting group.

"Mine!" Jak's voice rang out loud and clear above the noise of the donkeys and the panicky screams of the unwounded man, who yelped for mercy in Spanish as he scrabbled back toward the old gas station.

"I can..." Mildred began, as still as a statue at Ryan's side.

"No."

Jak's wrist snapped forward, and the thrown blade hummed through the air.

Ryan lost sight of the knife in the poor light, but the man kept running, stumbling over the rough ground, leading to the unthinkable conclusion that Jak had actually missed him.

Not that it made much difference.

To the gut-tearing horror of the fleeing man, the earth moved in front of him and seven vengeful figures rose from the ground, all as pale as spirits of the night.

He skidded to a halt, looking as if he were about to fall on his face.

Before that could happen, the Navaho lifted their blasters and opened fire at him. He staggered to his knees, them tumbled over, rolling twice and finally lying still on his back, staring sightlessly at the dawn sky.

One of the Native Americans gave a whoop of triumph, and they all rushed to surround the corpse of their enemy.

"Had it not been for us, this one would have escaped to tell the tale and betray us all," Two Dogs Fighting shouted, shaking his single-shot rifle at the watching Anglos.

Ryan was about to acknowledge the possible truth of that, when Jak interrupted him.

"No!" he called.

Sleeps In Day was brushing sand and dust off his face, hair and clothes, but he stopped at the single word from the white-haired teenager.

"What?"

"Said you didn't chill him."

"This is madness. The holes in his flesh leak their blood. It cries out from the barrels of our blasters. How can you say such a thing?"

"Look." The albino walked straight up to the group of warriors and pushed them aside as though they didn't exist. Ryan and the others had followed him down into the hollow, joining him by the corpse.

Ryan stared down at the body, seeing that the man was young, probably around twenty. His complexion was dark, and his mustache was long and drooping. His shirt was torn across the chest by the impact of the bullets, the wounds scattered, none of them actually looking to be immediately fatal.

Sleeps In Day scowled, touching the dead man with the muzzle of his own gun. "If we did not kill him, then tell me, white-hair, who did?"

"Me."

"You?"

"Sure. Look."

He knelt and rolled the corpse onto its face. The man's back was ragged and sodden with blood, showing the impact of the Navaho bullets.

"There is how he died," Thomas exclaimed. "It shows your lies."

"None your bullets would've chilled him." Jak felt in among the long matted hair at the nape. "Here." He peeled the hair back to show everyone the hilt of the knife driven deep into the body, just below where the skull sat on the spine. "That killed him."

"He was still running," Sleeps In Day said. But his voice had lost its confidence.

"Like chicken," Jak replied, pulling the leaf-bladed weapon out and wiping it on the dead man's pants. "Like chicken."

Chapter Twenty-Nine

"How much time before the General works out something's gone double wrong?"

Ryan glanced at J.B. "Could be as long as four, mebbe five hours."

"Could be little as an hour."

"No." He shook his head at the Armorer's suggestion. "Gotta be longer than that. I reckon the bottom line on time is two and a half hours. Then he sends out a search party. By then we should've reached the caves."

J.B. had taken off his glasses to polish them. "That is, if Sleeps In Day and all his brothers don't decide to start another Indian war first."

It was a fair comment.

There had been a degree of tension and hostility within the uneasy alliance right from the beginning, a traditional dislike that probably had its atavistic roots at least three hundred years in the past.

The near fight between Thomas Firemaker and Ryan had simply been a case of glowing embers bursting out into an intense, flaring fire.

Though that had passed, it had widened the gulf between Anglo and Navaho.

Then the bitter argument over who had killed the last of the General's repair party had come close again to outright conflict, despite the fact that it had eventually become obvious to everyone that the mortal wound had undeniably been inflicted by Jak's throwing knife.

Ryan had discussed the problem with all of his own group of friends, and it had been agreed that they should try to avoid any further difficulties. At least until the caves were reached and the firefight won.

The uneasy truce had been resumed.

THE BLACKTOP WOUND up and over the ridge ahead of them, opening onto a wide valley, its sides studded with groves of tamarisk and live oak.

"Look, Dad," Dean said, reining in his mount and pointing to the right.

Doc was currently winning his battle with Judas, and he managed to stop the mule without too much of a struggle. "I observe that the General is a man who believes in leaving his calling cards at his own front door."

There had been a series of billboards set along the road, on steel frames. Only one of these remained, carrying the message that it was only a half mile to the J. C. Wright Caverns, where "An unforgettable experience is waiting just for *you.*"

The remaining stark frames were all decorated with corpses, in varying stages of decay, ranging from dislocated skeletons, desiccated by the Southwest sun and wind, to bloated bodies, swollen by the rotting gases of the stomach.

As they heeled forward, constantly keeping an eye on the skyline for any sign of danger, the party fell silent at the horror of the mutilations.

Some had been crucified upside down, many of the bodies showing the clearest evidence of having been tortured by fire. Most of them lacked fingers and toes, and not one of the weathered skulls was complete.

"Bastards," Mildred whispered. "Be good to make the Earth a mite cleaner with their passing."

The two most recent corpses, nearest to the entrance to the caverns, looked as though they both might possibly once have been female. But it was difficult to tell, as the breasts had been hacked off and the genital areas were simply patches of scorched and clotted blood.

Most of the hair was gone, and the carrion crows had already taken the eyes and the soft tissues of the face.

But Thomas Firemaker gave a great cry of agony and hurled himself from his pony, running to stand beneath the bodies, his head thrown back, mouth open.

Sleeps In Day called out to him in a harsh burst of their native tongue.

"What's he saying, lover?" Krysty asked.

"Looks like the poor son of a bitch just found a couple of his relatives that the General and his men took along with them for sport."

A quiet word with Sleeps In Day revealed that the corpses were those of Thomas's sister and the sister of his mother.

It took all of the Navaho leader's persuasion, backed by the threat of the blasters of the Anglos, to prevent Thomas from galloping off to charge the gates of the enemy base.

THEY ALL AGREED to stop there, leave the horses and carry on to the caverns on foot.

The argument came when Ryan again appointed Dean to stay behind and watch over the animals.

"No."

"Not asking you, Dean. I'm telling you to stay and guard the horses for us."

"No, Dad. I've had enough of being left out of the action all the time."

Ryan closed his good eye for a moment and struggled to control his anger. And failed. He suddenly swung his right hand, open-palmed, and knocked his son clean off his feet. "This isn't some fuckin' stupe game."

The boy got unsteadily to his feet, unshed tears glistening in his dark eyes. The livid mark of his father's fingers flared on his cheek.

"Bastard!" His hand fumbled for the butt of his big Browning Hi-Power.

"Draw that and I'll kill you, Dean. You're my son and I love you deeply, but never, ever go for a gun against me. And don't ever argue with me when I tell you to do something. You hear me? Someone has to stay with the animals in case there's a sneak attack, looping around us. You're good with the horses and you're quick and alert. I trust you with this, Dean."

"You always give me shit jobs." The hand edged away from the blaster.

"Not true. You don't have the age or experience or simple physical skill for some situations. That isn't the case here. You're my best pick for it."

The boy turned from his father, his face sullen, the narrow shoulders slumped.

Krysty reached and touched him on the arm, but he pulled away from her. "You have a choice," she said softly. "You believe what you say, then leave us now. Go away on your own and don't come back."

He looked up into her green eyes and flushed. "You mean that, don't you?"

"Course. I wouldn't lie to you, Dean. I know Ryan is telling the truth. There isn't time to go into this. So, do like he says, but without looking so pissed. Or don't do it at all and go off on your own."

Dean hesitated, looking around, face by face. Mildred nodded to him. Jak gave no clue at all what he was thinking, the crimson eyes steady on the younger boy.

"Doc?"

"The difficult part of growing up to be a man, Dean, my boy, is that being a man comes along a little before you're quite ready for it. And before you quite understand what it all involves. We all learn that."

Ryan looked down at his chron. "No time for any more of this talk."

"Not just a matter of doing it," J.B. said. "You've traveled long enough with us to know that. You do it. Do it as well as you can. And in the right mood. Sit here feeling sorry for yourself and you won't pay attention. Could mean you get chilled. Could mean we all get chilled."

"I understand," Dean said, managing a small smile. "Sorry, Dad."

"And I'm sorry too. For losing my temper. Not proud of that, Dean."

The boy held out his hand and his father shook it firmly, grinning at his son.

"I'll do it well," Dean promised.

ALL OF THE HORSES, including the pinto ponies and the mule, were tethered in a dense copse of sycamores, a hundred yards east of the overgrown blacktop.

Ryan glanced back once, seeing that Dean had his blaster drawn and was cautiously patrolling just inside the perimeter of the trees, keeping a good watch.

He lifted his right hand in a farewell wave, watching the boy respond.

THE LAYOUT of the J. C. Wright Caverns proved to favor the attackers.

The blacktop dropped, then rose again quite steeply toward a low, single-story building on the ridge ahead of them. Then it cut down to the right and vanished around the flank of a frost-shattered bluff. The trail of the war wag's wheels followed on past the building, out of sight.

With the death of Man Sees Behind Sun, the group had lost their best tracker. But the marks were so clear that even Doc could have followed them.

"Not even feet that way," said J.B., who'd been out at point. "Looks like they got their main entrance around the back there."

"Could there be a way in through that house?" Sleeps In Day asked.

"I reckon that must once have been the main Visitors' Center for the caves," Mildred said. "You figure it that way, Doc?"

"Possibly, madam, possibly."

"Don't risk coming off the fence, will you, Doc? If it is the Visitors' Center, then I'd expect there to be an entrance to the caverns close by. Maybe an elevator or maybe a path from above. I visited Carlsbad and I— Yeah, there was an elevator took you into the heart of the place. But lots of folks preferred to walk down a path. Maybe this is the same."

"One way to find out," Ryan stated.

THE CLOUDS HAD CLEARED away, and it was turning into a beautiful day. The only darkness was a bank of purple, far off to the south, lurking over the Grandee. The sunshine was bright, drawing the moisture from the ground, leaving a residual humidity that was fast burning off.

Once they'd left the blacktop, Ryan felt a sense of safety. It was as though the General and his forces had nothing to do with this particular part of the complex.

He turned to Krysty, close at his side. "You feel anything, lover?"

Her fiery hair was clamped tight around the back of her neck, a sure sign that there was serious danger in the area. But she smiled at him.

"Sure. It's close..." Krysty paused. "But it's not that close. I felt it right up until we quit the highway. The evil lies in that direction, but not up here."

"Looks like that diner we visited," Mildred said, right at their heels. "As if nobody's been here for a hundred years. No broken windows or anything. Like it was patiently sitting here, just waiting for us."

"Perhaps like the notorious house of Roderick Usher," Doc commented, trying to make his voice sound spooky.

"And what walks inside the caverns, walks alone," the black woman replied.

The Navaho were tightly bunched together. Since the agreement to go the center, none of them had spoken a single word.

The glass in the long windows that ran the length of the front of the building was tinted black, shutting out some of the bright New Mexico sunlight. It also made it utterly impossible to see inside the center.

"Could be fifty men with gren launchers watching us from in there," J. B. Dix pointed out.

"Thanks for that cheerful thought, John." Mildred took a deep breath. "Well, we going in or not?"

"We're going in," Ryan said.

The door opened easily, and the air inside had the familiar Deathlands tang to it. It tasted like nobody had breathed it for a century. There was a flatness to it, a deadly stuffiness as if one were swallowing lumps of sun-dried cotton.

"Welcome to the J. C. Wright Caverns," Krysty said, looking around her at the shadowed expanse of the atrium. "All we need now is to find that unforgettable experience that they promised us."

"I'd like to find some food," Mildred told her. "That'd be what Dean calls a hot pipe unforgettable experience. My backbone's rubbing through my belly."

"Nobody been here." Jak moved across the dusty floor, so light that his feet hardly seemed to leave any mark. "Nobody forever and day."

"Split up and check it out," Ryan said.

He turned to the Native Americans. "Should be a way from here down into the caves. Way down to the General."

J.B. had walked past the information desk, by a row of darkened vending machines.

Nobody spoke, the low-ceilinged building as silent as an Egyptian tomb.

Suddenly a voice boomed out, "Welcome to the J. C. Wright Caverns. The unforgettable starts now," followed by an echoing peal of maniacal laughter.

Chapter Thirty

Everyone had dived for the nearest cover. Ryan found himself flattened under a long bench that was covered in some kind of artificial deerskin. The SIG-Sauer was in his right hand, the Steyr tight across his shoulders where the strap had snagged awkwardly as he moved.

"What the fuck was that?" Mildred asked from somewhere to his left.

The laughter had stopped, but the voice came blaring out again. "So much to do and so much to see. Fun and education for everyone, from nine to ninety. Want to know more? Just select the topic and I'll be glad to oblige."

There was a taut silence, broken by J.B. "Dark night! Nearly won the order of the brown trousers there. You can relax. It's a machine."

"It was like the voice of the night spirits," Sleeps In Day said from near the entrance to a small bookstore.

Everyone was standing up, brushing off dust.

"I must've triggered it by standing close," the Armorer said. "Amazing the storage batteries still hold enough power to operate it."

"Can I make it work?" Krysty asked.

Ryan holstered the blaster. "Guess so. The General must be way out of hearing."

She quickly joined J.B. in front of a blank-screened console. "No picture?"

"No, Krysty. Guess that part of it malfunctioned back in the long winters."

There was a row of buttons. "Should I press one? This says 'Food facility.' I'll press that."

Once again the voice came out from concealed speakers. "Want to know about eating, pardner? Then I'm your man. Best burgers you ever tasted. Teriyakiburger. Mexicaliburger, with the hottest chili that ever blistered your lips. Kazooburger and Zapataburger and Jim and Carla's supaburger. You ask for it and you got it. With melts and subs and dogs and slushes and sodas in thirty-seven tongue-tingling flavors. It ain't just star-toppling, pardner, it's downright apocalyptic."

The voice had lost a little volume as the message ran on, and the last few words seemed to slur and drag.

"You have to pick the food message." Mildred sighed. "Cruel, sister, cruel."

"Want me to try another one, lover? Here's one for the gift shop."

Doc stopped her. "I beg you to let it lie, dear lady. Having heard about the range of edibles on offer, I believe I can imagine what attractions the gift shop will have for us. Hand-crafted genuine kachinas from Taiwan. Genuine mica wind chimes from Brazil. Genuine piñon candles from Toronto."

"What's Ronto, Doc?" Jak asked, interrupting the old man's flow.

"Toronto, sweet youth. A Canadian conurbation. The Naples of the north. The Venice of the tundra. Where culture ends and the frontier begins. Through its rooms the women come and go, talking of the place called Toronto." He rubbed his hand across the silver stubble that decorated his cheeks. "Or should that have been Michelangelo? I disremember."

Ryan and the others had all gathered around the silent machine, looking at its controls.

"Might help if it told us the way down into the caverns," Krysty said.

"What I was thinking."

"One button's called 'How to get there,' at the top." Mildred pointed to it.

"Should I press it, Ryan?" J.B. asked.

"All right."

"It is always better to leave the things sleeping that should not ever be woken," Two Dogs Fighting said from the back of the small group.

"Press it."

This time there was an appreciable delay. The voice sounded whispery and tired, like an elderly man awakened from a deep slumber in the afternoon sun.

"You come here for the miracles below the ground... ground... ground... ways of getting there. A pair of rapid-velocity elevators situated at the eastern end of the Visitors' Center...enter...to the heart of the Crystal

Room and the other to the Dry Ocean. The large illustrated map by the side of the information desk will show your position locationwise. For the sturdy-hearted and strong-shoed there is the mile-and-one-quarter winding path, past the exit orifice of the nightly bats' spectacular flight. This is not easy...easy..." They heard the faint hissing of the unwinding tape.

"Is that it?" Sleeps In Day asked. "Then we must take this long and winding path."

Ryan nodded. "I wouldn't—"

But the voice came back again, even quieter, whispering erratically like a dying pirate passing on the location of Flint's treasure.

"Bats are real messy at keeping house...in your mouth...injections available but call the medical...report anyone you see touching the stones inside...experience of..." Again they heard only hissing static.

"The path's over here," called Young Pony Runs.

For the last time, the long-dead voice murmured to the group of invaders.

"In...failure then no need to worry as...emergency nuke lights...throughout the caverns."

"Good news about having some emergency lights down there," J.B. said. "Let's keep everything crossed it works all right. Otherwise it's going to be a dark highway."

There were low walls on both sides of the winding pathway, with a bright yellow line down its center, making it simple for them to follow.

They emerged briefly into the open, at the top of what looked like an almost sheer drop toward the black mouth of the caves. But the trail zigged and zagged in an easier pattern.

"Must be where the bats come out at night," Krysty commented, pausing at one of the sharp turns.

Ryan stared out into the black funnel of rock. "Yeah. See the marks on the walls. Generations of shit down there. Hope we don't have to wade through it."

Sleeps In Day joined them. "Ryan Cawdor."

"Yeah."

"If there are no lights, then we shall not follow. We will return and pursue the marks of the wags, perhaps hold them between us, like the horns of the buffalo."

Ryan nodded. "Sure."

THE LIGHTS WERE WORKING. A string of flickering yellow bulbs set along the right-hand wall of the path gave just enough illumination to follow the painted marks.

"Are we off to see that wonderful wizard, ma'am?" Doc said to Mildred.

"How's that?"

"Following the yellow brick line."

"Sure, Doc, sure."

"Wish that there was proper lighting, so we could appreciate what this place really looks like," Krysty said as she walked close to Ryan, close enough for him to be able to catch the familiar scent of her body.

"See one fireblasted cave and you've seen them all. Just be glad to get to the other side and meet up with the General and chill him. Steal his wag and drive back to Jak's place. And then jump on again."

"Always jumping on again, lover."

He nodded slowly. "I know."

MILDRED SIPPED at her water canteen. "Not much left," she said. "Think this General's going to let us have our pick of his supplies? Sure he will."

Doc was breathing hard, finding that the constant up and down of the narrow path tired him. "I have managed to make out many of the signs that tell us what wonders we are passing by. But all is lost in the deepest and most Stygian blackness. A great, great pity, is it not?"

Jak was the only one there able to appreciate anything of the beauties of the caverns. The albino condition that seemed to have bleached all of the blood from his body had also left him with poor sight in the brightness of noon. But he saw well in the dark.

"Boring, Doc," he said. "Stalactites and stalagmites. All there is. Got stupe names."

"I observed we had passed by The Venetian Gondola, The Sleepy Giraffe—which I could just glimpse and bore precious little similarity to any giraffe I ever saw. As for London Bridge and the Endless Embrace... Well!"

"There is a map here." Thomas Firemaker, his voice still as taut as a drawn bowstring, called everyone to a place where several paths seemed to intersect.

It was a plan of the caverns, painted onto a sheet of clear plastic. In the dimness of the caves, the colors had hardly faded.

The overhead emergency lighting was just strong enough for them all to be able to see the map.

"That's where we came in," J.B. said, pointing with the muzzle of his Uzi at the top section, which showed the aboveground area of the caverns. "There's the one elevator. The other one not far ahead of us. And the underground eatery's there as well."

"Look." Jak ran his ivory finger across to the far side. "Says Stores, Personnel. Private. That's place."

Ryan considered it. He had always had an excellent sense of space and direction, something that had saved his life on several occasions. He could see the blacktop that had drawn them to the Visitors' Center, and the way it continued around the far side of the caverns, where the tire tracks of the last of the General's wags had vanished.

"Yeah," he agreed.

"Can we stop off at the restaurant?" Krysty's green eyes seemed to shine in the gloom like molten emeralds.

"Doubt there'll be any food worth risking." Ryan looked around. "Though I guess it could just have survived in some forms. Mebbe freeze-dried, if there's anything like that. Been kept in a dim light and a constant cool temperature for all this time. It's on our way toward that area around back."

THE DOORS OF ONE of the elevators were wide open. The others stood slightly ajar, with a skeletal human arm protruding between them, the fingers hooked into claws. The remains of the nails were jagged and broken, black with old blood.

"Poor devil." Mildred stooped and peered at the sad relic. "Must somehow have gotten trapped in the elevator at the time of the missiles. Power went out and she—or he—couldn't get the doors open enough. Miserable way to go."

J.B. was looking around the cafeteria area. "Not many good ways to go in Deathlands, Mildred."

"Suppose not."

Jak and three of the Navaho had already moved off, behind the serving counters and the cash registers, through the swing doors into the kitchen area.

It was Two Dogs Fighting who came out, his voice ringing beneath the vaulted roof and raw stone.

"Fine cold water and packages of soup and other things to eat. It is good."

"Probably got their own artesian well built in. Still functioning after all these years." Ryan called out to Jak, who had just stuck his head around the door. "Try mixing up some of the soup stuff. See what it smells like. See what it tastes like, but be triple careful."

"Sure. Eaten predark stuff before. Not cans. Shit. Packages all right."

"We'll take an hour's break," Ryan said to the others. "Get a chance to rest after the walk. Eat and drink."

"And be merry," Doc offered. "For tomorrow we shall surely die."

"Today is a good day for dying," Sleeps In Day stated. "We will see that."

"*CORDON BLEU* CATERING it isn't," Doc said, pulling a face as he considered the green plastic bowl of cold watery gruel on the table in front of him.

"Least I don't think it'll poison you." Mildred sipped at it cautiously. "Like a mixture of camel piss and grit."

"But it's *good* camel piss." Krysty grinned.

THE MEAL WAS OVER, and Ryan led the group along the path.

"Wonder why the General and his men haven't bothered to explore this part of the caverns?" Krysty asked the one-eyed warrior.

"No need, I guess. Looks like the door through to the service part of the caves just ahead of us there."

They were surprisingly solid, made from what seemed to be a good grade of sec steel. There were triple dead bolts in the center and massive bolts at the top and bottom. Their size and thickness went some way toward answering Krysty's question.

"Now it begins," Ryan said.

Chapter Thirty-One

Abe had gone hunting.

It was a cold, clear night, and the lights flickered like tiny diamonds all over the outskirts of what had once been the powerful ville of Seattle. Trader had been scouting down there a couple of times, finding what he expected to find.

Like virtually every other of the large predark urban sprawls, the ruins of Seattle were a killing ground for the freaks and the mutie butchers. The topless towers with shattered windows loomed over cross streets filled with the rubble of the ancient nukings.

Norms rarely strayed into those pocket of paranoid violence, unless they sought something that they couldn't get anyplace else, which normally meant either jolt or bizarre sex. The quest for either could seriously damage the health.

Trader had gone out of curiosity, mingled with his own natural arrogance that there was nowhere in Deathlands where Trader feared to set his foot.

"Never has been and never will be," he muttered, sitting by the small, bright fire and sipping at the remnants of a bottle of distilled mescal.

Abe had accompanied him along the meanest of streets, covering his old leader's back, his stainless-steel Colt Python questing at every twitching shadow.

It was late evening now, with a coolish breeze coming off the Cific. Trader had lost track of the days, something that he'd noticed seemed to be happening a lot more recently than it had in the old days.

He still wore a weather-beaten chron on his wrist. Won it in a poker game from a one-legged whore in Chimay—Barbie? Barbara?

Abe had only been gone for about an hour, after some of the plentiful deer that roamed the hills.

It crossed Trader's mind to wonder what was happening to the dozens of messages that they'd sent on their way through the breadth and length of Deathlands. The wording had faded a little from his mind, but the gist of it was that Abe had tracked down the Trader, proved he was alive, confirming the trickle of rumors that had begun within weeks of his faked disappearance.

"Not faked," he said. "Not the right word. Really meant it. Didn't want to be found."

The message had gone with every merchant and packman that he and Abe had been able to find anywhere in the vicinity of old Seattle.

The message had told of the success and warned that they would stay around that part of the Northwest for three months, urging speed in responding to the warning.

Mebbe Ryan Cawdor hadn't got the message.

Mebbe he didn't care.

Mebbe he was chilled, propping up six and a half feet of cold earth.

"No," Trader said loudly. He realized the bottle was empty and lobbed it away into the blackness, waiting for the satisfying tinkle of broken glass. But there was no sound at all. The bottle must have landed in a bed of soft moss.

Ryan wouldn't be dead, nor would J.B. Neither of them was capable of dying, no more than Trader himself.

"Live forever," he muttered, aware that his tongue had grown a little too large for his mouth. The liquor was burning at the ulcer that had plagued him for years, as if fifty red ants were biting all at once.

Unbidden, an image of the face of Ryan Cawdor swam into Trader's mind—the unruly hair, dark and curling, tumbling down over the one good eye, an eye of chillingly pale blue; the puckered scar seaming the right cheek from mouth to eye; the black patch tied over the missing left eye, destroyed many years ago by Ryan's older brother, Harvey; the lips, thin and cruel, capable of both humor and compassion.

"Son I never had." Trader nodded owlishly. In all of his rangings and his dealings he had always wanted Ryan to inherit his power.

But things just hadn't turned out that way.

No point in anyone weeping over the past, over all of the roads and choices not taken.

The hillside to both right and left of Trader's camp had once been scattered with expensive housing, aimed at the upwardly mobile young businessmen and women of Seattle. It had taken only one Russian nuke, slightly off target, confused by the defensive comp-scrambler system, to wipe the slopes clear, taking off roofs and folding the walls in like so many cardboard dominoes. The heat flash carbonized flesh, blood and bone into a human-shaped smear on a garage door, melting glass in window frames and turning the sand in play pits into rippled glass, exploding the Saabs and BMWs and Volvos in the manicured drives.

Now there was hardly any sign that there had once been a community of little boxes among the woods.

In the first few days that Abe and Trader had been hunting and camping in the hills above the ville, they'd been approached by a number of the locals, sounding them out. Who were they? What were they doing? They explained that there were dues to be paid for being on someone else's land.

Trader had done some explaining back, using his well-worn Armalite to emphasize some of his more obvious points.

He lay down flat on his back, knotting his fingers behind his head, aware of the misplaced and broken knuckles on both hands, relics from his early teen days when it was fists before knives. Before blasters.

"Where I step, the flowers die," he said, lips peeling off his teeth in a wolfish grin.

Trader yawned, suddenly feeling tired. The awareness that he wasn't as young as he'd like to be had come to him very gradually, beginning several years ago. A couple of kids had been enlisted into War Wag Two as general gofers. Neither was more than seventeen. One had been part Kiowa and the other black. The wags had been camping by a large nameless lake, someplace up in the Rockies.

The crews had been relaxing, skimming stones across the placid, mirrored water. Trader had always been the best at it, selecting flat, round pebbles, snapping them away underarm, watching them bounce fifteen or twenty times.

That evening the two newcomers had both easily outthrown him. Trader flexed his shoulders, remembering how he'd tried to do better. The spirit had been goddamn willing, but the flesh was treacherously weak.

"Where did they..." He tried to recall what happened to those two boys. "Jud and Skip." Poor Jud was certainly dead, his throat cut by a mutie woman in the backroom of a store-cum-gaudy west of the Mohawk Gap. Skip had just...

"Just vanished," he said, like so many of the faceless names and the nameless faces from the long years of the past. Just vanished.

The fire was dying and Trader sat up again, breaking some of the thicker kindling across his knee and tossing it into the heart of the embers, where it quickly flamed and crackled, bringing a wave of fresh heat.

Part of him was deeply unhappy that little Abe had managed to track him through his self-imposed exile, deep into the Cascades. While another, smaller, part of him was sort of flattered and pleased.

And it might be good to meet up once more with Ryan and John Dix.

There was a faint sound out in the blackness, and Trader picked up the Armalite. Cause and effect blurred in the lightning speed of his combat reflexes, reacting so fast that he didn't even realize that he'd moved.

"Come on then," he breathed.

Nothing happened and the noise wasn't repeated. But he still cradled his beloved blaster.

"Seen us some days, friend," Trader whispered, patting the butt of the Armalite very gently with the flat of his right hand. "Never let each other down, have we?"

The dreams were continuing.

Last night he'd been running desperately, arms pumping, along a winding path, between impenetrable walls of damp, dripping pine trees, trying to make it to a certain agreed rendezvous before the war wags pulled out.

It wasn't like some other nightmares, where one of the faceless, nameless things was pursuing him along dusty corridors through ruined shopping malls.

This time there was no pursuit.

Just racing against time.

Trader had somehow known, in his dream, that he was impelled to run beyond his breaking point. Yet it was all totally futile. However fast he sprinted, on his burning feet of fire, the war wags would always pull out a minute or so before he reached them, leaving him to stand and shout, emptying the blaster into the sullen sky, seeing the blue gray of their exhausts as they lumbered off along the deserted blacktop.

It would all be for nothing.

"Waste of fucking time," he said, looking down at the Armalite. "Waste of fucking time, friend."

He slowly lay down, wincing at the multiplicity of pains that ran through him. Mentally he ticked off where each one came from, each blade and bullet, each fall and fight. More years of blood and toil than anyone could imagine.

The pain in his lower stomach was particularly bad that evening, and he hoped that Abe wouldn't be too long with his kill. Even a rabbit or a squirrel would be welcome to ease the sharp discomfort he felt.

Trader closed his eyes, resting for a few moments, keeping all his fighting senses alert.

ABE HAD NARROWLY MISSED a clear shot at a resting roe deer, at the side of a stream noisy enough to cover the sounds of his own tracking.

Then he'd seen the light of another fire, in an abandoned line shack up near the top of the next hill along. It seemed safer to wait it out and not run the risk of attracting attention.

When he eventually returned to his campsite the fire was almost out, with just a thin column of watery smoke rising into the air. As Abe dropped the rabbit in the dirt, he noticed that Trader was sleeping like a baby.

Chapter Thirty-Two

J.B. pointed with the Uzi at the notice above the doors that led to the service area of the caverns: Private. Positively No Entry to Any Members of the Public. Service, Staff, Stores and Company Parking. All Passes Must Be Shown.

"We get the message," Mildred said.

Ryan glanced around at the Navaho. "We all ready for this?" he asked.

Sleeps In Day answered for the eight warriors. "We are ready," he said solemnly.

Ryan and the Armorer slid back the bolts and turned the keys in the powerful locks. There was a faint feeling of resistance, and a distant grinding sound, but everything seemed to be working.

"Slow and easy," Jak whispered, so eager to get through that he was pushing against Ryan.

There was a deeper darkness on the far side, but some of the weak, golden light from the emergency system spilled through the gap between the doors.

Ryan was first to peer into the tunnel beyond. It wasn't unlike looking into the heart of one of the passages that lay at the heart of most redoubts—a roughly curved roof, the walls hewed from living rock.

There were no lights in that section, so that it was possible to see only for about a dozen yards.

"Beware the Minotaur."

Doc's voice, low and sonorous, made Ryan jump. "Fireblast! My nerves are tight enough without you coming whispering in my ear, you double stupe!"

"My dear fellow, I am so sorry. It was just that the scene beyond yon portals put me most fearfully in mind of artists' representations of the great maze of Crete. Controlled by the followers of Minos. Wherein did dwell the fabled and murderous Minotaur."

"What was that?" Krysty asked.

"It had the body of a man, but the head of a ferocious bull, my dear. And it slew the poor souls who became lost within that dread labyrinth."

The Navaho had half heard what Doc had been saying and they now drew back, gathering together and whispering urgently in their own tongue.

"The old one tells of this monster," Sleeps In Day said. "Is it true?"

Doc laughed. "It might perchance have been true once. Legend tells that the labyrinth was built by... Let me see. By Daedelus, I believe. And the monster was eventually slain by the brave hero, Theseus."

"So the bull is dead?" Two Dogs Fighting asked.

"My goodness, yes. We may find other monsters in these pitchy depths, but I can guarantee that none of them is likely to be the Minotaur."

"Come on." Ryan was losing patience with all the time-wasting. "Follow close. We'll stop every thirty steps or so to listen for danger."

THE STONE WAS COLD to the touch, slick in places with damp. A couple of times Ryan found his hand brushing against some sort of fungus, sticky against his skin, disintegrating into a stinking cloud of spores.

After going about a hundred paces, stopping a couple of times, he called for Jak to come to the front.

"What, Ryan?"

"I can feel some fresh air from way ahead. Taste sagebrush, so it's coming from outside."

"Can smell it. There's triple-dim light as well. Want me go first?"

"Sure. But take it slow. Can't all see in the dark like you can, Jak."

The albino took the lead, Ryan close behind. Then came Krysty and Mildred, followed by Doc, with J.B. bringing up his favorite rearguard position for the Anglos.

The Navaho huddled along a few paces behind.

"Think they're frightened of the General, lover?" Krysty whispered.

"No. What I know about them, it'd take a lot more than the General to chicken them out. No, it's the dark and the fear that there might be hostile spirits that are bothering them. If we can get through to the action, then they'll be fine."

"Getting lighter," Mildred said quietly, her voice swallowed by the confining vastness of the tunnels. "I can see Jak's hair ahead."

"Getting wider, too." Krysty stopped, shaking her head. "Feel someone close, lover." Her voice sounded troubled. "Can't tell where they are, but close."

Ryan hissed out a warning to Jak, telling him of Krysty's feeling of danger. Looking ahead to the teenager, he was aware that it was considerably lighter. The roof glistened now, and he could see how the tunnel curved to the right.

Jak held up a pale hand, stopping everyone. He beckoned Ryan forward to stand with him at the start of the bend in the passage.

"Voices," he said quietly.

Ryan could hear them now that everyone was still.

"Close," he mouthed.

Jak nodded, making a delicate, almost-feminine gesture with his right hand to indicate that he thought they were just around the corner.

The time for hiding and waiting was nearly over.

Trader used to insist that when you had to go in against a hostile ville, you went in with everything, as hard and fast as you possibly could. No point in holding anything back in reserve for the next day.

Because the next day might never come.

Ryan knelt and eased himself forward, pressing his face flat against the slippery walls of the tunnel until he could squint around with his good right eye and see what was farther along the passage.

It was an open space, about forty feet across, that looked, from the ingrained oil stains on the stone floor, like it might once have been used as a motor pool.

Now it was brightly lighted. From somewhere farther in, Ryan could catch the pounding roar of an electrical generator, possibly powered by the water that flowed through the caverns.

There were shelves lining the sides of the room, half-filled with cans and bottles. Ryan's guess was that they'd stumbled upon a section of the General's larder.

Jak tugged at his jacket. "Who?" he asked.

"Nobody in sight. But I can hear voices and a gen, and there's a wag engine going. Reckon we must be inside the defensive perimeter for the base."

A woman, singing, froze them all in their places. It was a mournful tune, about someone called Adelita. Her voice was high and pure, like Sierra ice.

Ryan beckoned J.B. to his side. As an afterthought, he called up Sleeps In Day.

"No other way in. We passed no side turnings or doors that I saw."

"Nor me," the Armorer agreed, taking the chance to peek around the corner.

"We should go straight in," the Navaho urged. "If we lose, then it will be with honor."

"Rather win without honor," Ryan said. "Staying alive and winning come to the same thing."

"Dark night!" J.B. exclaimed. "When you said that you sounded just like Trader."

"That a compliment?"

The armorer hesitated a few heartbeats. "Well, yeah, I guess it is."

"What do you reckon the old bastard would do if he was here now?" Ryan asked.

"Go straight in, with all blasters firing."

"Probably would. Then again, Trader had the armaments and the number of trained shootists to take out most baron's sec forces. We don't have that."

"So?"

"So, we go in, all right. But a mite more careful than Trader would've been."

Time before they were discovered was measured, at best, in minutes.

"CAN'T WE STOP and eat?" Mildred asked. "This is sort of recent canned food."

"You sound like Dean," Ryan replied. "Do the business first, then think about eating."

The woman's singing had stopped, somewhere ahead of them. The large room had obviously once been a meeting of three main passages. One had a rusting door locked across it, with a notice warning of unsurveyed caves. The second one was dark, while the third one, on the right, was brightly lighted and seemed to lead in the direction of the caverns' rear.

"That one," Ryan said.

The tunnel curved a little, and Ryan again hesitated. There was the sound of footfalls coming toward them. He held up the SIG-Sauer and turned to face the rest of the group.

"Wait," he whispered.

Thomas Firemaker and Two Dogs Fighting glanced at each other, holding their blasters at the hip.

Krysty sensed it first. She opened her mouth, her eyes wide with alarm. "No," she began. "Don't do—"

Too slow and too late.

The two warriors charged forward, beginning to whoop at the tops of their voices, brushing past Ryan's belated attempt to stop them.

They were momentarily out of sight, but there was the sound of their yelling, and their ancient guns being fired, more shouting and a burst of automatic fire.

They heard a single choking scream, then a moment of silence.

"Fireblast!" Ryan said. "Come on!"

Chapter Thirty-Three

Ryan didn't go rushing toward the skirmish. He simply walked quickly the few paces that brought him around the bend in the vaulted passage and saw almost precisely what he'd expected—the bodies of the two Native Americans, blood-sodden, one of them still kicking his feet in his death throes. Ryan couldn't recognize which one it was, as their faces had been torn away by the bullets from the Kalashnikov assault rifles held by the three men standing in the center of the tunnel.

There was a fourth man, kneeling, hand pressed to a bloody wound in his left shoulder.

All of them looked as though they had their origins south of the Grandee, and all wore the black uniforms of the General's men. A red stripe down the pant leg was the only splash of color, from the black berets to the black steel-tipped boots.

Part of Ryan's combat mind analyzed the fact that the quartet had done extremely well to chill the two Navaho as quickly and efficiently as they had, since the attack must have come as a total surprise.

But the main part of his brain was concerned with taking out the armed men as fast as possible.

The passage wasn't all that wide, and J. B. Dix, at his heels with the Uzi, wasn't able to open fire immediately.

The AKs began to swivel toward Ryan as soon as he appeared, and he dropped to one knee, firing with the SIG-Sauer, seeing two of the General's men go spinning away, dropping their blasters.

But the third dived to one side, trying for the cover of a pile of old packing cases, firing as he went down. The fourth wounded man was no immediate threat and didn't enter into the mathematical equations of lethal fighting.

Ryan winced as a stream of 7.62 mm rounds poured from the full-auto Kalashnikov, ricocheting and sparking from the stone walls.

But the gunner had already used some of the 30-round mag on the two dead Navaho, and the hammer quickly clicked on an empty chamber.

"Stay down, Ryan," J.B. snapped, able now to bring the Uzi into play. The powerful submachine gun had a fire rate of six hundred and fifty rounds per minute at a muzzle velocity of around four hundred meters per second.

The Armorer poured half a mag into the pile of boxes, a spray of white splinters erupting into the cavern. There was a single short cry of pain from the man who had used the crates for cover. As the boxes fell, the body flopped lifelessly to the side, the Kalashnikov clattering on the stone floor.

Ryan put a single full-metal-jacket round through the head of the helpless, kneeling man, the tumbling bullet exploding his skull like a smashed melon.

Nobody else had a chance to fire. The remaining six Navaho stood in the stillness, looking in disbelief at their two dead comrades and the four corpses of the General's men. The air was smoky, tasting of cordite.

"They died well and very bravely," said Sleeps In Day. "Four of the enemy to accompany them into the dark beyond."

Ryan turned on the Navaho. "You stupe bastard! They died pointlessly and could have gotten us all chilled. They might as well have swallowed their own blasters for all the good they did. I took out three and J.B. wasted the other one. Your people died for fucking nothing."

Sleeps In Day drew a broad-bladed knife from his belt and thrust it toward the white man's stomach. But Ryan had seen the attack coming and taken a step back, shooting him once through the center of the chest.

The powerful handblaster kicked him three staggering paces backward, until he tripped over his own feet and went down, dropping his own gun.

"Shit," Mildred breathed.

The other five Navaho stood paralyzed at the shockingly sudden burst of violence upon violence.

"Don't," Ryan warned, covering them with the SIG-Sauer. "Don't make it worse."

"No time for talk," J.B. said. "Shooting'll bring men like blowflies to fresh horse shit." He paused, staring straight at Ryan. "Might have to—"

Young Pony Runs started to lift his single-shot musket. "It was badly done to..." he began.

"Yes!" Ryan said.

He, J.B. and Jak were ready and opened fire almost together in a devastating explosion of death, delivered at point-blank range.

Jak's Magnum boomed and blew away two of the Navaho. The Uzi, set now for single-shot, ripped into two more while Ryan's SIG-Sauer put down Young Pony Runs.

The bodies were still falling, the echoes of the shots rolling around the cavern, when Jak called a warning. "Someone coming this way, fast!"

Doc stood motionless, his jaw gaping, the ponderous Le Mat drooping in his right hand, pointing toward the crimsoned floor.

"That was most thoroughly damnable, Master Cawdor," he whispered.

"Later," Ryan said, already halfway through reloading the automatic.

"Jesus, that..." But Mildred was also ignored.

The far end of the killing ground was obscured by a tall metal cabinet. A figure appeared around it, then vanished before anyone could get off a shot. Ryan had a snatched image of blond hair and very pink cheeks, but the woman's reflexes were in good shape and she escaped.

"That's it," Jak said. "Now know here. Shit and fan together."

They could hear the woman screaming out a warning at the top of her voice. Ryan vaguely wondered whether it was the same voice that had been singing Adelita so sweetly.

"Ryan, that was simply murder to shoot down those poor devils like that." Krysty was as pale as ivory, her green eyes narrowed in anger.

"Stupe." J.B. threw the epithet over his shoulder as he ran forward, pausing by the cabinet at the angle of the passage. "No choice, Krysty."

"No choice! Gaia, there's always a choice."

Ryan was following the Armorer, but he snatched a moment to talk to the woman. "Chief tried to stab me. Chilled him. General's men were seconds away. Figured that Young Pony Runs and others might slap metal. They did. Rest was—"

"Silence," Doc offered.

IT WAS A STANDOFF.

Around the corner was an open area that looked like it might have been one of the service personnel's garages. The floor was stained with grease, and there was an inspection pit to one side and an overhead system of chains and pulleys.

The last of the General's war wags stood by the double doors that were the only exit from the section.

At around a hundred feet from side to side, it was too wide for Ryan and the others to cross it in safety or for the General to send any of his forces out after them.

From the passage beyond the garage, Ryan and the others could hear shouting and men running. A couple of times there were shots fired in their general direction, but everyone was well under cover and the futile exercise wasn't repeated.

"Could take the tires out on the wag with the Steyr," J.B. suggested.

"All goes well and that's our way out of here," Ryan said. "Things go wrong we can stop it."

Krysty had crawled alongside him, with Doc and Mildred sandwiched between her and the Armorer. Jak had volunteered to go back a short distance and guard their rear. Though the evidence was that the General's forces hadn't infiltrated into the tourist side of the caves, it wasn't worth taking any chance.

"Lover?"

"What?"

"The Navaho?"

He sighed. "Told you. There really wasn't anything that looked like a way out of it."

"It was cold-blooded murder, Ryan."

"That what you want to think?"

"No. I don't want to think that at all."

"So?"

They were lying within three feet of each other, but they were separated by an enormous cold gulf.

"You weren't surprised."

He half turned, keeping part of his attention focused on the far side of the cavernous room. "I don't understand what you're saying."

"I think you do. I think you were razor-ready for Sleeps In Day to make that play."

"He tried to gut me!"

Now everyone was listening to their argument, as both of them raised their voices.

"And you chilled him. Then you guessed the others would try to avenge him, and you were ready for that and you chilled them, too. You, John and Jak."

Ryan shook his head. "You know none of that's true. None of it."

But he knew that it was all true.

Once Two Dogs Fighting and Thomas Firemaker had flipped—he hadn't really expected that to happen—then Ryan had seen the path that would be followed, saw how his own anger provoked the Navaho leader to attack him, an attack he was tensed to repel. And after that he had also seen the strong likelihood that the other Native Americans would try to chill the Anglos.

He'd even had the confidence to be sure that J.B. and, he thought, Jak, would be honed and ready to come immediately to his assistance.

"Liar," Krysty said very quietly.

"How can you know that, Krysty?"

"I can feel it. Smell it on you. Taste it in your words. I'm not saying you planned it all like that. It's not the way you go about things, Ryan. But your mind was so far ahead of everyone else that it turned out easy as putting a .38 through a blind man's eye."

"Trader said a man who wasn't ready for living was ready for death," J.B. said. "You can't condemn Ryan for what he did, Krysty. Anything else—any other fall of the cards—and we could all be dead meat by now."

There was a long stillness while the six friends considered the situation and what had been said.

Doc broke the silence. "Someone once remarked that it was the biggest treason to do the correct thing for the wrong reason. Though I think that it might have been put with a little more elegance than that."

"What are you saying?" Mildred turned her head toward the old man, her beaded plaits tinkling softly. "You saying Ryan did right or wrong?"

"I am merely noting that all truth is perceived. As a consequence, all truth is fallible."

"Cut the Delphic Oracle crap, Doc, and climb down off the fucking fence. Right or wrong?"

"Both. Both and neither. The means of this are that six good men lie dead back there, at our hands. The end result is that we are all still alive where we might not have been. Thus, I fear that the end probably did justify those means. But that does not make me like it any the more or feel specially proud to be a party to it. Like so many things in this sorry vale of tears, it has turned out to be more than somewhat inconclusive. Does that answer your question, Dr. Wyeth?"

She didn't reply.

But the ethical discussion was brought to an abrupt halt by the hissing, booming sound of a powerful loud-hailer.

"Best we talk," the magnified voice said.

Ryan looked around him, lifting a finger to his lips to ensure silence.

"I am the General. That is what I am called by my people and by the poor of this region. I do not know who you are out there, or how many there are of you."

There was still no answer. Ryan considered trying to make it across the space to the cover of the wag. If the hatch was open, then it might be possible to get in and use it against the General. But it was a long shot.

"My work party has not reported back yet. I wonder why that is. And my other wag? My heart is filled with sadness and my spirits are low."

The voice was educated and gave little clue to the origins of the speaker. But Ryan felt he could just detect the faintest hint of a Mexican accent. Almost concealed, but still there.

"You want to talk or fight, General?" Ryan called on an impulse.

"Talk first. A gentleman will always talk first. Under a flag of truce, perhaps."

"Don't do it, lover," Krysty warned. "Strong bad feeling on this."

Chapter Thirty-Four

Judas paused from nibbling the stubby grass that lay in the hollow where he and the other animals had been tethered. His satanic head came up, and he sniffed at the cool air. There was rain on the way, moving from the far dark horizon. But there was something else. The bloodshot eyes rolled in their sockets as the mule considered what it was scenting.

A few yards away Dean stirred in his sleep. The sudden movement of the mule penetrated into his rest, but not quite enough to bring him fully awake.

Three hundred yards away, picking a silent path along the abandoned highway, were two young men, swarthy, with long mustaches, dressed entirely in midnight black, with a single crimson slash along each leg. Each held a greased Kalashnikov assault rifle at the ready.

As soon as the General realized that the caverns had been infiltrated from the far side—something he had always considered impossible—he had ordered the two men out on a recce, from the rear exit, scouting up toward the rectangular shape of the Visitors' Center on the hillside.

They were to find what they could up there, and chill anyone they came across.

They were about two hundred and fifty yards from Dean Cawdor. The sleeping boy was still invisible to them, in a shallow hollow, though they'd already heard the snickering of the restless horses.

Judas swung his head from side to side, disturbing a swarm of small gnats that had been feasting on the salt sweat that coated his skin.

Something was wrong.

THE SUGGESTION of a truce talk had surprised Ryan. He'd called back for them to have a few minutes to consider the offer.

Ryan had beckoned them all to join him, speaking first to Doc. "Go and tell Jak what's happening. Warn him to keep extra watch. Could be a way between their section of the caverns and ours. Then come straight back."

"Your wish is my command, Excellency," Doc replied, knuckling his forehead. "I shall spin a loop around the globe and be back at ten to three to find if there is honey still for tea."

"Just go, Doc."

The four companions sat still and quiet, listening to the resonant click of the old man's boot heels, diminishing in the distance.

"What do you reckon?" Ryan asked, looking at J.B., Krysty and Mildred.

"No," Krysty replied immediately. "I vote we get out the way we came. Pick up the horses and head north. Decide at Jak's what we'll do then. Make a jump. Move on. There's been too much death, Ryan."

"Sounds good to me." Mildred looked at J.B. "What do you reckon, John? Fight or run?"

The Armorer slowly unhooked his wire-rimmed glasses, holding them toward the overhead light, angling the lenses and then wiping away a tiny smear. "Nobody ever told me to take my blaster and run. Nobody tells me that now. I say we listen to what the General has to say. He's backed into a corner. Lost half his forces and one of his wags. I figure he'll want us to pay a price for that. One way or another."

"Jak needs his price paying." Ryan looked around as he caught the sound of Doc returning. "Have to ask him what he thinks we should do."

The old man was alone. "I fear you'll find it difficult to ask young Master Lauren anything, my dear Cawdor."

"Why?"

"Because he's disappeared."

"Where?"

Doc shrugged. "You can knock me down and step on my face, but I will still be unable to provide an answer to that. Just not there, is all."

"YOU WANT TO TALK, General. How do we do this without someone getting coldcocked?"

The amplified voice laughed politely. "I like the sound of you, stranger. You have a name?"

"Ryan Cawdor."

"Ah. One-eyed man. Used to ride with the late and lamented Trader?"

"That's me. I know you?"

"Long ago, Cawdor. In another part of Deathlands. Years past. Doesn't matter where. Well, I think you and I are men of honor. I'll step out in thirty seconds with one of my people carrying a white flag. No need to come too close to converse. You do the same with one of your people. Perhaps the pocket-sized J. Rix... No, Dix, wasn't it?"

"No," Krysty whispered. "Never heard a man's voice I trusted less than him."

"Mildred," Ryan said, "cover me with that revolver. Krysty, you and Doc watch and get ready. But keep a look out behind you. Any threat to me and J.B. and you shoot. No hesitation at all. Understand?"

Everyone nodded.

"I'll have the Uzi on full-auto," J.B. said. "First breath out of line, and I cut them down."

The voice of the General echoed across at them. "Are we ready?"

"Yeah," Ryan replied.

THE TWO SCOUTS SQUATTED on their heels and looked down at the sleeping boy and the tethered animals less than a hundred yards away from them. One took off his black beret and wiped sweat from his forehead.

"Take him from here?" he said in border Spanish.

"Pretty boy," the other replied. "General didn't say nothing about us not havin' no fun if we could."

The other grinned, showing a mouth filled with spectacularly rotten teeth.

"Sure," he said. "Why not? No danger to us and some good sport as well. Let's go get him."

THE WHITE RAG, tied to the barrel of an assault rifle, was carried by a woman. Over six feet tall with flat, brutish features, she was dressed as the rest of the General's people had been. Her black hair had a beautiful sheen, like the underside of a raven's wing, and hung down past her waist. She emerged from the shadowy darkness of the far passage, walking out five slow, measured paces and then stopping.

The crackling voice of the General followed her. "I think it only fair that you reveal a token of your good faith, Señor Cawdor, by coming out yourself, or sending out John Dix. Then I can appear myself."

"I'll go," the Armorer said, holding the Uzi loosely at his waist.

"Cover you." Ryan had his eye to the sight of the Steyr, alert for any trap.

"Sure you will, friend."

After ten seconds, the General himself strode out, holding a silver-topped malacca cane, remarkably similar to that carried by Doc.

He was slender, with an olive complexion, sporting a trim goatee beard. There was a blaster holstered at his belt, and he wore a black uniform identical to the woman's.

"I await you, Cawdor," he called.

Ryan looked at Mildred, Krysty and Doc. "Watch behind as well as in front. I'm triple worried about Jak. If they got him, then they've got around the back of us. First sign of danger, start blasting."

He took a deep breath and walked out, having handed the rifle over to Krysty.

Trader had always preached the importance of never, never taking any chance that you didn't have to take.

Standing there, knowing that an unknown number of Kalashnikovs were trained on him, sent the short hairs prickling at Ryan's nape. His hand gripped the butt of the SIG-Sauer, and he was careful to keep it pointed toward the oil-stained floor of the old garage. It had already been agreed that J.B. would spray the tunnel where the General's forces waited, and Ryan would try to chill both the General and the woman with the flag of truce.

The man seemed totally at ease, despite the obvious razor-edged situation.

"Now, what is all this, Señor Cawdor? I should have known there was trouble. Scented it on the wet wind. Yet I didn't. My stranded wag and my relief crew... All chilled."

It seemed to be more of a statement than a question, but Ryan nodded. "Right. Gone where they belong."

"Ah, do I detect the bitter note of sought revenge here, Cawdor? There were Indians with you. Why should a man like you associate himself with people like that?"

"Get on with it."

"A sensitive nerve, perhaps, amigo? Well, what is this holy quest that brings you so far on my trail? Its roots must lie far north if there are Navaho involved." A smile of recognition flickered across the serene face. It was at that precise moment that Ryan realized he was dealing with a totally amoral madman, who would have to be chilled. There wasn't going to be any possible way of riding around this one.

"Think it's funny, General?" J.B. asked. Ryan had known his old friend long enough to be aware that the Armorer had also realized just what it was that faced them.

"Amusing, Señor Dix. Yes. I have ridden these parts for two years eight months and four days. Since the makeshift crew of *rurales* and so-called *federales* harried me from my ancestors' home below the Grandee. Since then I have lived off the land. This has meant the spilling of blood. But, we should not talk about chilling scum. Less than flies. Not men like you and I, Cawdor. It might even be blasphemous."

The temptation to open fire on the neatly urbane lunatic was almost overwhelming. But Ryan knew it would instantly produce a murderous burst of lead that would rip J.B. and himself to tatters of flesh.

"You been here in the caves long?"

The General nodded at Ryan's question. "One year and eight months and twenty-two days. It is an excellent base. There is nothing to attract pack rats and mercenaries to this desolation. But for me there was good shelter and a hidden supply of gasoline. My wag there is fueled up and ready to go. After we have reached our agreement, I shall go from here. Perhaps back over the border."

"What agreement?"

The General was making a weaving motion on the stone floor with the ferrule of his cane, the thin scratching noise the only sound in the oppressive stillness.

"You go away. I had not known it was possible to reach me from the other side. I never bothered. Lazy, perhaps. Get your horses or whatever you have and leave. I shall take my nine loyal comrades and depart in the other direction. Everyone lives and nobody dies. Is that not the best of endings?"

"Debt to be paid," Ryan said, finding it hard to force the words past his blind rage to kill.

"Indians? Or could it have something to do with gimpy old slut with the mewling brat? Ah, yes, that might be it. The venerable western Anglo tradition of guarding the sacred virtue of women and children. A man must do—"

Something that the General had said had rung a warning bell in Ryan's mind. But he couldn't spot what it was. There was a sudden, flaring danger. Jak? Where was Jak? But it wasn't the albino teenager that was—

"Horses," Ryan whispered.

J.B. turned to him. "What?"

Ryan couldn't swallow, his mouth was so dry. He breathed the words. "Horses. Bastard's sent someone to circle out front. Never thought of that risk. Hasn't rolled out like I wanted. Find Dean and horses. Chill him out there. Trail us in here, all the way from Visitors' Center. Feet in the dust. Get us like meat in a sandwich. Fuck it."

The frenzied, suicidal charge of Thomas Firemaker and Two Dogs Fighting had thrown away all his careful plans. The original idea had been to work their way in through the labyrinth of caves and try to chill the enemy without the risk of a major confrontation. Now things were horribly different.

Ryan was certain in his heart that his young son was under an immediate threat. And Jak could easily be dead. Otherwise, where was he?

It had gone appallingly wrong.

"How many are with you, Cawdor? Since Trader died... or did he? I heard word of you all over Deathlands. Nobody could travel that far and that fast to be in ten places in three days. Heard you got a woman. Red-haired mutie. An old-timer and a black woman kept appearing. And a mutie kid with white hair." The General slowly shook his head. "Not the class I'd have looked for from someone who was Trader's right-hand man."

"Ryan!" Krysty whispered from behind him. "Have to get out of here. I can feel a lot of blackness."

"Is anything wrong, my friend?" the General called, turning to whisper something to the statuesque woman at his side, who nodded slowly.

Ryan felt something close to a blank panic. "Got to move, J.B., or we lose it all."

"Not thinking of going, Ryan Cawdor? I think I would have to forbid that. I realize that would go against the rules of the flag of truce we stand beneath. Don't go." This time the snap of command was in the voice.

"Try anything and you get to be dead as well." Despite the cool damp of the caverns, Ryan found himself blinking sweat from his good eye.

The General threw back his head and laughed, sounding genuinely amused by the threat. "Think it worries me? Think I'm bothered at the risk of death? The fires of hell have been stoked for me these twenty years."

Ryan's index finger tightened on the trigger of the SIG-Sauer. He spoke to Krysty over his shoulder. "This is it, lover. Get out and try to save Dean."

J.B., at his side, was as calm as if they were discussing whether it might snow tomorrow. "Expect us to go back. Only chance is to go forward. Aim for the wag."

Ryan nodded. "My thought, too."

The General was tapping the stick in a regular rhythm, faster and faster. Now the madness was out in the open. The man genuinely didn't mind dying himself as long as Ryan perished at the same moment.

Mildred, her voice trembling with the tension of the moment, said, "I can take the sicko bastard's head off with the rifle. Just give me the word, Ryan."

It might be enough to throw the hidden marksmen for a vital split second, to have their leader chilled in front of them. Ryan couldn't come up with anything better.

His mouth opened to give the word, every muscle tensed for the dive for life.

When the shooting began.

Chapter Thirty-Five

Carlos, and his cousin, Jesus, had crept within thirty yards of the sleeping Anglo, who lay on his back, one arm thrown over his eyes. It had been the decision of Jesus to circle around, keeping the line of tethered horses and ponies between them and their intended victim as cover. Neither of them had paid any particular attention to the big raw-boned mule that had stopped eating and was now watching them through bloodshot eyes.

Carlos had the Kalashnikov cocked and ready, while Jesus had drawn a slim-bladed knife, carrying a loop of thin rawhide in his teeth, to be used to bind their tender young prisoner. The General had also told them to check out the Visitors' Center, but that could wait. He wouldn't know how long it took them to subdue and chill the guard on the animals.

Both men had swelling erections with the anticipation of plucking the little chicken in front of them.

THE SHOOTING CAME from somewhere behind the General and his flag-carrying lieutenant, the repeated boom of a powerful handblaster, echoing around the caves.

"Jak!" J.B. shouted, recognizing the distinctive sound of the albino's .357 Colt Python.

It was a lifesaving diversion. The woman with the white-flagged Kalashnikov had turned around, her jaw dropping, the blaster wavering toward the far wall of the garage. The General had reacted faster, starting to draw his blaster, while simultaneously dodging and running toward a small half-open door to his right.

But J.B. and Ryan were vital splinters of a second ahead of the enemy.

They were only a few paces from safety, directly behind them. J.B. opened up with the Uzi, aiming into the mouth of the tunnel where they knew the concealed guns were covering them. Ryan dropped to a crouch, running in a way that Doc had once remarked greatly reminded him of someone called Groucho, though he'd never explained why he thought that was highly amusing. As he darted back toward Krysty and the others, Ryan snapped off two rounds from the SIG-Sauer, trying to pick off the scurrying figure of the General. But both missed.

Blasters chattered from the far side of the garage, bullets howling and ricocheting off the raw stone, but nobody was hurt. Ryan and J.B. landed together in the passage, rolling between Krysty and Mildred, who stood holding the Steyr, unfired.

"Why didn't..." J.B. began, answering his own question as he scrambled hastily to his feet. "Course. Me and Ryan were in the way."

There was more shooting from the hidden Kalashnikovs, but the aim was wild. Since the first burst of shots from the Colt Python, Jak's blaster had been silent.

"What in the name of perdition is happening out there?" Doc asked.

"Jak," Ryan replied. "Must've worked around behind them somehow. Gave us the break we needed."

"Where did the General go?" Krysty asked. "I lost sight of him in the confusion."

"Hidden door on the side opposite the wag." J.B. peered around the corner of the passage. "Can't see a thing. Woman's gone as well."

"Now what?" Mildred handed the Steyr back to Ryan. "Still a standoff?"

"No." Ryan grinned. "Not with Jak Lauren behind them. I know the kid well enough. Nothing'll stop him in a maze like this. General said he had nine men. How many rounds, J.B., fired by the Magnum?"

"I counted four. Or five. Not certain. Jak's not the best shot in Deathlands, but I'd guess he could have sent three or four off to buy the farm."

Ryan considered. "I'm triple anxious about Dean. Reckon the General's likely sent some of his force out back to loop around. We have to get this over quickly."

"Two of us could go through the caverns and out into the Visitors' Center." Krysty ran her fingers through her tightly coiled red hair.

"Take too long. We must be close to the rear exit." Ryan glanced around. Once we clean them out, the wag'll be the fastest way."

"Listen." J.B. held up a hand. "That's Jak at work again. Hitting them from behind."

There was a cry that could have been pain, fear or anger. Or all three. It was noticeable that the silk-tearing rattle of the Kalashnikovs seemed to have ceased.

Ryan looked at the Armorer. "Worth moving in?"

"Could be. Run a feint and see what happens. Draw any fire if there's any fire there to draw. But they've seen the General doing a runner out the side. Captain jumping first off a sinking ship doesn't do a lot for the confidence of the remainder of the crew. Know what I mean?"

There wasn't a whole lot of choice.

Ryan sniffed. "Now, friends. I'll go right, toward the other main exit from here. J.B. goes for the wag. Full red power all down the line. You three wait and see what happens. We get chilled, you'll know there's no hope of getting out that way. So you go back through the caves and out to Dean and the horses. If they're still there. If we make it, then you all come at once. Mildred for the wag. Doc as well. Krysty follow me. Questions? No? Count of three. One and two and three!"

THE NAVAHO PONIES WERE more restless than the horses of the Anglos. But Jesus and Carlos were patient, moving slowly, setting down each foot with infinite care, avoiding the sharp snapping of a dry branch.

Now they were in among the line of tethered animals, pushing past them, whispering Mexican endearments, pausing to blow up the nostrils of a spirited black gelding, quietening the animal. They could still see the sleeping boy as they worked their way closer and closer.

The last animal they had to get past was tied a little way off from the rest of the line, a large mule with mean eyes and cocked ears.

"Take care of him, Jesus," Carlos warned in a breathless whisper. "Son of a bitch has a face like a devil."

His cousin grinned confidently. "No mule in the world frightens me," he said.

Judas watched them and waited.

RYAN KNELT, panting, on the far side of the garage, glancing behind him. There hadn't been a single shot fired at him or J.B. as they made their jinking dash across the vulnerable, exposed space.

The Armorer gave him a quick wave, crouched alongside the last of the General's war wags.

Krysty, Mildred and Doc were all waiting for the signal to move.

"Yeah," Ryan called, beckoning for them to come across, turning himself to face the darkness of the tunnel that he guessed would lead out to the open air at the rear of the caverns.

"Want me to get into the wag and start her up?" J.B. shouted.

"Give us ten, then drive her straight out the back. Wait for us out in the open, as long as you think. Should be easy to find the way."

"How about you?"

"Going to find Jak and then try and get the blood debt settled."

THREE WERE DEAD and one dying, within the first twenty yards of the corridor. The overhead lighting was good enough for Ryan to be able to see immediately that they'd all been whacked with a large-caliber blaster. It didn't need much deductive genius to work out that it was likely to be Jak's satin-finish Colt Python.

One of the dead was a woman, slender with short-cropped hair. The rest were male. One had been hit from behind, through the small of the back, ripping a hole out of his belly that you could have driven a semi through. He was leaning against the side wall, both hands clutched to the scarlet loops of intestine that gaped from the monstrous wound.

"*Por favor,*" he whispered, his eyes already looking into the unknowable distance.

"Don't have the time," Ryan said, hardly pausing, running on, Krysty at his heels.

"General said he had nine of his people left with him, lover. If he's telling the truth, then he's down to five, including that giant woman, the one who looked like her elevator didn't go all the way to the penthouse."

Ryan laughed. "Nice line, Krysty," he said over his shoulder. "You make it up?"

"Uncle Tyas McCann used to say it. Said he read it in an old book way back when."

The passage was running straight and the air was fresher, though it was overlaid with the smell of gunfire and the too-familiar scent of death.

There were two more corpses a little farther on. One had been shot, but the other had a neat little knife wound in the side of the throat, into the artery. Blood was still pumping, slow and feeble, from the gash.

"Three left," Krysty said. "So General claims."

"I wouldn't believe that bastard crazie if he told me the sea was wet." Ryan slowed down. "Light ahead."

DEAN DREAMED that he'd been driving a chrome-plated predark wag, but the front of it had mysteriously broken away and gone rolling down a steep hill, crashing into an eatery, leaving him in the rear half. The mechanic who was helping him with the repairs was a woman of eighteen, with blond hair all the way to her cute little ass, a cute little ass that was hardly contained by the shortest, tightest cutoffs that Dean had ever seen. She was smiling a lot.

It was a good dream.

"Little fuck won't know what hits him," Carlos breathed, looking at the sleeping boy, less than a dozen yards away from them. The child had a big handblaster at his side, but there was no way he was going to get time to use it.

Despite its hostile appearance, the mule didn't seem to mind the two men standing right beside it. It was even letting Jesus pat it affectionately on the side of the neck, pushing its long head against the man.

"Ready?" Carlos asked.

"Sure. Fun time, here we come."

J.B. HAD CLIMBED into the turret of the wag, checking carefully first that there wasn't one of the General's men or women skulking inside. While Doc and Mildred followed him, he checked the controls, finding that the LAV was fully gassed and ready to roll.

"Are we about to bid a fond farewell to this abode of Pluto?" Doc asked, a little breathless from the scramble. "I would not wish to encounter Cerberus or any of the other followers of this dark lord."

"Said ten minutes. Only four so far. Give Ryan the time we agreed."

RYAN STOPPED, and Krysty slipped in a patch of dampness and nearly fell.

"Gaia! What did you do that for?"

"Listen."

"Can't hear anything. Oh, I get it. Why can't we hear anything?"

"We figure there's three or four more of the hostiles around. The big woman. And the General himself.

Jak's doing good work in the shadows. So, where the fuck are they all?"

The caverns were as silent as the tomb that they had bloodily become.

Ryan checked his wrist chron. "Six minutes done. All goes well, then J.B.'ll fire up the wag and head for the back door in four from now."

"We go on?" Krysty was holding her snub-nosed Smith & Wesson .38, looking all around her.

"Sure. Not over till it's over."

A large red vending machine stood to the right of the tunnel, with white lettering emblazoned across it, proclaiming "Coke."

Opposite was a half-open doorway. Ryan pointed to it with the SIG-Sauer. Krysty nodded, moving forward slowly on the right-hand side of the passage, Ryan keeping level with her on the left.

They both heard a scuffling noise far off, like someone quietly moving a heavy piece of furniture. In the maze of passages and tunnels, it was impossible to tell where it had come from, but Ryan's guess was from behind the door.

Krysty took a few cautious steps, her back against the wall, reaching the Coke machine, flattening herself against it, while Ryan readied himself to dive for the doorway.

There was a thunderous crash, and the vending machine toppled forward, knocking Krysty over beneath it. Ryan started to turn, seeing the figure of the tall woman behind it, her Kalashnikov ready at the hip.

Chapter Thirty-Six

The blond mechanic had fallen to her knees, her thick-lipped, pouting mouth opening, the tip of her tongue glistening between pearly teeth.

Dean reached down and—

A terrifying, harsh noise shattered the stillness, jerking the boy from the heart of his languorously erotic dream. The noise was overlaid by another sound, someone screaming in terror, pain and blinding shock.

Dean's eyes opened abruptly and he sat up, part of him scared and angry with himself for having dropped off to sleep when his father had trusted him with the job of watching over the horses, their lifeline out of the desert hills.

There was a man—two men—both in the black uniform of the General.

Dean struggled to make sense of what he was seeing, only a few yards away.

The horses and the Navaho ponies were all spooked, tugging at their bridles, trying to break free. One of the men was on his knees, mouth open in a gasping shriek of agony, blood pouring in a gouting cascade from the side of his face. His left arm was jammed between the teeth of Doc's mule, Judas, who was rearing back, blood splattering its chest and forelegs.

There was an assault rifle lying in the puddled, trampled dirt by the kneeling man's feet.

The second man was limping sideways, hopping on his left foot, cursing in Spanish. He was holding an identical automatic rifle, but firing it was obviously a long way from the focus of his attention.

Dean fumbled for his Browning Hi-Power, nearly dropping it at his first attempt, grabbing it and thumbing back the hammer. The man who seemed to have been kicked by Judas had finally realized the potential danger of his position and was trying to get his balance and bring the blaster to his shoulder. His comrade was still preoccupied with the fight to wrench his arm from the mule's savage jaws, shaking his head in an attempt to shake away the blinding veil of blood from his eyes.

"Look out, Jesus!" The Kalashnikov was finally finding an aim in the vague direction of the sitting boy.

"Bastards!" Dean shouted at the top of his voice, ignoring the way it cracked and soared out of his control. He was angry, confused and frightened.

But the Browning was steady. He braced one hand with the other, like his father and J.B. had drilled into him.

"Bastards," he repeated, but much quieter, the word drowned out by the boom of the 9 mm automatic.

The jolt ran clear to Dean's shoulder as he squeezed the trigger, the force of the recoil coming close to spilling him flat on his back.

A puff of gray dust erupted from the standing man's chest, about the center of the fourth rib, halfway across on the right side.

He yelled, staggering back several paces, narrowly avoiding a vicious sideways kick from the enraged and murderous mule. The rifle was pointing at the dirt and his finger tightened on the trigger, pouring a futile stream of lead around his own feet, kicking up a hail of pebbles and sand.

Dean shot him again, this time the bullet smashing the man's left elbow, sending the rifle spinning away.

"We wanna be your friend, kid!" Jesus yelled. "Don't you killing me no more."

"Bastard." Dean stood and walked a few steps toward the wounded man, leveling the Browning and shooting him twice more through the chest, the second bullet going high and opening up the front of his throat, exiting through the cervical vertebrae and nearly severing the head from his shoulders.

Jesus dropped dead, and Dean turned his attention to the other one of the General's men.

Carlos was demented with his suffering. One moment he'd been pushing the mule away, ready to rape the pretty curly-haired Anglo boy.

Then the beast had snapped at him, slicing his ear off, fastening its incredibly powerful jaws in the side of his face and ripping away a chunk of flesh from his heek. The man had only realized the severity of the wound when he raised trembling fingers and found hey penetrated right through the torn skin and touched is blood-slick teeth, exposed to the air.

He'd pulled away, dropping to his knees in shock, ushing feebly at the mule, which had then bitten him adly in the shoulder, holding him helpless.

Now the kid had shot his cousin to death and was dvancing toward him, holding the handblaster with a nuzzle that looked bigger than a railroad tunnel.

"No," he tried to say, but his mouth was filled with lood and he could hardly see through the crimson nist.

"Yeah, you bastard," Dean said gently, shooting im three times at point-blank range through the middle of the chest, the 9 mm bullets destroying heart and ungs and chilling him instantly.

Judas felt the life fleeing from the target of his venomous spleen, and he opened his crimsoned teeth, lropping the limp, flopping corpse to the dirt. He norted triumphantly at it, pawing with his front looves.

"That's it, Judas." Dean was trembling with the violent tension, trying to reload his warm blaster, but inding that his fingers weren't strong on obedience. 'You done good, Judas. Real good."

He moved in, with the vague feeling that he might eward the mule with a hug or a pat. But Judas gave a issing, angry bray and snapped out at him, making im back off.

Dean grinned. "Hot pipe, you mean son of a fucking bitch, Judas." He nodded. "Yeah, fucking mean."

A MILE AND A HALF AWAY and two thousand feet deep, Dean's father was staring into the face of death.

The tall, powerful woman had her Kalashnikov braced at her hip, drilling straight at him. The range was less than a dozen feet and he was off balance, the SIG-Sauer pointing toward the doorway on the wrong side of the tunnel.

Krysty was pinioned like a netted bird, the weight of the Coke machine trapping her to the stone floor, her dropped blaster a yard away from her groping fingers.

Ryan had lived most of his life with the central awareness that the hooded man with the scythe could be waiting right around the next bend in the trail. Trader always said that living was a one-shot operation.

But he had never thought it would be in such a bizarre way and in such a strange place.

"Adios," said the woman, granite-faced, in a deep, grating voice.

The machine hadn't been emptied in a hundred years, but half a dozen Cokes still remained locked in the mechanical depths. As it fell, the front panel came away and the red cans rolled onto the tunnel floor.

Krysty snatched at one and hurled it, clumsily, upward and behind her.

It was one of those bizarre moments when the whole structure of time becomes fractured and stretched.

Ryan watched the bright-colored can as it tumbled slowly into the air, toward the hulking figure of the woman with the AKM. He was beginning to turn with the SIG-Sauer, but it would take hours before he was ready to shoot.

For the first time since he'd seen her, the General's lieutenant was showing some sign of expression. Her dark brown eyes were narrowing and the lips pulling back and up in a ghastly parody of a smile, a mask of gloating delight in her power and ability to cause pain and death on a helpless victim.

The Coke can hit her left hand, nipping fingers against the underside of the Kalashnikov. Not hard enough to break bone, but hard enough to make her yelp at the sudden sharp pain, jerking the rifle away from the injury, simultaneously squeezing the trigger.

The bullets missed Ryan's left shoulder by a good yard, bouncing and whining away, kicking a fountain of sparks off the vaulted roof and walls of the passage.

Time resumed its normal speed.

The blunt snout of the SIG-Sauer centered on the woman's body, and Ryan fired three times.

For a moment it seemed like flicking pebbles at a mountain of dough. The 9 mm rounds seemed to disappear into the black-clad bulk, as though the woman's body had simply swallowed them up.

But the stream of lead from the Russkie rifle stopped, and the barrel of the Kalashnikov began to droop toward the floor of the tunnel.

"Again," Krysty gasped, still pinned down helplessly by the machine.

The sadistic leer remained on the woman's face, oddly frozen, so Ryan carefully put a fourth bullet through the middle of the half-open mouth.

She was so tall, looming over him, that the full-metal jacket angled upward, splintering teeth into dancing fragments of bone, tearing the soft palate apart, and driving on through the front part of the brain. The bullet was rolling and distorting, causing terminal damage before it exited through the top of her head, shattering a chunk of the skull.

Her feet, in combat boots, were still twitching, the broken nails of her fingers scratching at the dusty stone, when Ryan holstered the blaster and stooped to heave away the fallen vending machine.

"Thanks, lover," he said, as he helped Krysty up, dusting her down.

She looked at the dead woman and the can of Coke that had saved both their lives.

"Like they used to say," she said, smiling. "There's nothing like the real thing."

"FIND JAK," Ryan said.

"Found you," an eerie voice replied, floating from behind the door at the side of the tunnel.

"You did good, friend," Krysty called. "Saved this one-eyed old fart from becoming coyote lunch."

The albino appeared, holding his big blaster, his white hair like an extra light in the main passage.

"Got her," he observed.

Ryan nodded. "Yeah. How many the rest you got? And how many left?"

"All and none," Jak replied. "Just General someplace running and breathing."

On an impulse, Krysty took a step forward and hugged the teenager, who stood still and endured the embrace, showing no trace of emotion.

"You did well, Jak," she said. "Truly."

"Chilled the pack but not leader."

Ryan looked around him, hearing the roar of the war wag's powerful engine coughing into life, not far behind them. "J.B., Doc and Mildred are on their way," he said. "General could be anywhere by now."

Jak looked at him intently. "You going," he said flatly, accusingly.

Ryan rubbed his hand over his chin. "Look, these caves run for miles. Bastard might be anywhere. Might know another way out. It's not worth—"

"Not worth Christina's and Jenny's lives, Ryan? Anyway, no other chance out."

"How do you know?"

"Heard talk 'fore chilled them. Two ways. One there—" he hiked his thumb behind him "—and Visitors' Center. General hasn't come this way. Reckon cutting back and out front."

"Dean's there," Ryan said. "I got a serious fear that the General might've sent a scouting party around the front and caught him cold."

"Get the wag and drive around. Only take about quarter hour," Krysty suggested. "And if Jak's right, then we can cut the General off before he escapes into the hills."

"Jak?" Ryan said.

"Yeah. But if doesn't come out then, I stay. You go, fine. Meet back spread. But I stay until look in General's face and chill him. Understand?"

Ryan nodded slowly. "Sure. Might even stay a spell with you here myself. Getting a real taste for those caverns. Here comes J.B."

THE CLOUDS HAD VANISHED, and the sky was a light blue from east to west and north to south. J.B. had switched off the engine of the wag, and it was cooling and clicking softly to itself.

Dean had hailed them, eagerly waving both hands above his head, rattling off the story of his adventure and the part that the sullen mule had played in it. Ryan, in turn, gave the boy a capsule version of what had been happening since they parted a few hours earlier.

"I swear that I'd plant a kiss on Judas if I didn't reckon he'd take off my face." Mildred laughed.

"I cannot convey the delight felt in my nether regions at the thought that I will never again have to straddle that saw-backed equine from Hades." Doc reached out with the tip of his sword stick and scratched Judas behind one ear. Amazingly the mule stood still for it, almost looking pleased with itself.

"All we need do now is wait for the General to put in an appearance," J.B. said.

"Still think we should have put a watch on the scuttle door out of the warren." Ryan looked at Jak. "Would've been safer."

"No." The young man's eyes were flaming like ruby torches. "Got feeling. Like Krysty."

"But if you're wrong..." Ryan glanced around. "Not all that long before dark. He can slip out past us. Be thirty miles away by the dawning. In any direction. We're double close to the Grandee. General gets over that and he's safe forever."

Jak stepped so close that Ryan could feel his breath on his face. The teenager was the best part of a foot shorter, but he managed to come near to staring directly into Ryan's good eye. "Can run. Can fight. Can try hide. Not forever, friend. Nobody runs forever. Promise."

"You really know he'll come?" Krysty said. "I can understand that, Jak. Hope it's a right feeling."

Chapter Thirty-Seven

Three-quarters of an hour later, the black-clad figure of the General appeared at the glass door to the Visitors' Center. He was hatless, showing a small crown of baldness as he made a mock bow toward the watching group, standing around sixty paces from the doors. His silver-topped cane had vanished, and he looked disheveled and dusty.

"I should have known, amigos," he called. "Maybe waited for a week or a month in that ghostly labyrinth and then you would have gone away."

"Not in a thousand years, butcher," Jak shouted.

"Ah, you must be the one who has an interest in that woman and the little one. I see."

"Drop the blaster," Ryan said.

"I think not," the General replied. "Thank you for the suggestion, Cawdor. But I will need it for a short moment or two longer."

"Looks like a Smith & Wesson," J.B. commented. "Seven forty-five Model. Eight round."

"Take him out with the Steyr, Dad," Dean suggested, recoiling at the way Jak spun around to face him.

"No fucking way, kid!" he spit with a bitter and ferocious venom. "I chill him. Nobody else!"

"Sure, Jak. Sure. Be a hot pipe that way. Let it swing, Jak, all right."

The General watched the exchange with a casual interest. "Dissension in the ranks? Strange that after this time I am ended because of a dead baby and a useless, crippled woman. Me, like that. For such a trivial and pointless reason. But I am forced to admit that you and your team are very good, Cawdor. Trader taught well. I had some passing pride in my men and women. Trained them hard and, I thought, enough. Yet, they have all been sent ahead to that limitless room in the basement. Now, I shall be joining them there. But first..."

He drew the automatic from its holster, and they all heard the click as he worked a round under the hammer.

"Down," Ryan said.

"No need." J.B. pointed.

The General had leveled his blaster at the serene sky above him and fired it in a burst of noise.

"Was that eight?" Dean asked.

"Eight," J.B. confirmed.

The General stood, legs spread, holding the blaster in his right hand. "One for the money and one for the show, is what I believe was once said. One for the baby and another one for the road."

He brought up the Smith & Wesson and placed the muzzle beneath his chin. Jak started to move quickly forward, but J.B. called after him. "It's empty, Jak. He can't—"

"Goodbye cruel world."

They heard the sharp sound of the hammer dropping on an empty chamber. The General lowered the spent handblaster very slowly, seeing the albino closing on him. He threw the weapon into the dirt and opened his arms, like a smiling priest receiving a candidate for benediction.

Ryan watched the final scene, a vague unease sliding across his mind. It was a rare business, pursuing a swift and evil bastard like the General, hardly even coming face-to-face with him. Most of the men and women that Ryan had chilled in the past couple of years had been people that he'd eventually gotten to know something about. But this was different.

He didn't even know the General's name.

Jak was twenty feet away from the man, and the unease became certainty.

"Hideaway, Jak!" Ryan yelled.

It was a .32 over-and-under derringer, hidden in the sleeve. From the speed of its appearance in the General's right hand, it was probably held there in a quick-release rig.

Ryan winced, waiting for the shot, powerless to do anything to stop it.

But it never came.

In the space of a single heartbeat, Jak had thrown two of his concealed knives, one with his left hand and the other with his right.

The first knife sliced into the General's right hand, severing the tendons in the wrist, so that the fingers opened spasmodically and the derringer slipped away to the ground.

But the blaster hadn't even begun to fall when the second throwing knife struck home.

At the last moment the General saw the blades glittering in his direction. An uncontrollable reflex closed his eyes for a fraction of a second. But the knife cut through the closed lid, driving through the dark pupil, into the optic nerve that was a direct channel into the brain.

The General had no time even to realize he'd been cut on the wrist, before feeling a punching blow in the face.

In the eye.

"*¿Quien. . . ?*" he began.

Something streamed down his face, warm, dripping off his chin, and clouds veiled across his mind.

Jak watched the man drop slowly to his knees, hands reaching out blindly in front of him. A pink mixture of blood and aqueous liquid trickled from the taped hilt of the knife that protruded from the socket of the right eye.

The albino pursed his lips and spit in the dying man's face. Twice. "For my wife and my baby, you bastard," he said with an infinite gentleness.

The General slid forward onto his face and lay still.

Jak stooped and retrieved his knives, wiping them on the man's black shirt.

"Shame so fast," he said, turning to the others, managing a grim smile. "Now go home."

Chapter Thirty-Eight

The journey back north was surprisingly free from any major incident, with one notable exception.

After some discussion outside the Visitors' Center, it was agreed that all of the animals should simply be let loose.

"Navaho's pinto ponies'll probably run free and wild," J.B. said.

"My horses should find way home." Jak looked at the line of animals. "Mebbe ride them as string myself."

"Let them go, Jak," Ryan urged. "Too many two-legged wolves between here and your ranch."

The teenager nodded, smiling. "Guess that's right."

Doc cleared his throat. "Forgive me, ladies and gentlemen, but I do have a small problem with this decision. Worthy and wise though it probably is."

"You want to shoot Judas yourself before we go." Mildred grinned.

"Quite the reverse."

"Hot pipe, Doc!" Dean exclaimed. "Why not ride the booger all the way home again?"

The old man smiled, a little thinly. "I fear that my altered attitude toward the beast doesn't quite extend to enduring physical suffering, dear boy."

"You want Judas to ride along on the wag with the rest of us, Doc?" Ryan laughed, feeling the release of the tension of the past few days. "Crowded enough as it is."

"No." Doc turned to the albino. "Jak, do you think the wretched beast will be able to find its own way home again, without harm or hindrance?"

Jak thought about it for a moment. "Doc, know any living thing stop Judas doing what wants?"

"No, I believe not."

"So, he'll make it."

THE SUN SHONE as they rattled northward, out of the hills by the Grandee, into the New Mexico desert.

Once again the engine overheated, and they had to stop for a couple of hours to allow it to cool down again. But the trip was easy and relatively pleasant.

When they were about forty miles away from Jak's spread, J.B. called from the driver's console that the engine was playing up again.

"Could do with water," he said.

"Small ville dozen miles east," Jak shouted from his perch astride the long barrel of the 25 mm Bushmaster cannon.

"Water there?"

"Yeah. Called Patriarch. Friendly."

THE TOWNSHIP of Patriarch was a dozen houses with the clapboard ruin of a church and a single store. The arrival of the clattering wag brought out the whole population, which seemed to consist of an immensely tall and powerful black man and his white wife, along with what looked like two or three dozen children of varying ages.

"See why the place is called Patriarch," Krysty shouted in Ryan's ear. "Looks like they're trying to repopulate the entire southern plains on their own."

"Haven't had so many strangers in many a long week," called the man, whose name was Fred Zero. "Got a packman from up north staying the night is all."

"Enough beds for us?" Ryan asked, looking down at his absurdly elongated shadow. Another half hour and it was going to be night.

"Sure. Sure."

THEIR BED WAS MADE from hollow tubes of old brass, and it tinkled and chimed every time either Ryan or Krysty made the slightest move.

"Sorry, lover," Ryan said. "Just can't concentrate with all this fireblasted noise going on. Wait until tomorrow when we get back to Jak's. Then we can bounce each other's bones without the musical accompaniment."

She kissed him gently on the cheek. "Be nice to have some quiet time together. And I don't just mean for making some good, slow loving. Rest up at the spread.

No need to make any fast decisions that we might regret later. I'm really looking forward to it, lover. Really."

Her hand had been lying across his chest, but it started to feather its way a little lower.

Lower.

In the end, the noisy bed didn't matter that much.

RYAN ROSE EARLY and walked down to find Fred Zero's pretty wife, Penny, preparing breakfast in a huge iron skillet.

"Hash browns, eggs over easy and some home-cured ham? How's that sound?"

He grinned at her. "Sounds like I've died and gone straight to heaven. Thanks."

"Go on through. Packman's just finishing and getting ready to hit the highway."

The trader was sitting at a small table, smoking a noxious cigar. As Ryan came in he looked up. "Sorry about the smoke, friend. I'll put her right out so you can enjoy the fine food that the lady of the house provides."

"Thanks," Ryan replied.

"Name's Kenny Friedman, and I cover the whole of Deathlands and I offer a range of... Hey, just wait a goshdarned moment there, my friend."

He was a typical packman, effusive and eager to prove he was the nicest guy who ever drew breath. But now his jaw had dropped, and he was fumbling in the breast pocket of his tweed suit.

"Something wrong?" Ryan asked.

"I don't... Your name wouldn't be Ryan Cawdor, vould it, friend?"

"Could be."

"Traveling with a redhead and a kid and an old man ınd— Hallelujah, but I hit the paydirt."

"How come you know me?"

"I got a note for you."

"From?"

"Couple of really mean... But, I guess I might be vrong, Mr. Cawdor, seeing as how they're likely riends. One was small and skinny with a long musache. Other was older and sort of scary."

Ryan nodded, his mind flooded with the news. Abe ıad done it. He'd damned well done it.

The piece of paper was crumpled and stained, but till totally legible.

"Success. Will stay around Seattle for three months. Come quick. Abe."

"How long ago were you given this?" Ryan asked.

Friedman wrinkled his face, counting back on his ingers. "Great Lakes was... Missoula... Billings... Butte... then I stayed a coupla days with... Right, I ot it. Give or take a day or so. Must have been up in he Northwest, by the sea. About six weeks ago from ow."

"Six weeks," Ryan said. "Leaves us another six veeks. Thanks, friend. Thanks."

Chapter Thirty-Nine

Two of the graves were large, the middle one much smaller. All three lay in shade, beneath a wall of red rock that rose vertically and vanished into the deep blue of the morning sky.

It was a place of great quiet.

Ryan opened his eye and looked up into the still air watching the ghostly shadow of the large white egret floating past, high above him.

Krysty stood with her back to him, looking down at the three markers.

He sat up and she turned, and he could see tears glistening on her cheek.

"I'm sorry, lover," he said.

"I know. We've done all the talking there is. I'm talked out, Ryan."

"I have to go."

"Sure."

"Can't make it with a jump. No control. Have to travel on foot. Start with the wag and see if we can get gas. If we can, then it shouldn't take more than a few days."

Krysty wiped angrily at her eyes. "A few days, Ryan A few days? How far is it?"

"About fifteen hundred miles up to Seattle. If the wag holds and the creeks don't rise, we can be there in under a week. Find Trader and Abe and get back here in the same sort of time. Call it a total of three weeks."

"Call it forever, Ryan."

He shook his head, joining her in front of the graves, staring at the carved names: Christina Lauren, beloved wife of Jak and mother of Jenny. Murdered; Jenny Lauren, dear daughter of Jak and Christina. Murdered; Michael Brother. Good friend from another time.

The faint scent of sagebrush came drifting up from the mouth of the canyon. Ryan put a hand on Krysty's shoulder, half expecting her to shrug it away. But she let it lie there, not moving. Not moving closer.

"J.B.'ll keep an eye on me. You know that, lover."

She continued to look away from him. "I told you. Talked right out."

An elegant yucca towered near them, its pearly white flowers clustered in a long spike. A Chamisa and tamarisk were a little farther away.

When they had first buried Christina, Jenny and Michael, a scant few days earlier, it had occurred to Ryan Cawdor that this must be one of the most beautiful places in all the world to pass the remainder of eternity.

Now there had been so many more deaths, all linked to the paying of the blood debt.

"You're still leaving at dawn?"

He nodded. "Yes. We are. Food and ammo. We've got a last night together."

That turned her around, her emerald eyes like blank pools, ice covered. She pushed away his hand as though it were an offensive insect. "Thanks a lot, Ryan. I can hardly wait for this 'last night together' you tell me we got. Can't wait for the last time you touch me and kiss me. And enter me. Every single thing you do tonight is going to make me more and more aware about it being the last time. Can't you... Gaia! Can't you see, Ryan, what you're fucking well doing to me?"

"I'm sorry. I have to do this. Trader was the man who raised me and then made me the man I am. Mebbe you should think that whatever love you have for me is owed, a little, to Trader. I can't change that. I can't just take a big square of linen and wipe all my memories away."

"I know that." Krysty closed her eyes. "Oh, I feel bone-weary, lover. Part of it's selfish. I wanted these quiet days together here. And you've robbed me of them."

He leaned down and hesitated. But Krysty responded, lifting her face to him. Their lips met, in the familiar, gentle kiss of two people endlessly in love with each other.

"I am truly sorry," he said as they broke apart.

"I know you are. It'll pass. Everything passes in the end, lover."

"We going to walk back to the house and join the others? Should be some supper there."

"Thinking about your stomach, lover." She smiled up at him. "Eat well. Could be the last good meal for a while."

"J.B. cooks a terrific dead snake pie."

They stood close, holding hands, looking one final time at the trio of graves.

Krysty broke the silence. "So long, Christina. Bye, Jenny. Sleep in peace, Michael."

"Amen," Ryan said.

Then they walked together, out of the shadows of the canyon, into the afternoon sunshine.